Whatever
We Are

Whatever We Are

NAOMI EAST

Charleston, SC
www.PalmettoPublishing.com

Whatever We Are

First Edition

Hardcover ISBN: 978-1-68515-331-1
Paperback ISBN: 978-1-68515-332-8
eBook ISBN: 978-1-68515-333-5

Dedicated to my husband and number one supporter: couldn't have done it without you, babe. And to the friend who knows me better than anyone else, thanks for being as crazy as me–you know who you are.

Whatever We Are Playlist

Collide – Howie Day

Fix You – Coldplay

What Becomes of the Brokenhearted – Jimmy Ruffin

Yesterday – The Beatles

Here Comes the Sun – The Beatles

Creep – Radiohead

Fire and Rain – James Taylor

Clean – Taylor Swift

Maybe I'm Amazed – Paul McCartney

I Can't Make You Love Me – Bonnie Raitt

Hold Me While You Wait – Lewis Capaldi

Mr. Brightside – The Killers

I'll Stand By You – The Pretenders

Angels Like You – Miley Cyrus

Dark Side – Bishop Briggs

Exit Wounds – The Script

Follow You – Imagine Dragons

Golden – Harry Styles

Bruises – Lewis Capaldi

Remedy – Adele

I Always Knew – The Vaccines

Dog Days Are Over – Florence + the Machine

Make You Mine – PUBLIC

Shallow – Lady Gaga & Bradley Cooper

Baby I'm Yours – Arctic Monkeys

Play with Fire – Sam Tinnesz

Burn It Down – LINKIN PARK

Love U 2 Death – The Darts

Fire and Flood – Vance Joy

Stubborn Love – The Lumineers
Home – Phillip Phillips
Fire Meet Gasoline – Sia
Welcome Home – Radical Face
Before You Go – Lewis Capaldi
Be Your Love – Bishop Briggs
Runaway – AURORA
Lost? – Coldplay
Dream a Little Dream of Me – The Mamas & The Papas
Creep – Duomo
Happy – Duomo

Table of Contents

Prologue

When they met for the first time, it wasn't special. There were no fireworks, sparks didn't fly, and bells were not going off. Not all love stories work that way; some take more time. Some people need to find a way to love again after being scarred by their past. That's not to say Grace didn't notice him. He was hard not to notice. Over six feet tall, soft brown hair that fell just right, and kind blue eyes. The eyes were what really made her take notice. Most men these days either leer with clear intent or ignore you, but genuine kindness without a hint of creepiness—that is rare. Men often made her skin crawl of late. It wasn't always their fault, to be fair. Having recently unlocked repressed memories in therapy helped explain this.

Grace had always had an odd feeling that she couldn't shake, that there was a gap in the memories of her childhood. There were things she knew about sexuality at far too young an age that she had no explanation for having learned. Now she knew how her far-too-young brain had learned those things. Still there were blanks, a shadow where there should be a face. Not knowing who the abuser was might be the hardest part of all. Having to doubt and question everyone in your past. It made trust crumble. Sometimes she wished the memories had stayed repressed, but it was too late now; the only way through was forward. After years of multiple bad relationships and finally learning how to be happy on her own, it was rare for Grace to notice a man this way.

So while fireworks weren't a thing, still there was something just in the fact that Oliver had caught her attention without twisting her stomach in knots. Not that she would do anything about it, but it put a small smile on her face as she walked home from Whole Foods. All the while thinking how nice that guy seemed who had picked up her dropped bag of basmati rice and smiled kindly.

The funny thing is she had no idea that Oliver had noticed someone for the first time in two years. Two years. That's how long he had been a widower. What a stupid word, Oliver often thought: "widower." It should be something more like "lost man." That reminded him of the Lost Boys from Peter Pan and was somehow comforting. In all honesty, when you married your best friend and high school sweetheart at twenty-two years old and had fifteen years together, only to lose them completely out of the blue…"lost" was the word that described his life these days. So yeah, the woman in the store—noticing her was strange. He didn't want to notice women. It usually made him angry more than anything. He didn't even think he could actually recall what she looked like; it was more the feeling he had gotten from her. Like she had been prepared to bolt away from him, then instead had changed her mind and smiled with a sweet "Thank you." That was literally the extent of their interaction, and for some ridiculous reason, he was still thinking about it. Weird.

Whatever We Are

So on a whole planet full of people, two of them had locked eyes for a split second and shared a tiny connection. Two people who hurt, two people who weren't looking for anything, two people who never asked for this to happen. Maybe, just maybe the universe had decided it was time for them to heal. Time for them to believe in love again.

Catalyst

Oliver

Ally,

Today I noticed a girl in Whole Foods. I am telling you this because it made me feel guilty. I couldn't even tell you what she looked like, really, if I'm honest. Isn't that ridiculous? I think she had blond hair, or brownish-blond maybe. She wasn't as tall as you. All I know is she didn't remind me of you, and that is why I feel so guilty, I think. You were bold; you were vibrant and happy. You would never have seemed skittish about a stranger helping you pick up something you dropped. You would have flirted or laughed. She could barely get out a squeaky thank-you. So baby, what would you have to say about this? Would you be laughing at me right now? Yeah, probably. That is one of the noises I miss the most: your laugh…you had a few different kinds, and I'm starting to have a hard time remembering them all, and that really pisses me off. So I guess now I'll have some scotch and try not to think about you and your laugh all night. No, just kidding, I will be thinking of you all night, Ally. Because you're still my wife. I'm not letting you go, baby, not yet.

Pouring my drink, I think about writing to my dead wife. Is it weird? Eh, who knows. I've done weirder things in my life. It wasn't a shrink or a therapist who suggested I do this. It was something my grandfather said, the only other widower I know. He wrote letters to my grandmother after she died. His are all handwritten and probably much more interesting than these ones I keep on my iPad to Ally. But they've helped, as much as anything can help with an absolute shit situation. Being married for fifteen years was not always perfectly smooth, of course, but we were best friends. I never imagined a future without her. Never envisioned a life where she wasn't lying on the couch next to me. Her feet in my lap, those honey-brown eyes sparkling with mischief at something, as usual.

Now I'm drinking alone and wondering why I can't react like a normal man when noticing a woman today. I should turn on some TV and try to distract myself, but I'd rather try to figure this out in my brain somehow. I've never purposely decided to be celibate for the rest of my life, but I still can't stand the thought of being "unfaithful," which is pretty messed up considering I'm no longer a husband. Not a husband. I haven't thought those specific words before. It sounds so wrong. I have been a husband since I was twenty-two. That doesn't just go away, does it? It has been two years, yes, but I still feel Ally here. In myself, in our home, in my head and heart.

A nervous-looking girl dropped something, I picked it up for her, our eyes met, and she seemed...relieved? I was intrigued, I'll be honest. Feeling intrigued was something; it was so much more than I had felt about another person in so long. What drew me to still be thinking about this girl hours later? Maybe I just need to get laid? No, that's not what this is though. If it was as simple as a bodily reaction, I would understand it easily; I am still a man, after all. I know how to handle my own urges. I still keep that between me and Ally. No, this is something else. I actually think I just want to know new people again.

Wow. Lightbulb moment here...I think I want human connection. OK, that I can handle. I pour another drink, proud of myself for thinking this through and figuring something out about myself. I pick up my phone and open the group text I have going with my two siblings.

—Ready to go out into the world and be a person again, guys...need your help. Where does a man start?

My older sister Jess answers immediately as usual.

—Whoa, who is this speaking? Wait, are you drinking?

I chuckle to myself. Of course she thinks it's the drink talking. She has been trying to get me out of my own head for so long; this is definitely unexpected.

—Drinking, not drunk. Been doing some thinking is all, it lead to an epiphany. I think it's time. So what should we do?

—Ummm Milo, are you believing this? Woo-hoo! Sibling night out, I say.

My younger brother Milo will probably take a few minutes to see his phone, but I know he'll be happy too. I wait to hear from him with a half smile on my face.

—I'm here. Well, well, well, good on you, big bro. Ally would be proud. Yes, let's do it. This Friday night? I know a nice place for drinks…quiet but still cool. We can talk without shouting, so good for old folks like you two.

—Oh ha ha, like you're so young and hip.

—Thanks, guys, it means a lot. Talking will be nice. I feel like I'm making some personal breakthroughs. I hope Ally would be proud. Appreciate it. Love you both.

—Love us, huh? Ok, you definitely are drinking, but I'll take it XX

—Of course you love me, dude. I'm the best brother ever. See you guys Friday. I'll send the details later.

So I guess I'm taking my first step back into "normality." Funny, all it took was a smile from a stranger to make me want to be alive again.

Coincidence

Grace

I'm at work and again my mind wanders to him. It's kind of absurd how often he keeps popping into my head, that guy with the kind eyes who picked up the dropped bag of rice. Such a silly kind of crush for a thirty-four-year-old woman to be having. Not that I want to be having a crush on anyone these days. I guess that's why it keeps taking me by surprise that I am thinking about him so much. I wonder what he's like, and I hate to admit it, but I bet he's married. He had that vibe. Maybe that's why he made me feel at ease. He wasn't a creepy single guy looking for his next conquest. Just a nice, normal husband to some lucky woman. I'm convinced that's where all the nice men are these days: already married. So that decides it. I'll forget about him. I need to get my head straight for this meeting we have with a client anyway, so no more daydreaming about tall strangers with nice smiles. It's just so juvenile anyway.

"Grace, what is that look on your face?" Kyle is smirking at me in that way he does.

"Nothing! I'm just trying to mentally prepare for the meeting, that's all."

"Yeah sure, that's totally what it looked like."

I do consider mentioning it to Kyle. He's actually a good friend, but what is there to even mention? I mean, I want to talk about Whole Foods Guy (what I call him in my head) but what's the point? Fuck it; life is boring lately.

"I'll tell you about it after work. Want to get dinner and drinks?"

"Oh, dinner and gossip? Yes, please! Should we invite Tara?"

"Yes, but no one else. I hate hanging out with these people after working hours when I don't have to. I can just about stand you two." I wink and smile sweetly.

"Ha! Nice, glad we make the cut. Thai or Mexican?"

"If you want me to be talkative, give me margaritas."

"Las Flores it is!"

The meeting runs late, of course, because the pain-in-the-ass clients hate all of our ideas and want to tell us how to do our job. So we spend three hours going back and forth to convince them to leave the marketing to the professionals (aka us). Now I really need that drink! By the time we get to Las Flores, a hip Mexican cantina, it's packed. Friday night is always busy like this here. Good thing Kyle called for a reservation earlier. We have a cozy corner booth by the bar, and even though there's chaos everywhere, it's somehow intimate. The three of us melt into it with a relieved sigh.

"God, I need this!" Tara breathes.

"Ugh I know, what a hellacious week." Kyle agrees.

I can't help myself though. Despite feeling the same way, I have a grin on my face in anticipation of talking about Whole

Foods Guy. Just thinking about him again makes my stomach do a small, girly little flip. I am forgetting work, stress, and everything and being ludicrous, but I can't seem to help it.

"OK, there's that face again!" Kyle points at me. "We're ordering drinks, and then you are spilling!"

"Oh yes please, anything to get work out of my head." agrees Tara.

"Well now I feel stupid because it's not actually anything. You're going to be so disappointed when you hear my lame little story," I say, feeling about thirteen years old all of a sudden.

We get three preposterously large margaritas, and I tell them my sad little tale.

"You guys know me; I've sworn off men recently. Not trying to meet anyone. I have no idea why it even made such an impression on me. I just can't stop thinking about him," I add, feeling the need to clarify that I understand my own foolishness. Hearing it all out loud has made me feel sillier than ever. "Besides, he's probably married or something, and it's hardly like I'll ever see him again."

Tara laughs, "Stop being such a Debbie Downer! It sounds cute, and if that's his local grocery store, you very well could run into him again one day."

"People meet in all kinds of awful ways these days. That one is actually relatively normal if you think about it," adds Kyle.

They're just being good friends. They aren't aware of all the details of my messed-up past, but they are aware of vague issues I'm dealing with through therapy. So I know they are being kind.

"You guys are too sweet. I know that I'm being silly, but it's put a smile on my face all week, and that's something to appreciate. It was a nice encounter at least." I shake it off, ready to forget all about it. It was fun to have talked about, and now I'll let it go. I'm relaxing with friends, the tequila is starting to work, and I'm actually happy with being single. Those are the god's honest facts.

That's when I look over to the booth on the opposite side of the bar, and he's there. Whole Foods Guy is sitting there, deep in conversation with another guy and a girl. What. The. Hell. I blink and think I must be more buzzed than I thought, because this is way too much of a coincidence. I must be manifesting him in my head because of the conversation we just had.

"OK, guys, this is freaking me out," I whisper after a minute.

"What?" Tara and Kyle both say in unison.

"That's him over there in that booth. I swear it is."

"No way!"

"Are you sure?"

"I mean I'm like ninety-nine percent sure. It's just too crazy though, right?"

"Oh my god, this is karma or fate or some shit like that," Kyle slaps his hand down on the table. We all burst out laughing at that—and oh crap—now he's looking over here! I think I want to die of embarrassment right now. I'm just going to pray he doesn't recognize me.

Collide

Oliver

J ess, Milo, and I are close siblings. We lead separate lives in the same city, but we text regularly, and usually at least once a month, the whole family is all in the same room at some point. They have all been so supportive since Ally died, each in their own way. Jess is the oldest and takes her big sister role very seriously, always looking after her little brothers. Now that she is married herself, the constant attention has toned down a bit, but just a bit. Milo is the typical baby, used to getting his own way, being all independent and the self-proclaimed "fun one." Me? I was the steady one, always knew what I wanted in life and got it. Settled down young and had the ideal life in a lot of ways. Ally and I had dated since we were teenagers and married while I was still in college. We just believed that once you had "the one," there was no reason to wait. Now I'm suddenly single again at almost forty years old, and it's strange to say the least. But with these two, every time the three of us get together again, the dynamic goes right back to normal, and I love that. Of course Milo picked a cool Mexican cantina; tequila is his thing lately. This place is nice though, and it's relaxing to be here with my two favorite people. Jess is still a newlywed but tries to act like she's not because she hates the thought of making me feel sad.

It's not like I haven't gone out anywhere in the past two years. It's just that tonight it feels different because it feels like I chose this. I actually want to be here. I'm feeling kind of light headed just thinking about turning a page in my life and starting to genuinely live again. Well, that and the tequila that Milo keeps putting in front of me. I haven't done shots in years, and it's undoubtedly affecting me more than my usual slow-sipped whiskey.

"So, Ollie, are you going to tell us what the incentive was for this breakthrough?" Jess is narrowing her eyes at me in that knowing way she does.

"There actually was something, but it's going to sound stupid," I say.

"Stupid and tequila are perfect amigos, man. Why do you think we're here? We are your family, and we already know a lot of stupid about you," Milo snorts, taking the seriousness down a notch. His special talent. He's right though; if I can't be stupid in front of these two, I've got nothing. That's the great thing about siblings: no matter how old you all get, you can act like kids together, and it's just right. So I'll just tell them the story.

"OK, so it was Sunday afternoon, and I was grocery shopping; you know, wild weekend stuff. I had an encounter. Well, not even, just ran into a girl or woman, whatever. She dropped something, and I picked it up and handed it to her, and for some reason I was struck with a feeling. I have no idea what, honestly. Curiosity, maybe? She seemed kind of nervous or wary, but then when she looked at me for a second, it was like

I made her comfortable or something. She smiled, thanked me, and walked away. That is literally the extent of it. But I kept thinking about her for some reason. So it got me thinking about myself then, and I came to the conclusion that I wanted to rejoin humanity, so to speak. Meet new people; learn their stories. Like that girl: Why did she react to me the way she did? I was interested. Does that even make sense?"

Milo is looking at me like he's still waiting for the punchline, a crease in his brow. Jess just leans back looking at me, though, and says, "I think it makes perfect sense."

"You do?" Milo says incredulously. "I'm so lost."

That makes me laugh.

"Look, Ollie, you've been living so deep inside your own head and grief for two years that you probably could have run over a little old lady in the grocery store and barely noticed. But this is progress. It's like the fog is lifting, in a way!" Leave it to Jess to put it in a way that makes complete sense.

"So does this mean you're ready to meet someone new?" Milo is nervous even saying it; I can tell. He is always putting his foot in his mouth, but I just laugh again. Jess reaches out and smacks him in the side of the head. "This isn't about sex, you idiot!"

"Ouch! I mean, I know that, gosh. I guess I'm just not good with words. I just mean, is this a turning point in terms of moving on from Ally? Wait! Shit! No! I didn't mean that either." Milo has a deer-in-the-headlights face now.

"It's OK. Relax, man." I shake him by the shoulder. "I'm not about to start dating, no. I suppose I'm just glad to discover I have an interest in humanity again."

"Well you say 'humanity,' but I heard a story about a woman. Just saying." And he holds his hands up in a gesture of innocence. I laugh at my idiot brother again. Maybe it's the tequila, but I feel so relaxed and happy. I let the night just wash over me, appreciating how much I've laughed and how much I've been smiling. I'm thinking about the girl from the store again now. "You know it's funny, but I can't even say for sure what she looked like. It was more about a feeling I got from her."

"Well if she's ugly, then it's a good thing you'll never see her again," Milo says.

"Ugh, Mi, you are so shallow!" Jess grimaces.

"No, Jess, I'm just not afraid to be honest and realistic. Look, we come from a good-looking family. Ally was beautiful. Your husband isn't a dog. It's just a fact of life that pretty people are drawn to other pretty people."

I'm barely listening to them now as they bicker. It's like pleasant background noise when your siblings fight, so nostalgic. Familiar background noise that's been playing in the soundtrack of my life, and I love it. In truth though, I'm silently pondering what Milo said about never seeing her again. I am aware that the likelihood of randomly running into her again is tiny, even if I did recognize her. Somehow the thought is souring my happy mood all the same. I don't like it. That's when a group on the other side of the bar in a booth laughs loudly all together, and I glance over. And I keep looking... because I can't be sure, but I could swear it's her. I mean, of course it might not be, because I hardly remember her face, but the hair looks right. Also, she's looking back at me, and she blushes furiously. I'm frozen for a minute. Do I want it to be her? Suddenly all I can think about is Ally. No, I'm not going to do this right now. I want to be out in the world, alive and interacting with people. Later, at home all alone, that's when I'll think about Ally. Instead, I pick up another tequila shot and drain it.

"Whoa, old man, better slow down. Don't even try to keep up with me. We both know you can't do it," Milo jokes.

"Hey, I have to go to the bathroom. Be right back." And just like that, I get up and walk away because I can't over-think this. Heading to the bathroom will lead me right past her booth, and the tequila is making me feel bold. I want a closer look.

Big City, Small World

Grace

"Crap! Crap! Crap!" I hiss under my breath. "He's walking this way!" It's not just that; he's looking at me, and there's plainly recognition in his eyes. Those gorgeous blue eyes, they're still kind, but tonight they're also smiling. I don't remember that from before.

"Oh, wow. That is a tall man," Tara observes matter-of-factly.

"He's looking right at you, Grace. That has got to be the same guy!" Kyle whispers.

"What should I do? Acknowledge him?" I'm surprised to find that I feel very light and easy in this moment.

"*Yes!*" demands Kyle.

"Get up and go to the bathroom so you can bump into him," Tara suggests.

There's no way I'm doing that; I'm not chasing him down. Instead I allow my eyes to meet his and smile slightly. I just know my pale skin is blushing like crazy and wish I could hide it, but there's nothing I can do about that. He nods at me and a broad smile breaks out on his face then. Wow, the things that does to my insides. Well, no going back now, I think to myself. He veers away from the bathroom hallway and heads toward our table instead.

"Hi, I thought I recognized you. From the store, right?" He holds out his hand, and I take it, really hoping my palm isn't sweating.

"Yes, hi. That's me, clumsy girl on aisle twelve," I joke nervously.

"Wow, big city, small world. I'm Oliver."

"Grace. Nice to meet you officially." He glances briefly around the rest of the table, so I quickly introduce my co-workers, and he greets them both politely. "I don't want to interrupt anything. Just wanted to see if it really was you."

Now things could get awkward, and I know I'm doing that weird lip-biting thing I do when I'm anxious.

"Oh gosh, no, you aren't interrupting anything at all. We just came here to unwind after dealing with some awful clients all afternoon," Kyle assures him, always so good with putting people at ease.

Oliver glances toward me again. "Grace, could I buy you a quick drink at the bar, or is that really rude? Sorry, I don't get out much. I'm not sure if there is protocol about these things."

"Sure, I think that's fine. You guys don't mind, do you?"

"No!"

"Of course not. Enjoy!" Tara and Kyle both hurry to assure us as I slide out of the booth.

I feel so nervous and yet excited all at the same time. We find two barstools to perch on, and the bartender asks what we want to drink.

"Is it weird if I just get a club soda and lime? The margaritas here are pretty lethal. I don't know how much more I can take in one night."

Oliver lets out a little chuckle and says, "Oh good, me too. I didn't want to look like a wimp, but my little brother has given me multiple shots in the last hour, and I am not used to that kind of thing."

I laugh, relieved. "Is that who you're here with?"

"Yeah, my brother and sister. Siblings' night out."

"And you abandoned them to talk to me? Great, now I feel like I better say something interesting." I didn't mean to say that out loud, but yeah, I did. That's what I do when the nerves take over...no filters.

He laughs. "No pressure. Actually, tonight is just me getting back out into the world of humanity a little and seeing what it's like. Seeing the same person twice in the same week felt like some kind of sign."

"Hmm, interesting, so why don't you get out much, Oliver?"

"Long story really, but the short version is I lost my wife two years ago, and it's been...hard. Very hard...to care about stuff like going out or just meeting new people, that kind of thing. I guess eventually things change, but it's that first step that's the hardest to take." He goes quiet then, and man, I need a second to think about this. Not what I was expecting.

"That explains the married vibe." I blurt out. Oh great, Grace, you are such an idiot.

"Married vibe?" He raises his eyebrows.

"Oh, well, I got a nice feeling from you that day in the store, and I thought you were probably married." I try to explain my weirdness. "I mean, you weren't creepy or sleazy, that's all. Sorry, I'm a little crazy."

"Ah, that explains the look."

"Look?"

"Yeah, you had this startled look at first, like you wanted to bolt away from me. Then it kind of changed, like you calmed down or something. It intrigued me."

"Oh that, well like you said, long story." I try to laugh it off, but it sounds too flustered. "I don't mean anything like what you've been through, of course. Just some stuff that has come up in therapy. They have me feeling sort of off-kilter lately. But it's a good thing that I'm dealing with it all." I puff out a breath and realize I now probably sound like a complete basket case. To shut myself up, I concentrate on my straw for a while and drink the lime-flavored fizzy water, wishing I had ordered some vodka in it.

Oliver looks down at his hands. I notice them then too. Big hands, smooth and tanned; god, he really is sexy. With a solid gold band on that third finger of the left hand. He twists it a little in an automatic gesture that he clearly does all of the time.

"It's nice to know I'm not the only person with issues. If that's not a rude way to put it. Sometimes I feel like a freak: thirty-nine years old and ready to retire from life because my wife died."

"How long were you married?"

"Fifteen years."

"Wow, you guys married young. That's so sweet. Of course you feel that way after so long. It's only natural. It's also quite an accomplishment, you know. I've never had a relationship that lasted more than three years. Lots of people haven't."

"Yeah, I guess so. For us it just felt effortless and natural. We were best friends, high school sweethearts…it went by so quickly. Marrying that young wasn't always easy going, of course. We had bumps along the way and ups and downs like everyone. But I wouldn't change a single thing—except the ending, of course."

"I'm so sorry." It's a totally useless thing to say, I know, but I mean it. He looks so terribly sad, and my heart aches for him.

"No, I'm sorry." He says firmly. "What kind of a guy invites a girl to have a drink and does this?" He runs his hand through his hair in an agitated way.

"Hey." I reach up on an impulse and lay my hand on his arm. "It's OK. It's your first foray out into the world of the living. You are allowed to think about her. It's actually a beautiful thing that you are."

He looks at me for a few seconds and smiles a little sadly. "Maybe I'm not as ready as I thought."

"That's OK. My therapist says I should stay away from men for a while. So we both have no clue what we're doing," I babble, decidedly oversharing.

"We're a great pair, then!" he laughs.

"Perfect." I clink our glasses together in agreement.

"Seriously though, Grace, thank you so much for this. I know it seems like nothing probably, but it's meant a lot to me to meet someone new and just feel comfortable talking."

"Well I feel the same, so thank you too."

"Would it be weird if I asked for your number? Not in a sleazy way. Just, you know, in case we want to talk again as friends sometime."

"Sure, we can exchange numbers. I mean, there's no guarantee we'll keep randomly running into each other, right?"

We exchange phones and each put our numbers in the other person's phone. It somehow feels so normal and not date-like at all. That's a little disappointing on my end because he's so damn good looking, but he clearly isn't looking for anything more than a friend. Still, when we say goodbye, there's a feeling deep down inside that something about my life has just changed.

Tequila and Signs

Oliver

I sit back down without looking either of my wildly grinning siblings in the eye.

"Good trip to the bathroom?" Milo mocks.

"What was that?" Jess demands immediately.

"That was the grocery store girl, believe it or not. Strange timing, huh?"

"She's not ugly." Milo looks over at Grace with an appreciative look on his face.

"It's not like that." I glare at him.

"Are you sure? Because we saw numbers being exchanged…"

"Yes, I am sure. We took each other's numbers because we actually enjoyed conversing." Then I sigh and hang my head, squeezing my eyes shut. "I kept talking about Ally. I feel like a jerk."

"Oh honey, you aren't a jerk at all." Jess squeezes my shoulder.

"Dude, she listened to that and still gave you her number? Weird!" Milo says.

"She isn't looking for anything like that. Guys creep her out or something, I think. I'm not really sure. Look, can we just pay the bill and go? I think I've lived enough for one night."

I honestly just want to be home now. I need to ground myself with the familiarity of it all. We wind up our night with lots of promises to keep in touch and get together soon. All the same old things. The minute I step into my apartment I breathe a deep sigh of relief. Kicking my shoes off in the corner near the door, I smile, remembering how much Ally hated me doing that. Now it doesn't matter anymore. I head for the bedroom, strip off my clothes, and get into some old sweatpants. So much better. Stretching out on my couch, I automatically reach for the iPad where I write to Ally. Surprisingly, I want to tell her about Grace. Is that messed up? Oh well. What in my life isn't?

Ally,

I ran into her again. Can you believe it? What were the chances of that? Her name is Grace, and for a few seconds, I actually considered if I could ask her out. Then I started talking about you; guess that answers that. But she didn't seem to mind. She listened to me and genuinely seemed to care. I can just imagine what you would say to me right now: "Ollie, how pretty is she?" I can hear the smirk in your voice and everything. Well I can't lie to you, baby, even now…she is very pretty. But she isn't you. No one can ever compete with you because you got to die in your prime. You will forever be young and perfect. The pinnacle of beauty for all time. I can only say shit like that to you. Can you imagine how people would look at me if I said that out loud? I did get her number, but only because I haven't talked so freely to someone new in a long time, and it was nice. Besides, she wasn't the flirty type. So I'm letting you know now: I think I have a new friend, and yes, it's a girl. Also, I miss you just as much as ever, baby. Life goes on, it's true, but I'm not letting you go, not yet.

I flip the lid shut on the iPad and continue to think over the night. I have a strange desire to find out more about Grace, to talk to her more. We only spent a few minutes talking, but it felt so easy and natural that I wish I had lingered for longer now. I look where she programmed her number in my phone and silently curse to myself. She only put Grace. I'm such a dummy for not getting her last name. At least then I could see if she has social media. This makes me wonder what my social media looks like to outsiders, just in case new people will be looking at it soon. I open my Instagram. At one point years ago, I'm fairly certain I had a Facebook account, too, but it's so long ago I doubt I could even get into it anymore. The Instagram account is pitiful. Ally always used to laugh that I never knew what to post. There are pictures of us, of course, and they cause a small pain in my chest but also bring a smile to my face. The last time I posted was three months ago, Gramps and me sitting in lawn chairs in Mom's backyard holding beers. I captioned it "Grumpy Old Men." Well—that seems kind of lame. I wonder if I should put something new.

Then I recall that Jess made us take a "sibling selfie" at the bar tonight. I text her asking for it. When it comes through, I'm surprised to see how relaxed and happy I look.

Before I can overthink it, I post the picture with a short caption, "Tequila and Signs." I'm not entirely sure what I even mean by that, but it feels exactly right.

Real People, Real Pain

Grace

Lying in bed on my phone that night, I look again at the number he programmed in. Oliver Bekker...wait, that's a whole name. I could google him. I bite my lip, wondering if that's a good idea. What's the point? Do I really need to obsess even more about this guy? I may or may not ever see him again. Should I keep feeding my ridiculous crush like this? He clearly isn't over his wife even now, so he doesn't want anything from me. I'm doubtlessly setting myself up for disappointment yet again. I just can't seem to stop myself, though, as I type his name into the search engine. It pulls up a few hits, and I know right away that the first one is him because there's his picture. It's from his work website. It's a civil engineering company that seems to specialize in bridges. Well, plenty of those in the city. I go back to the google results and click on the Instagram profile, hoping it's the right Oliver Bekker.

Bingo. I sit up now, stuffing the pillows behind my back. He posted a picture from Las Flores with his brother and sister tonight. I read the caption. Then I read it again. "Tequila and Signs." Surely he can't be referring to what he said about seeing me twice in a week seeming like a sign, can he? I feel my heart begin to beat faster and try to remember exactly what he said. "Seeing the same person twice in a week felt like some kind of sign." I could swear that was it. How odd that he would reference it. He looks happy in the picture, smiling broadly, and I notice he has a dimple on one side. "*Ugh!*" I groan loudly to myself. Damn, this is really the last thing I need. *Why?* Why does this man have to spark something in me? He is a widower in love with his wife. *His wife*. That thought makes me curious to see her.

I start scrolling through his pictures, looking for one with her in it. When I find one, I pause. They are standing on a dock holding wine, and there's a marina behind them. The caption says, "Happy Fifteenth Baby!" It was their anniversary. Their last one. I wonder, How long after this did she die? She is beautiful, almost as tall as him with a stunning smile and long, silky hair. Not super skinny but definitely fit, like she was athletic. She's smiling contentedly, leaning on Oliver's chest with his arm around her shoulder. I can't help but suddenly feel a deep ache at how sad it all is. How did she die, I wonder? I suppose I could keep digging online and probably find out, but abruptly I realize I'm not going to do that. This isn't just some fascinating news story. These are real people with real pain; I saw it tonight in Oliver's eyes. I don't want to go digging around in their private lives like this.

I close the app and put my phone down on the bed, feeling more depressed than ever. I can't imagine having it all like that and just losing it out of the blue. What does that do to a person? How do you ever get over that? Or do you? Maybe it's better to never have it all. Then you won't experience the pain of losing it. That's what I tell myself. I'm better off how I am: happy on my own, nothing to lose. In the back of my mind, though, that caption pops back into my head unbidden, "Tequila and Signs." I lie down and close my eyes. Tonight I go to sleep with a smile on my face despite myself.

Starting
Something

Oliver

I haven't stopped thinking about Grace all weekend. It's freaking me out a little, and I can't help but wonder what it means. I can't overanalyze this though. Not if I'm really determined to reenter the world of the living, like I keep telling myself. As I sit on my couch with mindless sports on the TV and a beer in my hand, I try to think of something I could say in a text to her. In my mind I go over the options:

—Hi, Grace, it's the sad guy from the bar Friday night. (*Lame.*)

—Hey, what's up? (*What am I, nineteen?*)

—Hello, how are you this evening? (*Are we business associates?*)

—Hey, you, how's Sunday night treating you? (*No, just no.*)

What the fuck? Those are all idiotic. I remember how easy it was to talk to her in person, and it brings a smile to my face. I should just say what I would to her face. I pull up the number she gave me and start typing.

—Hi. I've been thinking about you. It was really nice meeting you the other night. Hope you've had a good weekend.

I send it, my heart pounding a mile a minute like I'm running a marathon. Within a minute, I see three dots dancing around showing that she's typing back. I sit up straighter... this is suddenly much more real and nerve wracking. My leg starts bouncing up and down as I watch those gray dots.

—Oliver, hi! So nice to meet you too. My weekend has been good, mostly just spent cleaning my apartment and reading books...you know, like a really cool person. How about yours?

I smile to myself (again), picturing her curled up with a good book.

—Well, I got kind of crazy myself. Went for a run, cooked for one, visited my grandfather, and now ending with a bang—on my couch watching TV. I should find a good book. Got any recommendations?

—Not unless you like romance or fantasy haha. I'm not very highbrow.

—Do I seem highbrow to you?

—Hard to say. Your suit was pretty fancy on Friday night. I can't help but picture you in an elegant robe, sitting in your leather chair with a whiskey glass, cigar, and maybe a *Sherlock Holmes* book.

—Well I'm flattered—that beats the gray sweats I'm actually wearing at the moment. Although I can often be found with a glass of good scotch, so I guess you got one part right. No smoking for me though.

Insanely I have the urge to ask her what she's wearing. Stop, Oliver. Get a grip.

—Ah good to know. I can't stand the smell of cigarettes.

—By any chance would you want to get coffee sometime? Not a date, just to talk again. I enjoyed it a lot last time.

I wonder what she thinks of this. It confuses even me. It isn't like I want to ask her out, but at the same time, I want to see her again. I hardly know what I'm asking for myself.

—Of course, when did you have in mind?

God, this girl, she makes everything so easy. I wasn't even prepared like the dumbass I am. Now I need to think. All I know is I don't want to wait.

—How about tomorrow morning? I don't know what time you have to be at work. Maybe we could meet up beforehand. I can get to work anytime as long as it's before eleven. I have a meeting then.

—Sure. How about 8:30 at Cup of Joe on Sixth Avenue? That's near my office.

I almost type "It's a date," but catch myself with a jolt. No, it's not a freaking date. Instead I just say,

—Perfect, and thanks! I'm glad you don't mind sad strangers who are socially inept.

—No problem, as long as you don't mind weird women with no thought filters. See you then.

—I much prefer unfiltered people. Have a good night.

***

Grace

I hate how giddy it makes me, texting with Oliver. He's made it clear he just wants a friend to talk to. I just can't make my silly heart seem to get the message. Usually men are so cryptic, playing head games and having silent power struggles with you. Not this man. He says what he's thinking, and it's the most refreshing thing. I get to see him again in the morning, I think to myself with a grin. I hadn't dared to hope it would be so soon. I need to be careful with my feelings though; as much as he is a breath of fresh air, he is also undeniably attractive, and I'm only human.

Ever since my last disaster of a relationship, I've been avoiding another one anyway, so I can do this. Especially after what I uncovered about my past recently. I sought out a therapist after I finally got myself out of an abusive relationship I had been in for nearly three years. My boyfriend was insanely controlling and even hurt me, but for some crazy reason I had allowed it. That angered me so much in hindsight because that wasn't who I was. I was a little spitfire Irish girl who took no shit from anyone. So why had I allowed this man, who didn't even know the meaning of the word "love," entrap me in a horrific situation like that? I wanted answers, and more than that I wanted to make sure I would never allow it to happen again. So I got myself help.

My therapist is great. She eventually helped me remember something, though, that my mind had repressed. Something that had happened when I was very young; it was an unexpected revelation, to say the least. A whole new issue I was still in the process of dealing with. Apparently when a child experiences abuse or trauma, their brain will sometimes repress the memory in order to help them cope. Having those memories suddenly come back was beyond jarring. I still cannot remember the identity of my abuser, though, and that's been the hardest part. I have this giant blank space full of fear and doubt. Questioning everyone I ever knew and trusted.

I just wish I could be sure of who it had been. It does help explain many things in my life nevertheless, and how I ended up thinking I deserved a horrible relationship like the one I was in. I am grateful for that, at least; understanding is half the battle.

I guess in a strange way, the fact that Oliver only seems to want friendship from me makes me extra comfortable around him and even more attracted to him. Ironic. I sigh deeply and get up to prepare for bed. At least tonight I'm going to sleep with something happy to look forward to in the morning. I often have nightmares, reliving the newly unburied memories, and sometimes going to bed is honestly terrifying. Not tonight, though. Tonight I might have good dreams, I think.

Coffee and Confidences

Oliver

The fact that I made sure I looked my absolute best this morning is something I'm not going to think about too much. I can't help myself though. Grace is so very pretty, and I am a guy, after all. I wore a fitted blue suit that I know brings out my eyes, and I even broke out my Armani cologne that I almost never use anymore. As I sit at the table with my coffee, my leg is bouncing nervously yet again, and I'm actually biting my thumbnail. Biting my goddamn nails: seriously, this is pathetic. I got here closer to eight than eight thirty, so I'm already well into my morning caffeine, I'm sure that isn't helping my nerves. Every time the door opens, I hold my breath, but it's still early and she isn't here yet, so I take out my phone and open the notes. I have a few minutes, and to calm my thoughts, I decide to write to Ally.

Ally,

It's not a date, I promise. I know you would tell me it's OK if it was, but it isn't. I just want to stop being such a loner. She's a new friend, and you have to get to know someone to really be friends, right? OK, so I'm nervous, which makes it seem more like a date. Also, full disclosure, I wore the cologne you bought me for the first time in a long time, but it's just anxiety about making a nice impression, I'm sure. I'm still not ready to let you go, baby.

I exit out of the notes, and when I look up, there she is. She's ordering her coffee, talking to the cashier with a bright smile on her face. She notices me watching and waves at me. God, she looks good. She's wearing a black pencil skirt that really hugs her curves, and I know her green blouse matches her striking eyes because I remember them well. I swallow hard, trying not to notice every little detail. Instead, I focus on my coffee. Yeah, coffee is good; think about that. When she walks over, I get up and for a second, I don't have a clue what to do, so I pull her chair out for her.

"Thank you. Men don't often do that anymore these days," she says sweetly.

"I get the feeling you hang out with the wrong type of men," I say with a laugh.

"I will one hundred percent agree with that. Maybe you can tell me where all the good ones are hiding?"

"Ah, true, I'll give you that. I guess they aren't super easy to run into on the streets of New York these days. Maybe check out Whole Foods." God, why did I just say that? What the hell is wrong with me? She gives a low chuckle, and well damn, that's a cute laugh.

"Good plan. I'll have to go back there soon." She twists her coffee idly as she smiles at me. I like how she isn't shy about making eye contact when we talk.

"It's nice to see you again. I'm glad you agreed to meet me again so soon. I was afraid you'd think I was being too pushy."

"Not at all. I think it's great you are feeling like going out more! It's what you wanted, right? To open yourself up a little more?"

"Yeah, I think it's good for me. I've gotten to be such a loner these last couple of years. I am really getting sick of my own company, to be honest. I have my family, of course, and a few friends and workmates, but it's nice meeting someone completely new with no connections to my past life, you know." It's a truth I hadn't realized until this moment, Grace is the exact breath of fresh air I needed.

"I bet. You know, I've never lost someone close to me, so I won't pretend I know what you've been through, but I do know what it's like to want someone to talk to. Everyone needs that."

I nod at that, thinking how right she is.

"It takes you by surprise, all the other things you lose besides just the person. We had a lot of friends that were other couples, and they aren't in my life as much now: not on purpose, just naturally. It got awkward for me to be with other couples a lot, and it was painful, too, of course. And I just miss the constant conversation. Ally was a talker. We talked all the time, and then my life got so quiet all of a sudden. Only me and my own head 24-7. I was so surprised how easy it was for me to talk to you. I guess that's why I wanted to meet up again."

"I know what you mean; you're easy too. Wait, no. That doesn't sound right. I mean easy to talk to!"

I laugh because her blush is adorable when she says something that embarrasses her, and I just can't help but tease her.

"I seem easy, huh? So, highbrow and easy. Wow, I am complex."

"Oh gosh, I told you my mouth has no filter!" She places her hand over her face and shakes her head.

"I think that just makes you one of the most real people I've ever met."

"Oh, I'm real, all right. No one would fake this awkwardness."

"So, Awkward Grace. You clean for fun on the weekends, you read very classy literature, and you like basmati rice. What do you do for work?"

"I'm in online marketing. I work on social media campaigns and designs for ads, things like that. It's good; I get to be creative, which I enjoy. Of course it can be stressful, like anything, but overall I'm happy with my job. How about you?"

"I'm an engineer. I work mostly in bridge design and maintenance, which is important in the city. Keeping them all safe and strong. I enjoy it too."

"You must be very smart." She wrinkles her nose. "That seems like it involves a lot of math. I hate math. I just don't have that kind of brain."

"I think math is easier to understand than life. At least it's full of inflexible rules. It's predictable and sensible. Life is never predictable, that's for sure."

"Tell me about it." Grace looks lost in thought for a minute. I want to know what she's thinking about.

"What unpredictable thing has happened to you lately?"

"Hmm, I could tell you, but then I'd have to kill you." She shrugs and gives me a smile that makes me feel all kinds of things I don't want to.

I adjust myself in my seat and lean in closer. "Oh, really? You do realize that just makes me want to know even more. You've heard my pathetic sob story. I think it's only fair you give me something in return. Don't make me play the sad widower card, because I'm not above it," I tease back.

She chuckles wryly at that and shakes her head. "You play dirty, Bekker. Well I'll say this much, have you heard of repressed memories?"

"Like something you forgot and it comes back?" I ask.

"It's more than forgetting though, more like your brain won't let it come to the surface to protect you. But then out of the blue it will come back sometimes. I recently discovered some suppressed memories from my childhood, and I didn't see it coming. I'm dealing with the fallout; it was most definitely unpredictable. But it's OK. I can handle it. That's life. Bad stuff happens all the time, at any age. We don't always get a choice about when we're going to deal with it, that's all." She plays with the sticker on her coffee a little, lost in thought. I wait, knowing she isn't done telling the story. "Honestly the hardest part has been that it hasn't all come back to me, so I don't know who to be angry at. I feel like I can't trust anyone from my childhood because I can't remember who the culprit was. I almost think it would be a thousand times better if I did. I could find closure from the answer somehow, you know?"

I don't even think about it; I just reach out and take her hand in mine, squeezing tight. "Grace, I'm so sorry. I shouldn't have forced you to share that if you didn't want to. That's terrible."

"Don't be sorry! I like talking to you. It feels like we've known each other for a lot longer, for some reason."

"It does," I agree. We drink our coffee in comfortable silence for a minute after that, just sitting, enjoying each other's company. It amazes me that I feel so at ease around this woman. I hardly believe it.

Then I realize I'm still cradling her hand in mine, and my thumb is slowly rubbing circles in her palm. Well shit, why does that feel so right? I look down pointedly and say, "OK, I should probably stop doing that now. I'm sorry, I don't know why I was doing it." We both laugh slightly awkwardly, but I don't let go yet, and she doesn't pull away either. After a few more seconds, I clear my throat and slowly remove my hand.

"You did it because you're sweet, Oliver. Thank you." And just like that, she makes me feel at ease again. Checking the time on her phone, she says, "I actually have to head to work now, but thanks so much for this. I haven't enjoyed a Monday morning so much in as long as I can remember."

"Me either. Coffee is better with a little Grace. What's your last name?"

"Murphy."

"Grace Murphy. How very Irish."

"Ah, yes, well, couldn't you tell by the paleness and freckles?" She laughs, gesturing to her face.

"It's a good look, I like it." We get up and walk out to the street.

"Well, have a good day in online marketing, Grace Murphy."

"You too, Oliver Bekker. Keep the city's bridges safe for us, OK?"

"Will do." I lean in for a hug. It feels good, and I find myself wishing there was a reason to linger, but there isn't and I need to walk away. So I turn away and force one foot in front of the other, blowing out a long breath, hating that I don't want to leave. All I can think as I walk to work is how screwed I am because my new "friend" is a little too special.

***

Grace

All morning at work I feel like a moron because I know I'm smiling for no reason. No, that's not true. The reason is Oliver. Having coffee with him this morning felt so surreal, like sitting down with an old friend and meeting a hot new love interest all at the same time. But he isn't in fact either of those things. I need to check myself.

"Get a grip," I say under my breath. That's when I get a notification on my phone from Instagram: "Oliver Bekker has started following you." Well, shit. That makes it a little harder to get a grip. Every time I talk myself away from him, something pushes me closer. I guess that's why he wanted to know my last name, I smile to myself as I think it. I open the app and press the blue "Follow Back" box. Then I feel silly for doing so immediately. I should have waited longer. No, I hate playing those kinds of games. That isn't who I am. I get the feeling he isn't like that either. I take a deep breath and let it out slowly. I just need to be myself. Only I do need to be careful and guard my heart with this man. It would be ridiculously easy to fall for him. He wants a friend, I remind myself for the hundredth time today. I need to learn how to be friends with men and not have it be sexual anyway, don't I? It's a problem I've always struggled with and something I've discussed with my therapist. So this is good for both of us. He still loves Ally, and I'm a psychological mess, in all truth. OK then, friends it is.

I just wish he didn't smell quite so delicious when he hugged me goodbye this morning, because that cologne made it hard to concentrate. If I close my eyes, I can still smell it: woodsy with a hint of citrus and something else I can't put my finger on. I wonder what brand it is? I might have to walk around the department store on my way home and spray some samples to see if I can figure it out. Maybe I'll buy myself some perfume too. It has been a long time since I wore any. My horrible ex accused me of being a whore when I last bought a bottle and then threw it out, and I just let him. Makes me sick to think how weak I acted back then. Never again.

Macy's is not my usual idea of a fun evening, but once I started my investigation into the colognes, I began to realize how much I actually do miss having a man in my life. There is something about the smell of a man that is irresistible; nothing else compares. The sales clerk helping me out is young and having as much fun as me with the mystery. She brings me over yet another bottle.

"This one is dreamy. My roommate wears it, and I have to admit it takes him from about a six to an eight."

"Wow, that's some potent stuff, then." I inhale deeply, and bingo! It's Oliver's scent from this morning. "Oh my god, yes, this is it! That's what he was wearing."

She claps in triumph and gives me a high five.

"Armani for the win!"

"I'll take the biggest bottle you have," I say without thinking. "Also, I want to find a nice perfume for me. I haven't worn any in years. I just buy scented lotions and things from Bath and Body Works, but I think I need a signature scent. It's more grown up."

"Oh yes, you definitely do! Especially if you are going to drive Mr. Armani crazy." She winks at me. "Let me take a whiff of your natural scent, and I'll gather some options. I love this part of my job." She enthusiastically leans in without warning and sniffs my neck with her eyes closed; well that's awkward.

"I probably smell like the streets of New York," I point out, leaning back a bit.

"No, you have a wonderful natural freshness. I think you need something sweet and floral. How does that sound?"

"Um…good."

"OK, wait here! I know just which ones to try." She hurries off to gather sample bottles. After trying out Gucci, Valentino, Dior, Marc Jacobs, Tom Ford, Kate Spade, Versace, and last but not least, Tiffany & Co., I am fairly certain I will be able to knock out an entire subway car with fumes. Both the clerk and I agree that Kate Spade is the winner though; it is subtle but enticing. I thank her profusely and make my purchases. At least next time I see Oliver, he won't be the only one who smells delicious.

Can't Stop

Oliver

It's Wednesday, which means I was with Grace two days ago. So why does it feel like I need to see her as soon as humanly possible? Why am I itching for any excuse to talk to her? That brief morning coffee was over far too quickly, and now I'm trying to figure out how to spend more time together next time. I can't seem to concentrate on anything else either, which seems laughably juvenile. I decide to just do something about it because I'm not getting any younger, and life is too fucking short.

—Would you like to grab dinner after work tonight?

I text her hoping that it seems casual. She doesn't answer right away like she did last time, so I decide I need to distract myself. She's doubtless busy working, as I should be. Instead though, I pull up her Instagram profile again. I like it. It has an old-fashioned feel to it somehow. Maybe because she talks about books a lot. It seems like she used to travel a lot but then didn't for a few years. I wonder why. It's clear she's an artistic-type person, too, which makes sense with how she loves the creative side of her job. If I'm being completely honest with myself, I'm looking for signs of boyfriends also, because one thing I can't understand is why no one has snatched up an amazing girl like her. I know a lot of people don't keep pictures of exes on their social media, though, so it isn't always easy to tell. While I'm looking at her pictures, her answering text message comes through.

—Dinner sounds nice. I'd like that a lot. Did you have a place in mind?

—Do you like Greek?

—Love it.

—Meet at The Agora at seven thirty?

—It's a plan. See you there.

When I get to the restaurant, I ask for a rooftop table because they have a beautiful patio up there. The softly playing Greek folk music makes all the city noise sound charming. It also has a large grapevine growing over the tables, full of sparkling cafe string lights trailing through the vines. The night is nice and breezy, perfect spring weather. I realize how much I've missed little things like going out to dinner somewhere nice. Ally and I tried to have regular date nights, and it was always fun. I don't do that kind of thing alone, obviously; now I'm the takeout king.

I have arrived early again, and I text Grace to let her know I got us a table on the roof, then I order us a bottle of sauvignon blanc. As I sip mine and wait, my mind wanders to some of my date nights with Ally. We used to get pretty frisky on them, and god, do I miss that. She even had some tiny sex toys she would wear, and I controlled them from an app in my phone. It made us so crazy playing around like that in public. By the time we got back home, the sexual tension was off the charts, and we were ripping each other's clothes off. I should not be doing this kind of reminiscing right now, though, I realize, because I'm growing hard just thinking about it all. I take a deep breath and adjust myself in the seat. Shit, I need to get a handle on this. Now I feel guilty and wish I wasn't meeting another woman tonight.

What a horrible mess I am. And it's far too late for regrets because Grace appears at the top of the stairs just then, and I go to stand up. Then I remember my stiffy, so I grab a big cloth napkin and shake it out in front of my pants. I pull out the chair next me and pray she doesn't look down.

"Hey, how are you?" I lean in and kiss her cheek, noticing she has perfume on that I didn't smell the last time I hugged her. It is enticingly wonderful, sweet and floral and completely feminine. That's not going to help my pants situation, I can't help but think as I inhale it.

"I'm good. Wow, it's so pretty up here. I've only ever eaten downstairs. I had no idea the rooftop looked like this."

"It's nice, right? Like a little Greek oasis in the middle of the urban jungle."

"I love it!" She looks all around, and I'm looking at her. I need to stop doing that. The mixture of feelings raging through me right now are making me feel nauseous. Guilt, lust, anger, and sadness. It's too much sometimes. Trying to distract my overworking brain, I pour her some wine.

"I got us some sauvignon blanc. I hope that's good?"

"Perfect, thank you."

"I just realized that this place seems like a date spot. I probably should have picked somewhere more casual."

"It's OK. I think as long as we both know it's not a date, we can just enjoy the pretty atmosphere." She gives me an encouraging smile.

"OK, thanks. Sorry, I didn't mean to sound rude or insulting in any way. It's not that I wouldn't want to take you on a date...I just, I'm not there in my life right now." God, I sound like such an arrogant prick.

"I know, I really do understand. It's all good. I'm not trying to start a new relationship either, so don't worry about me."

"Why aren't you interested in a relationship right now?" I take another sip of my wine as I examine her, feeling strangely glad to know she isn't looking to date another man right now.

"Well, about a year and a half ago, I got out of one that was really bad. One that I had stayed in for three years even though I shouldn't have. It wasn't good in any way. I realized I needed to figure out some things about myself and why I had allowed that situation to go on as long as I did. Especially before I tried to start being with someone new. So that's what I've been doing, figuring out my own messy headspace. I need to be sure of who I am and what I want before I'm ready to try all that again, you know?"

"That's very wise. I'm glad you got out of it eventually."

"If only I had never gotten into it; that would have been much better."

"I guess in the beginning you probably couldn't have known it was going to be that bad though, right?"

"Exactly. He was a charmer at first. Said and did all the right things. He didn't start to change and show his true colors until after we started living together, and by that point he had already messed with my head so much I already felt trapped and didn't even realize it. I never knew a person could manipulate another person like that until I was living it."

"God, Grace, that sounds horrible."

She shrugs. "I was lucky. I survived. I came to my senses and got away before it went beyond the point of no return. Some women don't make it out of those situations alive."

"He was physically abusive?" I ask. She nods her head tightly and takes another sip of wine.

I feel my blood slowly turning cold and I clench my jaw. I am almost never prepared for when memories of Ally's murder will creep up on me, and this one really came out of the blue. I can feel my hand shaking as I place my wine glass down, and I feel tears spring into my eyes.

"Oliver? What's wrong?" Grace's voice is full of worry.

"I'm sorry, I feel like a bastard right now. I'm angry about what you went through, of course, but this is also bringing back how Ally died, and I just wasn't prepared for those memories. I'm a mess all of a sudden, I'm sorry." My mouth has gone dry and I run my tongue over my lips trying to breathe and orient myself in the flood of grief.

"Don't apologize! Do you want to talk about it?"

I clear my throat, take another sip of wine and think about that for a moment. Grace doesn't say anything or make me feel rushed to answer. She waits patiently, completely understanding that I need time to figure out if I can talk about this.

That patience is exactly the thing I need in this moment. I look right into her green eyes and say, "Yeah I think I do. If we are going to be friends, you should know what happened."

"OK." She refills both our wine glasses, then settles back into her seat, giving me all the time I need to gather my thoughts. The waiter comes by while I'm still preparing myself, so we both order, although I doubt I'll taste anything now. My mind races as I prepare to share the most painful event of my life.

When the waiter is gone, I start, "Ally was a paramedic. She was really good at it because she just had this way with people. She could calm anyone down, even in high stress situations like car accidents or childbirth. She really loved what she did too; for her it was more of a calling than a job. She used to say that humanity was at its most beautiful when people were afraid. She loved helping people, and in a way that gives me some comfort about how she died, because I know she died doing what she loved."

I feel my voice going then, and the tears are coming. I take a break and wipe away the tears till they stop. Grace doesn't say anything. She simply leans forward and takes my hand gently in hers, holding it like a mother or sister would. Nothing flirty in it at all. She waits, holding my hand, and it feels so comforting I can go on. I squeeze her hand tightly and continue.

"I guess on some level I knew her job had dangerous aspects, but I never really thought about it like that. She had been doing it for so long I suppose I had gotten complacent. From my point of view, she was more like a mini superhero, sweeping in and saving the day. I probably tried not to focus on her ever being in danger because I didn't want to. But that day she was called out to a domestic violence disturbance along with the police because there was a woman who had been shot by her boyfriend. It wasn't a fatal wound, and they thought the man had fled the scene already. The woman was in the front yard when Ally and her partner arrived. They started tending to her right away. The police entered the house, not realizing the man was hiding in the backyard. He knew they were coming and was just waiting to get another shot at his girlfriend; he was crazy and determined to kill her even with all the emergency workers there. When the police went in, he came around from the back and went nuts shooting. He killed his girlfriend and both Ally and her partner before the cops got back out and killed him." I stop there because that's all I can do. Those are the facts, and just telling them has drained me.

"Oh Oliver, that's so awful," she whispers when I'm clearly finished. I quietly nod in agreement and drink more of the wine.

"Ally sounds like a wonderful person."

"She was. She died using her body as a shield trying to protect that woman."

"Really makes marketing seem pretty damn inconsequential."

I laugh at that. "No, I don't think so. I think you have a way with people, too, like Ally did. It's a feeling I've gotten from you since the beginning. You always put me at ease. Not everyone is a hero in the same way. Some people can be heroes by getting a guy who thought he was done with this life to want to live again."

"You give me way too much credit." Raising one eyebrow at me, Grace makes a face that brings yet another smile to my face. And that's the proof right there. After reliving that hell, I am somehow smiling because of this girl sitting next to me. I shake my head in wonder and squeeze the hand she is still holding.

"You really have no idea, do you? Thank you for listening to me. I think it was good I told you about it. I wish you could have met Ally."

"Me too."

The rest of the evening flows along easy and light as we eat and chat. Somehow talking about it and crying for those few minutes make me feel like a weight was lifted off my chest. I'm surprised to find that I do, in fact, enjoy the food after all. In truth I enjoy yet another night of just *being*. Because of Grace. When it's time to say goodbye, my whole soul is reluctant to part ways yet again.

Later that night, lying in bed, replaying the night in my head, I realize I am possibly the world's biggest jerk. I grab my phone, not even thinking what time it is, and send a text to her.

—I'm a jackass. I owe you an apology.

—Oliver, did you know that you apologize way too much?

—Sorry.

—Very funny. So what is it you think you did this time? (You did nothing, btw)

—You were telling me about something awful that you went through, and I turned it around and made it about me and my big sob story. That's a total jackass move! I basically cut you off. You opened up about a painful personal experience, and I somehow made it about my life.

—I appreciate the sentiment, but you're wrong. I was done with my story. Believe me, you don't need to hear more about my garbage ex (THAT man is a jackass, not you). Also, I understand how it is when something brings back a memory. It's like a floodgate is opened, and nothing will stop the tide of memory in that moment. Therefore, I hate to tell you, but I cannot accept your apology.

—I hate that you had to experience a relationship like that. You deserve only wonderful things and someone who knows what a treasure you are.

I watch the three little gray dots dance around, stop, and then start again. Then they disappear and are gone again for a while. I worry that I crossed a line that made her uncomfortable, and that's why she can't decide on a reply. I don't know why I can't seem to keep myself in check with her. The dots reappear and I stare, waiting for her answer.

—Thanks, Oliver.

"Way to keep trying to ruin a friendship, Oliver" is more like it. At this point I should just put my phone down and stop texting. It's late, and I'm feeling inclined to say things I probably shouldn't. My fingers are hovering over the keyboard, though, because all I want to do is keep talking to her. It's addicting. I feel like I can't stop, and I know I don't want to. How can I be feeling addicted to someone who isn't my Ally though? Throwing my phone down in my very empty king-size bed, I groan loudly because I may be feeling more alive lately—but feeling alive is freaking complicated.

I haven't felt such a strong desire for another person's company in so long, I need to figure out what to do with it. Should I try to step back a little? I get up then because the jumble of my thoughts is not going to let me sleep anyway, so I decide I need to talk to Ally.

Ally,

Baby, I am confused about myself, and I really need you. Talking to you always made things clearer. I miss it so very much. Here's my dilemma…what makes someone just a friend? Wanting to be around them a lot, talk to them, and hear them tell me about themselves? Feeling happier when they are around? But if that person is an attractive woman, one who smells amazing and who makes me be more aware of how I dress when I know I'll see her…is that crossing a line? I don't want to be over you, Ally. I don't want to stop being your husband. Deep in my soul, that is still my identity. So when I feel those other things, it just gets me so bewildered. How can you still have my heart and soul, and at the same time I'm drawn to another? It's about now I can hear you cutting me off with a laugh. You'd give me that look…you know which one. You'd tell me that *you* died, not me. That life goes on, and I need to start looking to the future, not just the past. You were always so practical like that. I'm not quite as pragmatic as you are though; I'm more of a sap these days. Up until now I've been content living the loner widower life. Suddenly it isn't as easy to do though. I crave more. I have to be brutally honest with you, baby: I crave her company. But it's you I love. I will just cultivate her friendship for now and see what happens. Maybe one day I will be able to let you go. Just not yet.

Rambling to myself and pretending Ally is listening is my normal outlet, and I feel a bit more settled. I can try to get some sleep now. Hopefully I don't drive Grace away with my craziness and mixed signals.

Distractions

Grace

When I get to work on Friday, I conclude that a distraction is in order.

"What could we do this weekend for fun?" I ask Tara over coffee. I desperately want to try and see Oliver; I just don't think it's a good idea. If I don't manage to keep busy, though, it will only be harder.

"We could see a show or look up what concerts are going on."

"I think I need something more active. I have pent-up energy I need to burn off."

Tara lets out a big sigh. "We need men: that's the problem. We both have some pent-up energy, believe me."

"We don't need men! Let's do something active, kayaking or rock climbing. What do you say?"

"I say you think I'm in better shape than I actually am. What about a paintball course? I've always wanted to try that. Shooting strangers with paint seems like it could release some sexual frustration."

"Oh, that actually sounds really fun!" I love that idea. We have to get back to work, but I send Kyle a message over our office server and tell him our idea. Tara is in charge of finding a place with availability on Saturday, and I text her letting her know that Kyle is in too. Twenty minutes later, Kyle is at my desk informing me two of his friends also want to come, so I let Tara know we now have a group of five.

"Who are these friends of yours?" I ask.

"Sean and Mark. They are old friends from college, actually. I know I've talked about them. We keep saying we are going to get together, but then we get too busy, so this was the perfect opportunity. They both happened to be available. It might have had something to do with the fact that I mentioned I was going with two hot chicks."

I glare at him. "It's supposed to be relaxing and fun, not a setup."

"There's no setting up, I swear. I'm just saying they were motivated, that's all. Anyway, they're cool guys. You'll like them. It will be fun." He insists.

"Fine," I acquiesce with a sigh.

That night as I blast my music, sip my wine, and cook some stir-fry for one, I feel good that tomorrow will be busy. Keeping busy should help take my mind off a certain tall, handsome man. Just then I receive a text. From exactly the one I'm trying to distract myself from.

—What are you up to this weekend?

I need to think before I answer him. After our dinner Wednesday night, I was feeling determined to be more careful of the circumstances I found myself in with him. I decided that if I am going to remain friends with Oliver, I should do very casual things with him. Yeah, so maybe not dinner at a charming rooftop spot with wine, sparkling lights, and romantic music. That was too intimate, too dreamy. It misleads my pathetic heart, and I can't handle it.

I feel so honored that he shared Ally's story with me. It broke my heart listening to him, but it was an honor. I wonder how a person ever gets over a loss like that. How much time is ever enough? I don't think I've ever really been in love, not the way Oliver and Ally were, so there's no way for me to know something like that. Then I start to ponder if I will ever find love like that. I hate that in this moment, the only man my mind can conjure up who could make me feel something close to that is one still in love with his dead wife.

I don't want to always be having deep, meaningful conversations with him because that will only up the ante of my feelings. The closer I get to him, the harder it will be to not blur lines. So if I mention paintball to him, even invite him along, that will be a way to see him, and it would be fun and casual, low-key.

—Actually a group of us are going to play paintball tomorrow. I've always wanted to try it. The weather has been so nice lately we thought we'd do something outdoors this weekend. How about you?

—I usually go to the gym on Saturday, but you're right about the weather. I'd rather work out outside when it's like this. I haven't played paintball in forever; it is a lot of fun. You will love it.

—You want to join us? I'm sure there's room for one more. It's at twelve thirty. We could get a late breakfast first, then go.

***

Oliver

I wasn't planning on texting Grace; I just did it without really thinking it through. Was I hoping she would want to see me this weekend? If I'm honest with myself, that's exactly what I wanted. Now I have her invitation right here in front of me, and I freeze up. What the hell, Oliver? It's a group thing, not a one-on-one thing, so it's perfect, really. Just what I need: a way to be around her and not be feeling like we're on a date.

—If you're sure I'm not intruding? It would be fun.

—Of course you aren't! You already met Tara and Kyle who are going. I don't know the other two people yet—they are friends of Kyle's. Do you want to do breakfast or just meet at paintball?

—Breakfast sounds good. I can pick you up if you want. I know a good diner I haven't been to in a long time.

—Great! I'll send you my address.

Just like that, we'll be together again tomorrow. Smiling to myself, I feel a bit like an addict who just arranged his next hit. It's been a week since I first sat on a barstool next to her and got the feeling I had met someone who would play some important part in my future. I can't help but wonder what she thinks of me.

At breakfast Grace asks me all about paintball, since I've played and she hasn't. I can tell she has a competitive side and plans to try and win.

"I've been to a shooting range lots of times, and I love that, so I know I can aim. It just sounds so fun with the way the course is set up and the teamwork and everything." Her enthusiasm brings a smile to my face.

"You are going to be vicious out there, I can tell. Glad we're on the same team. What led you to a shooting range? That seems a bit unusual for a Brooklyn girl."

"Oh well, that was with Matt, my awful ex. He was in the military before we were together and still loved going there, him and his buddies. I started joining them, and I just loved the adrenaline rush of it. I haven't gone since I ended things with him though. I don't want to run into him or any of them. I miss it."

"You shouldn't let him stop you. Maybe find a place farther away where he wouldn't be."

"I should; you're right. I have been distracted by other stuff lately, but I want to start having more fun. Life's too short to not do what you crave." I look at her, thinking she has no idea how true that statement is.

"I couldn't agree more." I tell her.

When we arrive and join the rest of our group, I'm a little surprised to see the two guys Kyle brought. Kyle is most definitely what I think of as a metro guy. Well groomed, stylish, and very hip. His college friends Sean and Mark, however, are decidedly "guy's guys". Muscled, big, and clearly here for more than paintball as they look over Tara and Grace. Sean is about my height but beefier, and he's wearing a T-shirt so tight I think it might bust open at the seams any minute. Well, someone wants his muscles noticed.

Mark is less obvious. He has a closely trimmed beard, and he is a bit shorter but no less well-built. Am I interrupting some kind of blind date setup? Grace surely wouldn't have invited me if that were the case, though, would she? I think about it for a minute and realize there is no reason she wouldn't. I have made it clear I'm not looking for anything but friendship. Crap, this isn't what I thought today would be like. A small part of my ego is feeling a bit bruised, and I find myself standing closer to her than strictly necessary. I can't help but hope they noticed she arrived in my car; I'm feeling petty like that.

We get assigned our gear and start going through the safety instructions and practicing. I notice that Mark has been staying close to Grace, making funny comments in her ear and giving her tips like he is some kind of pro. Sean and Tara flirt, and he doesn't even try to hide his interest or how handsy he is. Does that leave me and Kyle as a pair? Hell no.

"I hope that Mark isn't stepping on any toes." Kyle breaks into my thoughts just then.

"What do you mean? Why would he be?"

"Um, well I just noticed the scowl on your face and thought maybe you and Grace were here as more than friends. Mark isn't aware of that if it's the case, but I can let him know."

"No, we are just friends. Sorry, I don't mean to scowl. I guess I didn't realize today was a setup."

"Well, it's not. It just so happens that I have two girl friends and two guy friends. I didn't plan it to be a double date or anything."

"It's fine."

"OK, I can run interference between him and Grace if you want. Just say the word." He gives me a knowing look. I just give him a laugh to play it off.

"Don't worry about it, man. It's all good." At least Mark is more subtle than Sean, but I gather my thoughts and decide I can run my own interference. I come up behind Grace, place my hand on the small of her back and lean down to whisper in her ear.

"It seems they think you're a sweet innocent little thing, not the bloodthirsty shooting-range fiend you really are."

"Shhh, don't give me away. I want to be underestimated." She gives me a playful shove.

I just shake my head. "Evil, pure evil."

Mark clears his throat, giving me a quizzical look over her head. I know what he's asking, but I don't give him an answer. Instead, I keep talking to her like no one else is there. I've watched about as much flirting from that guy as I can take. I really wish Kyle had brought some geeky, ugly friends.

***

Grace

Tara loops her arm through mine and announces, "We're going to hit the ladies' room before we begin. Be right back." As soon as we're out of earshot, she turns to me and drops her mouth open dramatically. "Kyle has been holding out on us. What the hell? Those two are hot!"

"Yeah, they aren't bad." I have to agree with her; I wasn't expecting his friends to look like that. Mark is olive skinned with black hair and a close-trimmed beard that makes me wonder what kind of sensations it could create.

"Mark looks just like Mutt from *Schitt's Creek*!" she says, and I realize that's who he has been reminding me of.

Sean is a bit too flirtatious for my taste, but Tara doesn't seem to mind at all. He also reminds me of the military type too much for comfort, with his buzzed blond hair and skin-tight muscle shirt and cargo pants.

"It's too bad you brought Oliver though. Makes it a bit awkward for you to flirt with Mark," she points out.

"Who said I want to flirt? I am here for the game, believe it or not."

"Hmmm, not." We enter the bathroom, and I choose to ignore her comment. As I wash my hands, though, I do take a minute to make sure I look my best. Today has turned out a bit more intense than I planned, so I am not dressed as girly as I might have been. I wore an olive-green long-sleeve top and camo leggings with my comfiest hiking boots. My hair is in a low bun since I need to put a helmet on anyway. Tara looks much more feminine. I know she is more interested in flirting than winning, so that makes sense. Her hot-pink top and jeans are a good look.

"You aren't going to have a hard time impressing Sean." I tell her.

"I just hope he's not a sleazebag, but Kyle would warn us, right?"

"He better!"

"We'll have to corner him for more info later." She fluffs her hair and reapplies her lip gloss, then we head back out.

As we approach the guys, Oliver comes to my side immediately, and I see Mark glance between the two of us. It's clear he's confused as to what our relationship is. You aren't the only one, buddy, I think to myself. The worker comes over and asks if we are ready to begin. We are playing against another group of people, and we greet them briefly. Everyone gets into the protective gear, and we settle into our starting positions.

Once we actually start playing, I forget all about men and flirting. It's so much fun. I am a way better shot than anyone expected, and I am practically leading our team. Sean is definitely the most talented out of the guys, and we end up naturally taking over. Tara is the first out despite Sean trying to help her, then Kyle next. We get three of the opposite team's players out, and then I find myself hiding in a dugout ditch with Oliver. We lean our backs against the wall and take a breather.

"So Mark seems nice," he says suddenly.

"Oh yeah, I guess. Hard to tell in a few minutes, but he does, and Kyle's known him for years, so I'm sure he is."

"I wouldn't have come if I'd known I was interrupting a date for you."

"It isn't. I am here for the game. Kyle invited them." It's the truth.

"Mark seems to think something else."

"Well I told you I'm not trying to date. I can't help what he thinks. I am just out with a group of friends. That's it." It's a strange conversation to be having. Something about it feels much tenser than any of our other conversations ever have.

I lighten the mood by commanding, "Don't distract me anymore, Oliver. If you make me lose this game, I'll shoot you myself. I am here to win." Then I get up and start scoping out our next move. I hear him laughing behind me, then I hear a loud *plop*!

"Shit, I'm hit," he says.

"See? Distracted. It's not good," I point out smugly as I head out of my hiding spot.

It's down to me, Mark, and Sean now. I get the person who shot Oliver next.

"How many are left?" Sean asks as we regroup.

"Two," Mark and I both reply. He looks at me with a smile in his eyes, and I have to look away because now he's trying to distract me. These men.

"We need a plan." I tell Sean. At least he isn't flirting right now.

"OK. Grace, you're a damn good shot, by the way."

"Thanks. My ex was military, and we went shooting together," I admit.

"Should've figured," he snorts. "You go left with me, and Mark, you go right. We can come around behind them."

Mark gives him a look, then says, "I'll go with Grace."

"Dude, let's just win this first, then we can measure our dicks after, OK?" Sean just laughs and starts moving left, so I fall in with him.

"Jackass," I hear Mark mumble as he goes right. We only take another twenty minutes to wipe out the rest of the opposing team. The exhilaration of victory has us whooping and hollering. Sean lifts me up and spins around in celebration as the rest of our teammates head back out to join us in the win.

***

Oliver

Not only has Mark been buzzing around Grace like a bee to honey, but now as we head over to where the three survivors are celebrating, I see that Sean is all over her. I haven't felt these feelings of jealousy in more years than I can remember. As much fun as I have had today, I have also wanted to throw a few punches. Not that I have any right to feel that way about Grace. It pleases me immensely that as soon as her feet touch the ground, Grace puts space between herself and Sean. We all head back toward the shelter to enjoy some victory beers, and I'm gratified that she walks by my side again.

"This was so fun," she comments. "Did you enjoy it?" She looks over at me, and her beaming smile is contagious.

"I did. I just wish I hadn't let my distractedness get me out like that."

She chuckles. "Hopefully you last longer next time, Bekker."

"Oh, I can last." I throw back at her.

At that moment, unfortunately, Mark comes up on her other side to engage her in conversation. I listen as he compliments her aim and form. Yeah, I bet you like her form. It's glaringly obvious he's working toward asking her out, and I can't help but wonder what she'll say. She's single, after all, and even I have to admit he's good looking. She says she isn't looking to get into a relationship, but a date is just a date. The thought of the two of them going out, of them touching and kissing, is getting me angrier by the minute. I wonder if I can get her to make plans with me for tomorrow so she won't be available then, at least. As we crack open the first beers, I try to think of what I could invite her to do with me.

I go sit next to her. "What have you been reading lately?" She looks caught off guard by that but happy at the same time.

"Oh, you don't even want to know. It's a fantasy romance series, and it's embarrassingly addictive."

"I was serious about you finding me a good book, you know. I'm open to anything. You want to hit some bookstores together tomorrow?"

Her beer is halfway to her beautiful lips as she pauses. "You're serious?"

"Yes, I like reading. I used to read more, but I haven't been into it as much lately. I want to get back to things I enjoy. So help me out, won't you?"

"All right. I have a few favorite bookstores in different parts of the city. That would be fun."

"Good. I mostly like mysteries and thrillers. Maybe some sci-fi, but I'm open to new things too. Stock me up, Murphy."

She clinks her bottle against mine. "Deal."

Kyle comes over to us then and says, "Everyone is going to come back to my place after this, just to hang out for a while. You two coming?" Grace looks at me questioningly since we rode here together.

"I have to go visit my grandfather this evening, actually, but thank you for the invitation. Wherever you want to go, Grace, I'll bring you, of course."

"Well I'll just ride with Kyle, probably, but thank you. I'm so glad you were able to come do this, at least."

"Me too." I finish my beer and get up, ready to head off.

"I left my purse in your car, so I'll walk with you," Grace says. I say goodbye to the others, and we make our way to my Range Rover.

We both walk slowly, as if reluctant to have our time together come to an end. "If Mark asks you out, are you going to say yes?" I can't stop the words from coming out, as much as I know I should. We've reached my vehicle, and I lean my back against the passenger door, stopping her from being able to open it.

Grace looks at me. I can tell she is trying to understand why I'm asking. "I don't know. Why, Oliver?" She crosses her arms over her chest and doesn't back down in staring at me.

"I just wanted to know. I don't think he's right for you."

"Really, and what about him isn't right?"

I shrug. "Just a feeling I get."

Raising one eyebrow at me, Grace simply says, "OK, well, I'll certainly keep that nugget of wisdom in mind." She moves closer, reaching for the door handle near my hip. I don't move yet because I want her to be close. I want to smell her perfume again and see if her body reacts to me the way mine does to her. She's barely inches away now, and she looks up at me through her lashes, breathing heavily. "Are you going to let me get my stuff?" Her voice is quiet and moves over my skin like an actual touch. I just look down at her some more, using my body to say things my mouth isn't able to.

"I suppose I should." I say finally and move quickly until I'm standing behind her, and I open the door for her. I hear her give a small gasp at how close I am behind her, and a thrill runs through me knowing I do affect her. She bends down to get her purse from the floor, and suddenly the joke's on me because now I need to get away. Holy hell. I practically run to the driver's seat. As I get in, I notice a smirk on her face that tells me she's fully aware of my thoughts.

"Until tomorrow, then," she says and shuts the door. Well played, Grace Murphy.

What Becomes of the Brokenhearted

Grace

M ark did ask me out after a few hours of hanging out at Kyle's place. I told him that I just wasn't dating right now. He gave me a look that said he didn't really believe that for a second. I hope I don't regret turning him down, but it would hardly be fair to go out with him when my body was still on fire from that small encounter with Oliver in the parking lot earlier. It seems Mr. Bekker can't make up his mind, can't decide if he is still in mourning or not. I have to admit seeing him jealous made me feel giddy. I may have been with the others for the rest of the evening, but my mind was on him alone.

Walking around our third bookstore of the day, Oliver and I pass a shelf, and I notice one of my favorite books. Stopping, I take it out to admire this particular special edition.

"What's that one?" Oliver looks over my shoulder.

"It's one of my favorite love stories, a retelling of *Arabian Nights*. It's beautifully written, an enemies-to-lovers story, you know."

"Let's see what all the fuss is about." He takes it from my hands, opens to the middle, and starts reading out loud, "'What are you doing to me, you plague of a girl?' he whispered. 'If I am a plague, then you should keep your distance, unless you plan on being destroyed.' The weapons still in her grasp, she shoved against his chest. 'No.' His hands dropped to her waist. 'Destroy me.' The bow and arrow clattered to the ground as he brought his mouth to hers. And there was no turning back.'"

He clears his throat then, closing the book.

"See? It's beautiful," I say.

"I do see. Should I buy it?"

"I don't know. It's written for girls. It might be a bit too sappy for you."

"There's weapons in it. I think I can handle some sappiness. I'm going to buy it," he determines. That makes me laugh because I simply cannot picture this man reading such a romantic book. I reach past him and pick up the sequel, placing it on top of the other book.

"Well then, you have to buy the second one also, because it ends on a cliffhanger."

"Done."

I just shake my head at him. "You never cease to surprise me."

By five o'clock we have been to six different bookstores, and Oliver has about twelve new books. They are mostly thrillers and some sci-fi, but he also has the two romance ones that still make me chuckle. I, of course, had to buy some too; it's literally impossible for me not to.

"It's a good thing you decided to drive today," I comment. "Can you imagine if we had to walk around with all these books?"

"Do you usually order them online, or you always buy them in person?"

"I do both. I think it's important to support the local bookstores, though, because they are in danger of becoming obsolete if Amazon has its way."

He nods in agreement then looks at me in expectation. "So where to next?"

"I think that's enough books to last you a while. Are you hungry?" All we've had for the last few hours is some coffee, so I could definitely eat.

"I am. You know, we are pretty close to my place. Want to come help me put my books away, and I'll cook us something?"

"Are you sure? I feel like I've taken up a lot of your time lately."

"You mean I've been making you spend a lot of time with me, more like. It's me who can't stop asking you to do things with me." There's a moment of awkward silence at that.

Trying to not let his words have too much effect on me, I feign nonchalance. "Sure, let's go to your place."

When we arrive at Oliver's apartment, I find it's very stylish and comfortable. The brown leather sofa and chairs are obviously high quality because they are as soft as butter. The colors of everything are very modern: lots of black, white, and gray. It has the look of once having been decorated by a woman but falling back toward bachelor style now. Remnants of the feminine touch remain: throw pillows with bright flowers along with matching curtains, ornaments, and knickknacks here and there.

"I haven't had anyone in here but my family in as long as I can remember." Oliver is scratching the back of his neck, looking around as if wondering what he should do next.

"It's a really nice place."

"Thanks. Can I get you a drink? Wine or whiskey, or I have nonalcoholic options, too, of course."

"I think just water for now, thanks."

He goes into the kitchen, which is open to the rest of the main living area, and I start taking his new books out, placing them onto his coffee table.

"I was thinking of making omelets. Is that OK?" he calls out from where he stands looking into the open refrigerator.

"That's perfect. I love breakfast food."

"Good. Make yourself at home. I usually put on music when I cook. Do you have any requests?"

"That's what I do too. Anything you listen to is good. I like all kinds of music."

Oliver turns on his TV, opening up the Pandora channel, and starts one entitled Motown. The first song that starts playing is "What Becomes of the Brokenhearted" by Jimmy Ruffin.

"Good choice. I love this." I settle back into the deep couch, pulling my legs up as I flip through some of the books we picked out today. The sound of chopping in the kitchen is so soothing, and between that and the fabulous old songs, I'm fully relaxed.

I'm singing along to "Ain't No Mountain High Enough" when a laugh startles me. Oliver is standing in front of me, holding two wine glasses and a bottle, just looking at me.

"What's so funny?" I ask.

"You were really into that song. I have been standing here for like two minutes, and you didn't even notice."

"It's a classic. I can't help myself," I say defensively, flushing slightly.

"This is true. Look, I'm not going to force you to drink, but this pinot noir goes well with what I'm making, so I will leave it here." Placing it down, he walks back, still smiling at my singing. Well that is just going to make me sing louder. I may not sing well, but I do it with enthusiasm.

I pour myself a glass of wine, because pinot noir happens to be my favorite red, and get up to walk around the living room, looking at the few books that are on the shelves. There is a scattering of ones by Michael Crichton and some biographies, along with a couple by an author I also love.

"You read Blake Crouch?" I ask, heading toward the kitchen.

Oliver looks up from plating the food. "I do, yeah. He's good."

"I agree, *Dark Matter* is my favorite that I've read so far. I think it's brilliant."

"That one was my favorite too. The ending really got me."

"I think I finally believe that you like reading. I thought you might be just saying it." I give a small laugh.

"You thought I was just trying to impress you, huh?" He grins at me wickedly.

"You wouldn't be the first man to pretend to be interested in something, but I know you aren't like that."

"I might not be as noble as you seem to think, Grace. But the reading isn't a lie. Dinner is ready." He holds up two beautifully arranged plates, each containing an omelet and a small side of sautéed potatoes with herbs.

"Wow, that is impressive. No wonder the smells have been so mouthwatering," I say, examining the meal he made for us.

"Let's eat on the couch. It's more comfortable."

As the first bite hits my tongue, I can't help but let out a little moan. "Oh my god, Oliver. This is amazing. You're a real chef. So many hidden talents."

***

Oliver

When that moan escapes her lips, I almost choke on my wine. Almost. I somehow manage to contain myself, but for goodness sake. Does this girl have no clue what kind of effect she has on men? I haven't heard a noise like that coming from a real, live woman since Ally. I have to swallow hard and focus on my food.

"Thanks. I have always liked cooking. I don't have a huge repertoire, but I can make a few things pretty well," I finally manage to answer her.

"I saw Ally's picture. She was really beautiful." She nods toward the bookcase next to the fireplace, where there is a shelf of framed photos.

"She was. I was a lucky guy. When we first started dating in high school, I couldn't believe she liked a guy like me."

"Did you look very different back then?" she asks quizzically.

"Puberty was not my best friend. Acne and awkwardness were more my thing until about seventeen. That's when things got better. Besides the fact that I liked math a lot, I was even in a math club." I can't help but laugh at the recollection.

"Well, everything definitely worked out in your favor in the end."

"How about you? What kind of girl were you in high school?"

"Oh boy, I was trouble. I was boy-crazy and rebellious. And artsy. I was always part of the arts and drama crowds."

"I can only imagine."

"My freshman year I got suspended for breaking into the school at night with my boyfriend to graffiti the gym, mocking the jocks. I was so stupid back then."

"Sounds like you were fun and possibly a bit misled."

"Well I can't quite claim to be misled. I was the instigator." She snort-laughs then.

"Grace Murphy, you were trouble." I give her a mock reprimand.

Shrugging, she just says, "I acted out a lot. I hated my family and really just couldn't wait till high school was over and I could leave."

"You turned out pretty wonderful after all the teenage angst. I guess with enough time we all figure out who we are." We eat in comfortable silence for a while then, letting The Temptations and the Four Tops serenade us.

The wine goes down easily, and the more of it I have, the more I want to ask Grace what happened with Mark after I left them all yesterday. I know it's not any of my business, but I haven't stopped wondering. I try to bring it up in a casual manner.

"So did you have fun at Kyle's last night?"

"It was fine. We just hung around and talked, really."

That's not nearly enough information for my taste. "Did Mark ever work up the nerve to ask you out?"

"Eventually, yes." She is really going to make me ask her, isn't she? I wait, hoping she will elaborate. When she never does, I can't take it.

"And you said?"

"I told him I'm not really dating right now. He didn't seem to believe me though." She sips her wine and looks at me. Her green eyes give no indication of what she is thinking right now.

"I doubt he'll give up so easily," I say. She lets out a heavy sigh then. I can sense her frustration with me.

"I'm sorry for prying. It's none of my business, I know."

"It's not that. I just wish I knew why it matters to you."

I drink the remaining wine in my glass and pour more. "I don't know myself; it just does."

"That isn't much of a clarification." She reaches out to refill her own glass. I gather our empty plates and carry them into the kitchen, needing something to do. My mind races with contradictions. I want to touch this woman, I want to tell her to stay away from every other man, and I want to see her every single day. At the same time, I'm not ready yet, am I? I look down at the gold ring I still can't manage to stop wearing and close my eyes.

"Ally, what should I do?" I ask in my head. I'm incredibly attracted to Grace. I keep finding excuses to touch her; I know I do. I also want to protect her and make her see how beautiful and amazing she is. But is it fair that I try and do all of that if I am still hung up on my dead wife? I give myself a shake and tell myself to stop thinking so much all the time. Live in the moment, Oliver. We only get so many.

When I return to the couch, I sit closer to her than I was before. My body is turned sideways, practically encompassing hers. I know it's the wine and the jealous thoughts making me act this way. I lay my arm across the back of the couch behind Grace. Her face gets a little pinker at that, a fact I find adorable.

"I try not to care, Grace. There's just something about you." Lifting my wine, I never lose eye contact with her as I take another drink.

"But you aren't ready?"

"I don't know. I still think about Ally all the time. I need to figure out what to do about that," I admit candidly.

"Then maybe I should go." She shifts a little. The move causes our bodies to touch just the slightest bit more, but it's like an electric shock.

"Not yet. Please." I place a hand on her shoulder, trying to hold her here. Her head falls back, and she closes her eyes, clearly fighting something. I can't think of anything at that moment, though, because her neck is stretched out in front of me, and all I can think is how I want to bury my face in it, devouring all that creamy skin.

The opening notes of Mavin Gaye's "Let's Get It On" blare out of my TV speakers right at that moment. Grace's eyes fly open, and we simultaneously burst into laughter. I get up, and she does too.

"I'm going to go, Oliver. Really, it's for the best."

"OK. You're probably right," I concede at last. That was a bit of a wake-up call. If I'm not ready, why am I trying to play with fire? Because I'm a jealous asshole.

"I'm going to order an Uber. Can I just use your bathroom first?"

"Of course. It's that door there on the left," I point it out. Grace leaves as quickly as she can, thanking me again for dinner. I know I've crossed a line with her again, and it isn't fair. I need to get a grip on my behavior with this woman.

**

Grace

Monday, Tuesday, and Wednesday all pass with very minimal contact between Oliver and me. At night is the hardest because when I'm not busy, my mind wanders to him constantly. I don't help myself either. I spray the cologne I bought on my pillow because sleeping with that smell is so very satisfying. That moment on his couch Sunday night consumes my thoughts. I wonder what he would do if I made a move? I won't, though, because I don't want to be a regret he has to purge from his life the morning after. It would kill me.

It's my usual Wednesday night in. I have an episode of *Stranger Things* playing on the TV even though I'm not really watching it. I scroll through various things on my phone, and I think of him despite myself. As I scroll through Instagram, I come across a picture of Oliver's living room with one of the books we bought together and a glass of some amber-colored liquor. The caption says, "Inspired to read again. One of life's greatest pleasures." I smile at that. I'm so glad he's finding joy in little things again. He feels like a different man entirely than the one I met that first night we talked in Las Flores. I press "Like," then send him a DM through the app.

—Is the book good?

A few seconds later, his reply is there.

—It is. I started it Monday, and I'll probably finish it tonight. I forgot how great it feels to get lost in a story.

—It's the best feeling in the world, I swear.

—Have you had a good week?

—Pretty average. Just working. You?

—It's been the same for me, but at least now I have a good book at night. Thanks to you.

I exit out of the app abruptly then. I hate that every nice thing Oliver says to me seems to make me feel things I really don't want to be feeling. Why can't I just enjoy knowing this man without my dense heart trying to ruin everything? I send a text to Tara instead.

—You busy?

—Nope. What's up?

—My head is all jumbled. I need to talk. Want to meet up for a drink?

—Sure! O'Malley's in half an hour?

—Yes, thanks!

I get up, thankful I have a friend who can be as spontaneous as me. Throwing on some jeans and a hoodie over my tank top, I head to the Irish pub that's halfway between my place and Tara's. We settle in at the bar with our drinks, and I just dive right in.

"I am so confused by what Oliver wants from me. I mean, he isn't cryptic or anything like that. It's just that he's confused."

"He wasn't acting all that confused on Saturday," she snorts. "I thought he might punch Mark at one point, I swear."

"That's the thing: he basically told me he didn't want me to go out with Mark. At the same time, he makes it clear he isn't ready for anything and isn't over Ally. Then Sunday night he practically pounced on me on his couch—until he didn't. Then he was just done."

"Wait a minute. Why were you on his couch Sunday night?"

"We were out book shopping, and then we got hungry. He said we were right near his apartment and he would cook something, so we went there."

"So you basically spent the whole weekend together? But you're just friends?"

"Yes." I throw back the reminder of my drink because this isn't helping clarify anything.

"What about Mark?" Tara asks then.

"What about him?" I retort, confused.

"He is available and interested, not to mention damn hot. Why do I need to spell this out to you?"

"I have feelings for Oliver. How are you not understanding that?" I shoot back.

She just shakes her head sadly. "But look what that's doing for you: making you crazy. He can't decide what he wants or where he is in his life. How is that fair to you?"

"So I should just use Mark to try and get over him? That isn't fair to Mark."

"He probably wouldn't mind as much as you think."

"OK, well I came here to talk about Oliver, so can we just leave Mark out of it? Anyway, I already turned him down when he asked me out."

She looks at me like I have sprouted two extra heads. "Oh, tell me you didn't!"

"Of course I did. Speaking of that night, whatever happened with you and Sean?" Turning the tables onto her love life seems like a good idea right about now.

"Well we flirted, and he took my number, but I haven't heard from him, so I guess he didn't really like me after all." She shrugs it off.

"I'm sorry. I thought he really liked you."

"I think he really likes flirting. Maybe he could tell I'm not really a one-night stand type and that's all he was looking for; who knows? This city makes meeting good men seem literally impossible sometimes."

"Hear! Hear!" I raise my drink to that, and we both laugh.

"Maybe you should just try seducing Oliver. Once he succumbs, he'll realize he *can* get over Ally."

"Absolutely not! That is the worst idea in the world. He would regret it, and I'd ruin our friendship. If anything is ever going to happen between us, it will have to start with him. Only he will know when he's ready. In the meantime, I do want to stay friends. I love being with him. It is good for him too. He seems so much livelier and happier."

"Well just be prepared if you are determined to stick this through. You may end up hurt."

"I know," I groan and lay my head down on the bar. "We just need to avoid being alone in these intimate situations together. What can we do that won't get my foolish heart thinking amorous thoughts?"

"Well paintball was pretty good. It just brought out his jealousy, so that was a bit of a problem." She makes a good point: if the whole Mark situation hadn't been a factor, the paintballing was perfect.

"You're right. My usual go-to things for fun are adrenaline-pumping activities. That's always been my thing. I love a thrill. I bet it would be a good distraction for him, too, something diverting and active. I will stick to those types of outings; they will be good for both of us."

She switches to a more serious tone of voice then, pinning me with a look. "In the meantime, if you were to meet someone else, would you please just consider not rejecting them without even trying to give them a chance? I mean, what if he never gets over Ally? Will you stay single forever?"

"I'll think about it, yes. You make a valid point."

"I'm smarter than I look." She gives me a hug. We finish our drinks and head home. I think of some of the fun things I could do with Oliver that I consider "safe." So far it's always been him who initiates a conversation or an invitation, so I want to be the one to do it this time. Even though it's almost ten thirty, I consider texting him with my idea and decide to just do it.

—I want to take you somewhere fun and exciting next weekend. What do you say?

—I like fun. Are you going to tell me where?

—Nope. I want you to put yourself in my hands. Trust me?

—I trust you, but please be gentle.

—Big baby!

—OK, I surrender to you. Just tell me where to be and when.

—Deal. We have to get an early start Saturday, driving to Montauk. I'll pick you up, and you're in charge of coffee. I take mine black.

—Wow, OK. I like the sound of that. I haven't gotten away from the city in a long time.

I can't believe he agrees so easily to my plan without even knowing what I'm going to make him do. When he hears where I'm taking him, he may not feel so willing, but I guess we'll have to wait and see about that. He seems a little strait-laced, and I'm dying to see what happens if I pull on those

laces a little. I'm brimming with excitement now just thinking of this more and more: going somewhere entertaining
with him where we won't get all bogged down with heartfelt
moments like what keeps happening with us. We can just let
loose and relax, have fun together.

Dangerous Waters

Oliver

I'm waiting down on the sidewalk in front of my building with our coffees when Grace pulls up in a green Mini Cooper. When she comes to a stop, the top of the car barely reaches my waist, and I wonder how in the hell I'm going to fit in this sardine can.

I open the door and just look at her. "Um, Grace, do you think we should take my car?"

"What? Why?"

"Because I don't think I can physically fit in this thing," I laugh.

"Seriously? Let me push the seat all the way back and just try it." I hand her the coffees and start folding my body in half.

"OK, I'll try, but I'm bigger than you think."

"That's what all the men say," she jokes.

"Yeah, but for some of us it's true."

"Hmph." She makes a doubtful face at me. I manage to get in, and it's actually not as awful as I thought it would be with the seat pushed all the way back.

"All right fine, I fit in your tiny car. Let's go." I smirk.

"You sure you'll be OK, big guy? It is a long ride."

"I can handle it." We seriously need to change the subject because this entire ridiculous conversation is making me think dirty thoughts, and I need to not be doing that today. She just laughs and pulls out.

"OK I've been living in suspense for two days, and it's killing me. Are you going to tell me what we're doing today?"

"Not yet, it's a surprise! That's part of the fun. But...I can't stop you from guessing."

"Guessing, huh? I can do that. Well, we could be going to the beach, but that wouldn't really be a surprise, would it? So sailing?"

"No, not sailing, but a boat is involved at one point."

"Interesting. Give me a hint."

"OK, it will give you an adrenaline rush."

"Water skiing?"

"Nope."

"OK, deep-sea fishing?"

"How in the world do you think fishing gives you an adrenaline rush? It's one of the most boring things ever!"

"You've clearly never tried to reel in a giant swordfish."

"Oh, well that is true. I guess that's different. Still, we aren't going fishing."

"I'm at a loss. I don't know what you have in mind."

"Good! Just sit back and relax and let me steer today. I promise you'll have fun." She looks over at me with a brilliant grin, like it's giving her inexplicable joy to surprise me. So I decide to stop trying to figure things out and do as she says.

I drink my coffee with the window down and enjoy the breeze from the beautiful day. Grace has her music playing as she drives, and it's cute watching her sing along to all the songs as she sips on her coffee. It's peaceful and relaxing. I know my sunglasses are dark, so I use this opportunity to look at her unabashedly out of the side of my eye, hoping she can't tell that's what I'm doing. Her hair is braided back in two braids tight against her head. She's wearing a cute little black halter top and tight capris running pants. She seems so relaxed, and I can tell I'm seeing the most carefree side of Grace, enjoying her day off. I've heard about ten songs playing from her phone by now, and I can't help but laugh at the crazy variety. It goes from Dua Lipa to Elton John to Queen to Billie Eilish to Bob Marley to AC/DC.

"I'm getting whiplash from this playlist, I swear," I laugh.

"Oh, you haven't heard anything yet! Wait until NSYNC pops up."

"Oh god, no. Spare me, please, no boy bands!" I groan overdramatically.

"Hey, my car, my tunes."

"Yet another reason I will be driving next time."

"Rude." She chuckles and shakes her head at me. "And what kind of old man tunes would we be listening to if you were in charge of being DJ? Smooth jazz?"

"Not quite. I'm not an old man, thank you very much. I actually like a lot of this stuff you're playing. I just enjoy teasing you; it's too fun."

"Well my whole goal is for you to have fun today, so tease away. I'll take it."

Just then the next song to come on happens to be one of my all-time favorites: "Here Comes the Sun" by the Beatles. I reach over and turn up the volume.

"Now this is what I'm talking about. One of my favorite songs ever."

"Me too. I love the Beatles, but especially *Abbey Road*." And we both sing every word to the song as the sun shines on us. The words feel meaningful to this moment for me somehow. I can't help but feel like meeting Grace brought sunlight back into my life. I do feel like the ice is slowly melting in my heart. I also feel a little foolish for thinking these things, and yet at the same time, I don't care because I'm truly happy right now.

We stop for a quick breakfast at a diner about halfway there. By the time we arrive in Montauk, I am dying of curiosity for what she has planned for my adrenaline-pumping day. Then she pulls down a side road, and I see the sign. She is insane.

"Shark diving?" I look at her incredulously. Is she kidding?

"Have you ever done it?"

"Well, I've never been suicidal, so no."

"It's perfectly safe, and it's exciting!"

"Grace, I'm starting to worry about your sanity."

She guffaws, throwing her head back, and I swear her eyes are sparkling more than ever before. She is absolutely loving this. I feel the competitive side of me rise up. No way am I going to chicken out in front of this girl. I may think this is insane, but she clearly loves this kind of thing, and I am not going to look like the boring almost-forty-year-old who isn't up for an adventure. Instead I rub my hands together and say, "All right, bring on Jaws. Let's do this."

"Really!?" She looks triumphant. "You'll try it?"

"I'll try anything once." I shrug. Not true at all, but hey, I want to seem cool right now, so I'll go with that. I've been this sad guy who just mourned and survived for too long. Since meeting Grace I feel like a new person, one who isn't surviving but living, and it's exhilarating.

"Yay!" She celebrates her victory. "I called ahead, and they're ready for us. They rent the wet suits to us and have the air tanks and everything we need. We just have to get in the cage."

"Oh, just get in the cage, is that all? The flimsy little cage, and let them attract all the big bad sharks in the area over?" I'm also starting to doubt my own sanity at this point.

"I love sharks. They're so misunderstood. I know they can be deadly, but they're also magnificent. The first time I did this, the sense of awe I felt was amazing."

"So is danger your thing?" I ask as we get out of the car.

"I guess, kind of. I've always loved things that get the heart pumping and make you really feel alive. Even if it's just roller coasters, zip lining, or the more extreme stuff. It's also addictive, once you get a taste for it."

"You really would have gotten along with Ally." I shake my head. Those two would have been trouble together.

"Well she was clearly a woman of good taste." She gives me a sexy little smirk, and I can't help but wonder if she's talking about me. I can't help but hope that she is.

"Let's go be suicidal, crazy girl." I hold out my hand to her, and she takes it with a chuckle.

"So dramatic, old man."

"OK, if you are going to insist on calling me that, I'm going to need you to tell me how old you are. I'm fairly certain I'm not *that* much older than you."

"I'm a very youthful thirty-four. But age isn't about the number. It's about attitude, and you definitely fall into the 'grumpy old man' category," she teases.

"So I'm literally five years older than you, and you call me old man?"

"Stick with me, and I'll have you feeling young in no time." She winks.

"All right, then." I feel all sorts of things when I'm with her; no denying that.

The old man with the scruffy white beard looks like he did just step out of the movie *Jaws*. This guy is in charge of our safety for the day? Great. We're going to die. We get all the rules, watch the instruction video, change into our wet-suits, and practice using our air tanks. Now apparently we're ready; yeah, right. This boat taking us out into the sea has most definitely seen better days, and I can't help but feel like I'm at the beginning of a horror movie. You know the kind where you say, "They are such idiots. They're clearly going to get eaten by the sharks out there," and shovel the popcorn in your mouth while you wait for the blood and gore to start. I swear, if Grace weren't so damn cute and compelling, I would have put my foot down and said we're going to the beach in-stead. But no, here I am trying to act cool and collected, like I don't want to shit myself over what we're about to do. I also get the feeling that she would do this with or without me, and the thought of her doing it alone is not OK.

I look over at her laughing with White Beard, completely relaxed and excited about this. She looks stunning in her wet suit, and all the guys working on the boat wanted to "help" her get on. Pretty audacious, considering they don't know that she isn't my girlfriend. So yeah, I'm not leaving her side for a minute for multiple reasons. Not that she can't take care of herself, but men are dogs. Is that completely sexist and wrong of me to think? I don't give a shit. I get up and head over to where Grace is being entirely too flirty with the guys.

"How long till we get to where they drop the cage?" I ask her, drawing her attention away from those lecherous creeps.

"Should be there soon. Are you excited?"

"Yeah, sure, I'm excited. I'm also glad I have all my affairs in order, and at least I'm not going to die alone. I'll take you with me," I joke.

"I can hold your hand the whole time. I think you'll enjoy it once you get down there." She pats my chest, then takes my hand and twines her fingers through mine. I can't help but feel a sense of smug satisfaction as all the men who have been drooling over her take note of our entwined hands.

I lean in close and whisper in her ear, "Promise not to let go of me?" I don't know what possessed me to do that, but I don't regret it either. She looks up at me and nods in agreement, not saying anything out loud, but her eyes are saying a lot. Then her tongue comes out, and she licks her lips and swallows audibly. I realize I'm standing so close to her that she might actually be able to feel the physical reaction my cock has to what she just did, so I quickly shift sideways. Damn, she is too sexy. How am I supposed to be able to concentrate on not getting eaten by sharks right now?

"This is the spot," White Beard announces, breaking the moment between Grace and me. I'm relieved that we're here. Now I can try to distract my dick, and maybe it will behave itself.

My heart has probably never raced as fast as it is now as I'm preparing to jump into the cage in the water. I swear

I'm having an out-of-body experience because I do not do this kind of thing. Then Grace's small hand grips mine, and her fingers slide between mine, and our eyes lock. One, two, three—we jump. The cage door splashes down over our heads and is secured. Grace gives my hand a reassuring squeeze and a thumbs-up as the cage slowly lowers. The stillness and quiet of the water settles around us like a weight. It's bone chilling in its intensity, and Grace isn't wrong; I haven't felt an adrenaline rush this strong ever. There are no sharks in sight yet, but I can sense that they're getting closer, and I start to panic. I must be crushing Grace's hand with the death grip I have on it because she shakes it a little, indicating I need to let up. Then she must notice the sheer terror in my eyes, because she moves in front of me and pulls both of my arms around her, entwining all ten of our fingers and bringing our bodies as close together as possible. Her back is to my front, and I can feel her calm seeping through to me.

Like this we are directly in the middle of the cage instead of how spread out we felt side by side. I start to calm down gradually, focused completely on how perfectly her body fits into mine. I'm holding her so tight she can probably feel my heart pounding out of my chest. Then I feel her hand pat my arm, and she points outward into the water. I look and notice the shadows in the water all around the cage. They move closer, and they are sleek and beautiful. With Grace in my arms, I don't feel the dread I thought I would at seeing them. Instead I'm admiring their strength and elegant movements. Grace looks over her shoulder at me, her eyes full of delight, and I nod in agreement at the wonder of it all. They look peaceful, not aggressive as they glide by quietly. I can't help but marvel at how thrilling it is to see these magnificent creatures up close like this.

Once we are back on the deck of the boat, I feel a sense of elation. I conquered a fear, and it was glorious. I'm speechless, but I'm laughing because that was amazing. Grace is grinning from ear to ear, and we look at each other and just hug because it feels right.

"That was out of this world, Grace. You are insane, and I think I love it." I lift her off her feet and swing her around.

"I knew you'd enjoy it Oliver!" she squeals happily. Her arms are around my neck, and I realize I'm just holding her now. I don't want to let go, but I do. I step back deliberately and shake the water out of my hair like a wet dog. One of the guys working on the boat brings us towels. He lingers near Grace, asking if she needs anything else. I regret putting distance between us now, so I head over to her and grab her hand, leading her to a bench along the back of the boat, and we settle in to enjoy the ride back. I make sure I sit close and have my arm around her back.

"So what other crazy things should I try next?" I ask her.

"Really? You want to do other stuff like this?" She sounds shocked.

"Yes, I do. It felt amazing. I was absolutely terrified, and then I wasn't, and I felt like I could do anything. I can't explain it well, but I felt so alive!"

"I told you: it's addictive."

"I can tell." I'm looking at her, and all I can think is she's addictive. I don't know what I'm going to do with myself because I wasn't planning on her. I wasn't ready to be over Ally and meet someone new; at least I didn't think I was. I'm twisting the gold band on my third finger of my left hand as I look down and ponder this. My wedding ring to my Ally.

Grace looks at the ring I'm playing with. "Are you missing her now?" she asks.

"I should have done stuff like this with her. If I had known our time was limited, I would have made sure she experienced everything life had to offer. We thought we had all the time in the world. We were just so caught up with work and life and saving money for our future. Sometimes I wonder if I made her as happy as I could have."

"I am sure she was one of the happiest women ever. Do you have any idea how rare men like you are, Oliver? Ally hit the love jackpot, and she knew it, I'm sure. That's what all women dream of: a man who is faithful and loving. I can see in your eyes how much you loved her, and I know she was a lucky girl because of it."

"I hope she knew how much I loved her."

Grace takes my hand. "She did. A woman knows."

For a few minutes we just sit in silence, each lost in our own thoughts, as the sound of the water slapping the sides of the boat adds a sense of peace to the moment. The feeling of Grace's hand in mine is perfect, even though it's right over my wedding band. Before my mind can take that thought too far I decide to change the subject.

"No more sad talk," I say suddenly as I get up, pulling Grace to her feet also. "What's the plan for the rest of today? Dinner? We should definitely have seafood before we head back to the city."

"Sounds wonderful. I know a great place."

When Sparks Fly, People Get Burned

Grace

As the boat pulls back into the marina, I notice that Oliver has unzipped his wetsuit down to the waist, and I really want to get a good, long look at his torso; I can't deny it. I try to act busy collecting things and getting ready to get off the boat, but I'm just ogling the man. He's well built in a way that I didn't expect from a businessman. And he's inked. I don't know why, but I especially did not expect that. I can never resist a man with tattoos, and his are gorgeous and only accentuate the dips and swells of his muscles more. I can see some words on the left side of his chest over his heart, but I'm not close enough to read them. I wonder if they say something about Ally. On one shoulder there is a beautiful, artistic tree. Along the right side of his rib cage is more writing I can't read from here. My hand itches to run over that ink and read what's there.

Then he turns away, and I gasp because his back has the most gorgeous, sexiest tattoo I've ever seen. Large black wings appear to be sprouting out of his shoulder blades and dip down each side of his back, all the way to below where I can see past the wetsuit. Well damn, Oliver, you are a dark horse.

I quickly look away because I need to not look at that back anymore. My mouth is practically watering as it is. I need to get a handle on myself before I have to talk to him in intelligent sentences again. I give myself a mental shake and try to erase the image from my mind; yeah, that's never going to happen. I will be thinking about those tats later. Shit.

"Ready?"

I hadn't even noticed that everyone was waiting for me as I pretended to be busy.

"Yeah. Yup." Smooth, Grace, very smooth. Just avoid eye contact with him. When I do meet his eyes, they have a smirk in them that tells me he totally knows I was checking him out. Well he was practicing parading it around—it's hardly my fault! Oh boy, he does not want to challenge me to this game, because I am a master. I know I have my cutest bikini on under this wetsuit. I could easily distract him as much as he did me. However, out of respect for that gold ring he still chooses to wear, I'm not doing it. Not yet, anyway. But if he keeps it up, I may start playing. I noticed how many times he cockblocked all the flirty guys working on the boat. I would have had to be blind to not notice. This man is seriously confused about his feelings, and so I'm not going to push it. If anything is going to change between us, it will have to come from him. Only he will know when he's truly ready to move on from Ally. That's not a call I would ever try to make for someone. Keep reminding yourself that, Grace, I practically scream in my mind. I need to behave.

We get back to the main building, where we change and head for the car. I still feel awkward that I got caught admiring his body so obviously, so I've barely said anything.

"That comedown from the adrenaline dump has me starving," Oliver says, breaking the silence.

"The restaurant isn't far," I say.

"I need a stiff drink too," he huffs out.

"You enjoy. I'll make sure I only have one beer so I can drive us back."

"That seems unfair, not to mention you're going to be exhausted for that long drive. Maybe we should stay over somewhere tonight." My mind starts to panic at that a little; I was trying to avoid intimate situations with him.

"I wonder if we could even find anything. It seems pretty busy out here."

"Let me look online. If you don't mind staying tonight, that is. I'll pay for it. I don't want you driving tired, and I want you to relax and enjoy dinner and drinks. After everything you treated me to today, it's the least I can do."

I can feel my mouth getting dry, and my brain is spinning with all the reasons why this could be a really bad idea, but he's also right. We are both tired, and that doesn't make for safe driving.

"I should have thought this through better, huh?" I say, feeling a little guilty since this day was all my idea. "No way, you planned a great day. I think we're just going to be beat. I'll find us something."

"OK." I don't protest because it's the responsible thing to do. I just concentrate on getting us to the restaurant while Oliver is busy on his phone.

Driftwood is one of my favorite beachside restaurants. The deck on the back where most of the tables are hangs out over the water, and there is always a salty breeze. We get to our table and order our drinks.

"I'll be right back." Oliver gets up and heads back inside. I lean back in my chair and try to relax and not worry about staying somewhere overnight with Oliver. It's not like we'll be sharing a room or anything. The waiter brings my martini and Oliver's whiskey, and with the first sip, I start to relax. I close my eyes and just breathe in the briny air and the smell of seafood.

"I found us a place. It's above a bar down the street. The manager here helped me out. You're right: almost everything is filled up already. I checked, and there's also a pharmacy nearby we can stop at to grab some toothbrushes and things before we head over."

"Wow, you thought of everything. Thank you, that sounds great."

"It's all within walking distance, too, so if we have a few drinks, we can just leave the car here. The manager said that isn't a problem. There's only one tiny hitch." He takes a sip of his whiskey then, looking slightly uncomfortable.

"What's that?"

"It's just the one room; that's all I could find. Everything else is full. There is a queen-size bed, but I asked for extra blankets, so I can sleep on the floor. I don't want you to think I'm trying to be sneaky or anything. I can even sleep in the car if you'd prefer."

"Oliver, you barely fit in the car sitting upright. You aren't sleeping there." I give him a look like he's being insane. "I appreciate you offering, but I trust you. One room is completely fine. Don't worry." I sip more of my martini. Maybe some liquid courage will make me believe I'm as relaxed as I sound.

"Oh, thank god. That car is tiny," he says, clearly relieved I'm not going to make him sleep in my Mini. "No offense. It's a great city car, and it's perfect for you, but no grown man could sleep in that thing and not end up in traction." I laugh at that, just trying to picture Oliver squished into the impossibly small backseat of my car.

"I should have pretended to want you to sleep in the car just so I could watch you try to fit yourself in it," I say.

"Very funny," he deadpans. We order another round of drinks and settle in for a relaxing dinner.

Between the delectable seafood, strong drinks, and easy-on-the-eyes company, I can't remember ever enjoying an evening more in my entire life. We don't talk about anything sad or heavy, not tonight. We laugh; we just talk about anything and everything. By my third martini, I know I'm buzzed, but I am still well aware of everything going on, so I decide I've reached the sweet spot, and it's the perfect time to stop. Oliver seems so serene and carefree; he must be feeling his drinks as well. He tries to pay the whole bill, but I insist on going Dutch since he's paying for the room. It's a sublime night out as we stroll down the street toward the pharmacy.

"It's so nice to be out of the city and see the stars like this," I say, looking up at the blanket of sparkling diamonds all above us.

"It is. I haven't felt this laid-back for years. Thank you for getting me to do this today." He reaches for my hand, and we keep walking while holding hands.

"Um, excuse me?" We turn at the sound of a voice behind us. It's a teenage guy.

"Are you guys going in the pharmacy?" he asks us.

"Yeah," Oliver answers him suspiciously and ever-so-slightly moves in front of me. Ridiculous man. I could kick that scrawny teenager's butt easily, but it's cute he thinks he's protecting me.

"Would you do me a favor, man? If I give you cash, will you buy me a pack of condoms?"

"Why? You don't have to be a certain age to buy them," Oliver says, annoyed.

"It's not that. It's because my aunt is the cashier. I can't face her buying those."

I let out a very unladylike snort. "Sorry. That's not funny. I mean it is, but I didn't mean to laugh at you," I say.

"How old are you?" Oliver looks him over.

"Eighteen, and my girlfriend is too. We just need help because of my aunt, that's all."

"All right, dude, whatever. Give me the money."

"Thank you so much, man. You are saving my night!"

"What kind do you want?" Oliver asks.

"Um, I don't know, like the best for not knocking her up, you know."

"Oh dear god," I hear him mumble under his breath as we head into the store. I'm really trying to fight back my giggle fit that I can feel coming on, but I don't want to look like that drunk lady laughing loudly for no apparent reason. I head for the aisle with the travel-size toiletries and pick out what we will need for tonight. When I meet Oliver back at the registers, there's a pack of Trojans on the counter, and I add the rest of our stuff next to it. The cashier is a middle-aged redhead who apparently likes to chat. She comments that we must be from out of town and staying over, then wants to know where. Oliver tells her, and she nods and says that's a good place. Then as she rings up the condoms last, she gives me a wink and says,

"You enjoy your night."

"Thank you. I will!" I wink back conspiratorially and slowly run my finger down Oliver's muscular arm in a seductive move. Oliver clears his throat loudly, and I can practically feel the embarrassment coming off him in waves. It's hilarious, and I don't know how I manage to keep a straight face till we get outside.

Once I am out of the door, though, I burst out laughing. Oliver is laughing as much as I am while shaking his head at me.

"You are the worst." he grumbles.

"I'm sorry, I just couldn't help it! We gave her something juicy to think about."

The teenage guy comes running up to get his condoms. "You rock, man! I owe you! You want one? I can spare you one or two, maybe," he says, looking at the package like he's calculating how many times he's going to go in one night.

"No," Oliver says a little too loudly. "No thanks, that's fine. You enjoy."

We leave him to his night of debauchery and head into the bar we are staying above, and I still can't stop laughing.

"This town is highly entertaining after dark. I like it."

"You are the entertainment," Oliver huffs.

"Oh, the grumpy old man is back, I see." I poke him in the side.

He grips my hand and pulls me closer. "Keep calling me old, and I might just have to prove you wrong." His voice sounds deeper than usual, and I feel my skin break out all over in goose bumps. I'm not sure what to say, so I look over his shoulder at the bar instead and say,

"How about one more drink before we call it a night?"

He's still looking at me, and we are still standing very close. I don't move; I just wait for him to answer me.

"OK, one more," he finally says and lets out a breath like he wasn't breathing for the last few seconds. He doesn't let go of my hand as he leads me toward the bar. We sit down and each order a beer. I don't think another hard drink would be a good idea, and it seems he's thinking the same. It's a cute little place. The dark-wood bar is highly polished and clearly well loved. There's a hipster guy with a beard playing the guitar and singing in one corner, and a table of drunk girls in front of him is acting like he's famous or something. It's charming and relaxing.

As we sip our beers, the singer starts a new song, and I recognize the opening chords he's strumming but can't put my finger on what song it is exactly. Then when he starts singing, I know it. It's "Collide" by Howie Day, one of my favorites. Neither of us is talking, and the bar is quiet. We just listen to the song. It's beautiful, and the words make me feel all kinds of things about the man sitting next to me. I feel chills and rub my hands up and down over my arms.

"I'll be right back," Oliver whispers and gets up.

"OK."

He goes back out the door we just came in. I wonder if he needed to make a phone call or get something else from the store. I keep enjoying the song and my beer, soaking in the lyrics and how they make me feel. A couple of minutes later, I feel something being draped around my shoulders. I turn and it's Oliver putting a hoodie on me. I slip my arms into the sleeves and look down at it. It's a touristy-type blue zip-up hoodie that says "Hamptons" in hand-stitched letters.

"Did you just buy this?" I ask.

"You were cold," is his only response, then he continues drinking his beer.

"Thank you," I simply say and sip my beer again.

"The singer is good." He nods to the guy with guitar.

"He is," I agree. He downs the remainder of his beer, then pays the bartender and asks where we pick up the room key.

"I can get it for you, man," the bartender answers, then goes to retrieve it. I finish my beer, then search in my wallet for some cash and go drop it in the singer's tip jar. He gives me a wink and nod when I do, and when I turn back around, his table of groupies are all giving me death stares. Well hopefully I don't get stabbed by a drunk Hampton skank tonight, I think to myself.

When I reach Oliver again, he's just standing there watching me and shaking his head with a little laugh. "Causing trouble again, wild girl?"

"What? All I did was tip a good singer. How is that causing trouble?"

"That singer was eye-fucking you through the last two songs in case you didn't notice, Grace." He has leaned down till we are almost eye to eye, and I can feel him everywhere.

"Excuse me? No, I did not notice!" I scoff.

"OK, well I'm glad you aren't here on your own if you really are that oblivious to how men are with you."

I shake my head at him. "I can take care of myself, Oliver. And I can usually tell. I just didn't notice it with the singer, that's all. Do you notice every single woman that checks you out?"

"I notice ones on boats." He gives me a smug, crooked little grin.

I slap his chest and grunt. "Well maybe next time, wait until you're in the dressing room to start stripping, then."

"Fair enough." He holds his hands up in surrender. "Let's go up before those girls come after you for stealing all the attention."

He puts his arm around my shoulder in a proprietary way and looks over at the singer with a nod of his own.

"You're being trouble now," I whisper.

"Just making sure he doesn't try to follow you thinking you're staying here alone overnight."

"My big protector," I mock. Unfortunately, the joke's on me because my stupid body is singing with his touch right now, and I'm never going to be able to calm it down and get any sleep. When we reach the room, it's really cute, all white and beachy feeling. It's super small, though, with low ceilings that are practically touching Oliver's head and not much room in it around the queen-size bed. There are two tiny side tables, a wall-mounted TV, and a folding luggage rack, and that's it.

"This is barely bigger than your car," Oliver snorts.

"At least it has its own bathroom," I say, opening the door to the en suite. Oliver leans in, looking over my shoulder.

"Is there a bathtub?"

"Shower stall. Why? You feel like a soak?" I raise an eyebrow at him.

"No, smartass, for me to sleep in. There's hardly any floor out here around the bed."

"I'm not making you sleep on the floor. Don't be ridiculous. We can share the bed."

He sighs, looking at the bed. "I don't know."

"I won't attack you, Oliver. I promise," I say dryly.

He laughs slightly. "That's not it."

"Then what?"

"I was going to sleep in my boxers. These clothes are all salt crusted. I'm just thinking of practicality. You probably don't want to sleep in all your clothes either."

"That's true. I was actually thinking to shower and sleep in this hoodie you got me since it's big and comfy," I concede.

"OK, look, it's fine. You sleep in the big hoodie; I'll sleep in my boxers, it's not a big deal. It'll be fine. You take your shower first. I think I'll go listen to that singer a little more. Text me when you're done, and then I'll shower." He says all of this in a rush like he's trying to convince himself.

"OK." Before I can say anything else, he's already gone. All righty then, let's do this. I get what I need from the bag of stuff we purchased from the pharmacy and get cleaned up. Once I'm all clean and ready for bed in my underwear and cozy hoodie, I get under the covers on one side of the bed and text Oliver.

—Shower's free. Come on up whenever.

A few minutes later, there's a light knock on the door.

"Come in," I call out. I have my back propped up against the headboard and the TV on with an old 1950s sitcom in black and white. I love comfort TV like that.

"I'll be out soon," Oliver says as he heads to the bathroom.

"OK." God, this is about to get crazy awkward, isn't it? What am I going to do? Should I turn off all the lights and TV and just pretend to be sleeping when he gets out? That could work, I think. I don't want to make him uncomfortable, and at least one of us needs to get enough sleep to be able to drive us back to the city tomorrow. On the other hand, we are both in our thirties, for goodness sake. We should be able to handle a little close proximity. I mean, we were squished in my tiny car for hours, then shared a shark cage, for fuck's sake. This is hardly any closer than that. It's a lot farther apart than when he held my body tight against his in the cage, in fact. I can feel my body growing warm all over at the memory of how it felt being held by him like that. Not the time to think about that, Grace! I squirm in the bed, trying to rid myself of the memory and the fire it's igniting in my core right now. Shit. This is really dumb. I just made myself completely hot and bothered when I was supposed to be doing the exact opposite!

That's when the bathroom door opens, and he comes out in just his boxers, towel drying his hair. Dear god, save me. I keep my eyes glued on the TV screen, but I can't see anything. I've been blinded by his body. He sits down on the side of the bed with his back to me, and holy handsome hell, I forgot about that back tattoo. There are simply no words for it. I know I'm staring but don't even care.

"It's beautiful," I hear myself say softly, and *crap!* I did not mean to say it out loud.

He turns around and says, "What is?"

I look him dead in the eye and lift one eyebrow. "Seriously? You just gave me a full view of your huge back tat." I wave in the general area of his back.

"Oh, the wings. Sorry, sometimes I forget about them. I hardly ever see them." He chuckles.

"True, I guess, but I don't forget my tattoos, even if I don't see them constantly."

He twists fully around now and leans on one elbow. "Oh, really? Interesting. I haven't seen any tattoos on you." Now it's his turn to raise an eyebrow at me.

"You aren't very observant, then," I snort.

"What are you talking about? You don't have any visible," he insists.

"My neck is hardly a hidden spot." I pull my hair up and turn around, showing him the small claddagh symbol at the base of my neck. "It was plainly visible all day while I had braids in," I point out.

"OK, you win. I guess my fear of being shark bait had me a little too distracted to see it earlier. I apologize. It's very pretty, by the way."

"Thanks."

"Where are the others?" he continues.

"Nowhere you're going to see."

"Hmm, seems unfair. You can see all of mine." He sounds disappointed.

I laugh, "You really think playing ink show-and-tell is a good idea when we have to share this bed?"

"Oh, yeah, no, that's a very good point. Smart thinking, Grace." His tone is hilarious. I suddenly feel like I'm talking to my father.

"Thank you, Daddy. I'm glad you approve."

"Daddy?" He looks at me with wide eyes.

"Not like that, you freak!" I throw a pillow at his head.

He catches it and slams it down, saying, "You behave yourself, young lady. I'm warning you," in his most fatherly tone possible.

I groan loudly. "That's the worst dad voice I've ever heard."

"Yeah, no, I don't really do voices," he laughs.

"Clearly. Turn the lights off, Oliver. We need to get some sleep so one of us can drive tomorrow."

I click the TV off, and Oliver gets the lights, then climbs into the bed. It's funny how with a few jokes, I feel at ease with him again.

I snuggle deeper into the bed. It's actually super nice, with big, fluffy down pillows and a down comforter. I wonder how much he paid for the room. It couldn't have been cheap. I bite my lip, worrying that I should offer to go half on it with him.

"Oliver?"

"Yeah?" I'm slightly startled at how close his voice sounds. For some reason I imagined him hanging as far off the side of the bed as he could get, but instead he's practically right next to me.

"Oh, I was just thinking this room was probably expensive, and I want to pay half."

"No, Grace, you aren't paying anything for it. No discussion."

OK, well then. "I don't usually like being told what to do, you know," I retort.

I hear a deep chuckle seriously close to my own chest. "I'm not in the least surprised. Let me explain myself better, then. You booked ahead and paid for the shark dive and then wouldn't let me pay you back. You drove here, and you insisted on paying for your dinner even though I wanted to. I'm simply not going to negotiate about the room payment. It's done, and that's all there is to it."

"Fine," I huff.

"Good girl," he tells me.

"Oh no, you did not." I say indignantly.

His laughter is infectious, and I can't help but laugh also.

"You're really trying to get a rise out of me right now, Oliver Bekker, and I don't think you have any clue what you're playing with."

"As long as you don't get a rise out of me right now, Grace Murphy."

I take a second to think about that, and when it dawns on me what he means, I gasp.

"Oliver!"

"I'm sorry, you just set it up so easily. I couldn't help myself." Great, now I'm thinking about erections, in bed, next to Oliver. I groan internally.

"What was that?"

"What was what?"

"That noise you just made." Oh, did I do it out loud? Crap!

"Um, nothing."

"It didn't sound like nothing," he insists.

"OK, I just groaned. I meant to do it internally, and it came out accidentally. It's nothing. A groan, that's all."

There's a few minutes of silence, and I wonder if he fell asleep. Then he says, "I have a confession, Grace."

"What?" I can feel my heart practically thumping out of my chest as I wait for his answer.

"I think I'm drunk. I was nervous when you were showering, and I had a couple more drinks real quick. I think that it's making me want to say things and do things I shouldn't."

I have no response to that. I'm not afraid of him in the slightest, even if he's loaded. He just wouldn't ever hurt a person; I'm sure of that. No, I'm not afraid of Oliver. I'm afraid of myself because I think I could easily have sex with this man right now, and he would gladly do everything I want to. But he doesn't really want to. Sober Oliver doesn't want to sleep with me. And I don't want to do anything to screw things up. I want him to stay in my life. If he does something tonight that he'll regret in the morning, I could lose him completely. So I have to be the strong one right now. Well shit—I hate this!

"It's OK," I finally say.

"It is?"

I take a deep breath to steady myself, because every inch of my skin is screaming to reach out and touch him, but I can't. "Yeah, it is, because you're a good guy, Oliver. You won't do anything you'd regret, even when you're drunk. I truly believe that."

"I wish I wasn't such a good guy right now." Dear god, will this man not throw me a bone? I'm trying here, I really am, but I'm only human.

"Why?"

"I've always been a good guy. I'm tired of it. I've only ever had sex with one woman my whole life, and right now all I want to do is be the bastard. I want to be the guy who says, 'Fuck it!' and pulls the gorgeous girl lying next to him over and crushes her with kisses."

I'm breathing so heavily I have no doubt he can hear me, but I can't speak. If I open my mouth, I will beg him to do just that. I feel the bed shift, and I know he's moving. Even in the dark, I can make out the silhouette of his body rising up next to me, and I can feel him looking down at me.

"Oliver," I whimper, barely able to form a coherent thought in this moment.

"Grace, you're so goddamn beautiful." His husky voice rakes over my body like a physical caress.

"I don't think you really want to do this though. I'm scared you will hate me."

"Why would I ever hate you?" Slowly he touches my cheek, lightly running his fingers down to my neck.

"If you thought I tempted you to do something before you were ready."

He just stays there frozen and quiet, thinking about what I said.

"Can I just kiss you then?" he finally asks. I don't answer. Instead I surge up into his arms, and my mouth lands on his in the most frenzied, feverish kiss I've ever had. His large arms wrap around me, holding me up against him, and one hand tangles into my hair, gripping tight. He positions my head exactly how he wants it and delves his tongue in deep. It's like he needs this to keep breathing. I moan loudly, completely lost to him and unable to hold back. He pulls me even closer, and I'm seated in his lap now, my bare legs across his hard erection. The boxers provide barely any barrier between us. This is getting out of hand quickly.

"God, Grace, how can I resist you?" His voice sounds so full of desperation and confusion that I wonder if I should try to stop him for his own sake.

"I'm sorry, I didn't mean to make this happen," I whisper against his neck, drinking in his scent.

"You didn't do anything. It's me. I'm such an idiot." I can feel his regret come crashing in, and it's exactly what I dreaded. I desperately want to fix this before I lose him in my life altogether.

"Oliver, it was just a kiss. It's OK, nothing happened." I climb out of his lap and kneel next to him, holding his face in my hands.

"I'm sorry, you don't deserve this. I'm such a crazy mess." He hangs his head in his hands, and I know that this moment between us is over. He's regretting it.

"Oliver, lie back down." I gently push him back down to his pillow. Now it's my turn to lean over him. I gently run my fingers through his hair and don't say anything because there's nothing to say. His body wanted me, but his heart is so broken. I hate that he has so much pain. I wish I could take it away. I lie down beside him, still running my hand slowly through his hair over and over. I place my head beside his shoulder. I feel his arm come up and wrap around my waist as he turns into me and pulls me closer.

"Thank you," he whispers in my ear, and I can feel his tears as they fall hot on my skin.

"Anytime," I whisper back and place a chaste kiss on his temple. We fall asleep in each other's embrace, and somehow there's a deep innocence in it. I cry with him in the dark not because I know his pain, but because I care for him and I want his suffering to end.

***

Oliver

Whatever We Are

The sun steaming through the curtains wakes me up, and I become conscious of the fact that I'm holding Grace in my arms still. Memories of all the asinine things I said and did last night come flooding into my head as I lay there unmoving. I'm stunned at how amazingly Grace handled the situation; she is fascinating. What kind of woman would know exactly what I needed in those moments? How does she get me even when I don't get myself? Deep down I know she wanted me as much as I wanted her, but somehow she knew that I wasn't ready in my soul yet. I feel like the most selfish prick in the entire world for the way I keep blowing hot and cold with her. I really need to figure out a way to keep some distance if I'm truly not ready. My stupid body is the damn traitor that keeps messing up and making me think with the wrong head.

Closing my eyes tightly, I dig down deep, looking for the strength to detach myself from her warm frame. It's possibly the hardest thing I've ever done. Speaking of hard, the morning wood I'm sporting is aching so much I can barely walk the few steps to the bathroom. At the bathroom door, I turn and look at her one last time over my shoulder. She hasn't woken up yet, but she shifted and pulled my pillow under her and is now hugging it like she was my torso a second ago. Her light-brown hair is a beautiful mess, and her toned legs are peeking out from the blankets. Shit, I really need to make some uglier friends next time. The problem is Grace is gorgeous on the inside, too, and I am drawn just as much to her soul as I am to her body.

I head into the bathroom and decide I need to just handle this sexual frustration myself, or I'll never get through a day in that laughably small car next to her. I look down and see my wedding band still on my finger. Yeah, I'm not about to jerk off thinking of another woman wearing that. I slip it off, silently hating myself. It doesn't take long to shoot my load, with the smell of her hair and feel of her skin still invading my brain. I splash cold water over my face afterward and try to fight all my self-loathing.

"I'm sorry, Ally," is all I can think. I get ready for the day, slipping my ring on last of all. I take a deep breath and head out.

I don't wake her yet. Instead, I head out to a coffee shop and get us some breakfast. I send her a text letting her know where I am in case she does wake up while I'm out. By the time I return to the room, Grace is up and ready for the day.

"Good morning," I say, handing her the coffee. I place the bag of pastries and bagel options on the end of the bed.

"Sleep well?" I ask.

"Surprisingly well." She nods as she blows on the hot coffee.

"Look, I want to clear the air before we start the day, I know you think I apologize too much, but we both know it's owed this time." She smiles sweetly, which kills me a little. I almost wish she would be pissed at me. Maybe if she hated me as much as I hate myself right now, my guilt would be eased.

"OK, go on," is all she says. I sit down on the edge of the bed and pat the spot next to me. She takes a seat too. I'm glad because this is easier to do when we are both facing the wall and not each other.

"I think it's pretty obvious that I find you incredibly sexy." I start out brutally honest. I can feel her shift slightly. "However, my head is still apparently not right from losing Ally. I need to have better control of myself. I'm deeply sorry for how I acted. I can't blame the drinks one hundred percent because I was aware enough to know everything I was doing, and I did it anyway. I can't thank you enough for helping me stop last night. I really want you in my life, and I could have screwed that all up."

She takes in a deep breath and lets it out again. "I obviously find you attractive too. I have had issues with, um… men in the past. I don't usually have men as friends, especially ones that look like you. More ones that look like Kyle." That makes us both laugh a little. "But I want your companionship, Oliver. I really do. You are a special person, and ever since we met, I've enjoyed your company like no one else. If anything I did or said yesterday contributed to what happened last night, then I'm sorry, too, because I know that I can be flirty. But you have been completely honest from the beginning as to what this is and what it isn't, so I think we just both need to find the boundary."

I nod in agreement. "So no more sharing beds, probably?"

"Yeah, that would be smart."

"Just so you know, you didn't do anything to make that happen. I like you just the way you are. Fun, flirty, crazy. Don't change a single thing. If I'm not ready to move on from Ally, that's on me, no one else."

She gives me slightly sad smile then. "I hope your heart will mend one day, Oliver. I hate how sad you seem sometimes."

"Me, too, but I feel a lot less sad when I'm with you."

The drive back to the city is quieter but not awkward. I drive the toy car and let Grace relax this time. She puts her feet up on the dashboard and leans her seat back while we listen to the Beatles and sing along to all the songs.

When "Yesterday" plays, I decide to share another piece of my soul with Grace. "This song is the tattoo on my ribcage."

"It is?"

"Yeah, we played it at Ally's funeral, and it just meant so much to me when I lost her I got it done in her memory."

"Oh, I was wondering if maybe the one over your heart was for her."

"It is. That one is a song lyric too, actually. It says 'Lights Will Guide You Home' from 'Fix You' by Coldplay. Ally loved them, and that song was one of her favorites. We played that one at the funeral also."

"Those are beautiful tributes," she says softly. "What about the others?"

"The wings were Ally's idea. She planned them out. I guess she liked the look of them."

"Smart girl." She chuckles quietly, which brings a grin to my lips.

"The tree was one we got together after going through a rough patch. It was around our sixth anniversary, and we had been stressed and too busy with work. We just let things drift, but we worked hard and came out stronger than ever, so we both got tree tattoos. To symbolize bending in the wind with strong roots and never breaking, growing stronger. Hers was smaller, on her wrist."

"Those are all the ones you have?"

"Yeah, but you know they are addicting, too, so I'll probably get more. How many do you have?"

"Seven."

"Is that all the information you're going to give me?" I tease.

"Fine, I'll tell you about them. Some of them are silly, and some of them are dark, though, so don't judge." She gives me a pointed look.

"Hey, no judgment from me, I promise." I hold up my hands in a placating gesture.

"Well you know I like to read, so I have some *Harry Potter* ones. I love that series, it got me through some rough years. It will always mean a lot to me." She removes her shoes and points to a small word on the inside of each inner foot arch. "'*Lumos*' and '*Nox*', the spells for light and darkness in the books." Then she pulls back her hair and shows me a tiny lightning bolt behind one ear. "This one is obvious."

"Cute," I say, and it is. There's something about a geeky girl that has always been hot to me.

"So what house are you?" I ask, trying to impress her with my *Harry Potter* knowledge.

"Gryffindor, obviously, Oliver. If you know anything, you should have been able to guess that," she says sarcastically, and I laugh.

"OK, you got me. I don't know much. I've only seen the movies, not read the books."

"Yeah, well, the two don't compare." Her tone gets a bit more somber then and I sense her hesitating. "Anyway, there is a bird with a quote under my boob, and a saying in Latin too low for showing. I don't really want to explain those two today, sorry."

"It's OK," I say immediately.

"Thanks. You saw the claddagh on my neck, for my Irish heritage. And the last one is on my lower back, It's a bow and arrow with the arrow drawn back. I got that because I read somewhere that an arrow has to be pulled backward before it can shoot forward, and that's how life is sometimes. We have to go back before we get ahead. I loved the idea, so I got that."

"Those all sound very cool. I don't know why you thought there'd be judgment."

"Well, I didn't explain the dark ones, that's why."

I don't say anything as I think about that. I just drive and think about this girl. She astonishes me every minute I spend with her, and yet people have hurt her deeply. It makes me want to find those people and make them all very sorry for that.

Truth or Dare

Grace

Ever since that intense weekend to the Hamptons, Oliver and I speak almost daily. Even if it's just a text or a meme or something one sends the other online. I feel like I can't recall a time when he wasn't a part of my life, and it baffles me that I only met him recently. We meet for coffees, lunches, and dinners occasionally. It has been less intense, as we both try to behave, sticking to public places surrounded by lots of people.

It's a Friday afternoon, and I am at work wondering what kind of takeout I'm going to order tonight when I get a text from him.

—I feel like going out tonight. How about you?

—Got to be honest, I've had an exhausting week and was really looking forward to takeout and pajamas on my couch…I know, very boring. I would say you can join me, but that's probably a bad idea, right?

…at maybe not. We can handle it, right?

…rth a shot. Come over after work?

—OK, see you then.

I rush home, needing to clean the place up a bit and get myself mentally ready for Oliver coming over to hang out. This will be our first time alone since returning from that weekend excursion. I make sure I don't light candles, instead having plenty of lights on. We don't need a romantic setting, for goodness sake. I put the TV on to further distract myself and choose a sitcom that won't feel in the least heavy or sexy. I also carefully choose my thickest sweatpants and a long-sleeve Henley shirt for maximum coverage. When the knock on my door comes, I feel as ready as I can be for the platonic night ahead.

"Thanks for letting me crash your night. I wasn't in the mood to be alone tonight." He gives me a small hug in greeting as he walks into the living room.

"Anytime. Sorry I wasn't feeling up to going out. I hope this isn't too boring."

"Are you kidding me? This is my favorite kind of night, relaxing and just doing nothing."

I hand him three takeout menus. "Good. Here are the best local options for delivery. Tell me which you prefer." As he looks them over, I can't help but look him over a little. As always he looks incredible, in navy-blue jogging pants and a fitted gray tee with a zip-up hoodie open over it. He looks like he has a fresh haircut that's slightly shorter than usual, and damn, it's sexy. I decide I need to go into the kitchen and get us some beers so I stop staring.

"This place sounds good, Banh Mi Palace. I can really go for that."

I hand him a beer, taking out my phone to place the order. "Perfect, I love this food. Make yourself comfortable. We can watch whatever. I just put this on earlier for background noise."

"*Brooklyn Nine-Nine*, huh? Good choice. We can leave this."

He settles into the couch and leans back, looking completely at ease. I place our delivery order, and we just chill for a while, catching up with how our work weeks went. Once our food arrives, I devour mine, having hardly had time to eat all day. Apparently this doesn't go unnoticed, because I catch him smirking as he watches me.

"Are you hungry, Grace?" he asks with a laugh in his voice.

"I told you, this week has been awful! I had to work through lunch today and grab a granola bar. That's literally all I've had besides coffee today." I roll my eyes at him, feeling no shame.

"Poor baby," he commiserates, and I try not to focus on the term of endearment he used.

I swig my beer, then realize it's already empty. Going to the fridge, I grab two more for us. We finish up our dinner soon enough and get back to just chilling on the couch in front of the TV.

"Is this what they call Netflix and chill?" Oliver asks out of the blue.

I cough a little at that. "Um, well, kinda. But it usually means something a little less innocent," I try to explain without actually explaining.

He turns to me. "What, then? I never understand that phrase."

"Just google it, Oliver. I don't want to explain it." I feel my cheeks growing pink.

"Fine." He sighs and types something into his phone.

"Oh, I see." Now he's the one blushing, and I can't help but belt out in laughter.

"Oh my god, Oliver, your face! That is priceless. I'm sorry to laugh, but I can't help it."

I get a cushion thrown at my head for that. It's totally worth it.

"It's a good thing I looked it up. I probably would have told people that's what we did tonight if I never knew the true meaning."

Placing the cushion behind my head, I plop my feet into his lap then. "Yeah well, they probably assume that's what we do anyway. I mean, what man and woman do this?" I point out.

"God, you're right. Oh well, who cares what anyone thinks." He takes one foot in his big hands and starts giving me a foot massage.

"Good boy," I tell him imperiously. He just shakes his head at that but keeps massaging.

Another episode in, and we are still doing more chatting than watching. It's perfectly relaxing, and I reach for my beer to find it empty yet again.

"I'll get us more," he says, getting up and heading to the kitchen. "You're all out," he calls back a second later.

"Shit. OK, I can run to the bodega. What else do we want?" I get up and head for my shoes by the door, grabbing my wallet and phone.

"I'm coming with you, we can stock up on junk food for later." He starts putting his shoes on too. I can't help but wonder how late he plans on staying. Not that I ever want him to leave; I just need to keep a handle on myself alone with him.

We stroll slowly down the sidewalk toward my local bodega, enjoying the evening air.

"Truth or dare?" I ask him.

He doesn't miss a beat. He simply says, "Truth."

"Have you ever committed a crime?"

"Not that I recall. I mean, I don't obey the speed limit all the time. Does that count?"

I give him a look. "No, Goody Two-shoes, that does not count. I mean like shoplifting or something real," I laugh.

"I can't say that I have, then. Sorry to disappoint. OK, Miss Bad Girl, truth or dare?"

"I'll start with truth also."

"Favorite physical feature on a man?"

"Easy, his eyes. They tell you everything you need to know. If I had paid more attention to my ex's evil eyes, I could have saved three years of misery."

"What a very clean answer. I expected something much worse," he teases.

"Of course you did. You have a filthy mind, Oliver. Truth or dare?"

"Dare."

I give him an evil smile and rub my hands together gleefully. "I know exactly what I want you to do."

"Oh no, I want to change my answer."

"No, that's not allowed! You chose, and you have to stick to it. I want you to do something illegal."

"I'm not going to shoplift."

"It doesn't have to be that. It can be anything." I throw my arms out wide.

"Like what?" I ponder that for a while as we walk.

"Got it!" I say suddenly. "Come with me. We are going to take a detour." I take him by the hand, and we head down a side street to the left. It's a warm night, and we are both over-dressed, so it feels even hotter. I lead him to an outdoor community pool that just closed for the fall last week even though it could have stayed open with the warm weather we've been having.

"What?" he asks, looking from me to the pool.

"We're going to take a dip in the closed pool."

Throwing his head back in laughter, he says, "You really are the craziest girl. We will get caught. They have security cameras, no doubt."

"That is all part of the thrill. It wouldn't be half as fun if there wasn't that chance of getting caught."

He looks down at his clothes then. "What are we going to do, jump in fully clothed?"

"Are you not wearing underwear, Oliver?" I challenge. He inhales deeply, blowing it out and thinking.

"You said dare," I remind him. He grabs my hand then with a wicked grin.

"Fine, how do we do this? I need the criminal expert to help me."

"This way." I start walking along the fence, looking for the right spot.

"Bingo." I find a gap between a gate and a building. We manage to fit through it and wait on the other side for a min-ute to hear any sort of alarm being raised. It's completely quiet, still, and dark. The large Olympic size pool shines in the glow of moonlight. The surrounding area is completely deserted luckily, so we most likely won't be caught.

"Grace Murphy, what the hell are you turning me into?" Oliver hisses as we sneak toward the pool in the shadows.

"Someone less old and boring," I reply. I slowly peel off my shirt and pants, letting them drop without looking at him. In just my bra and panties, I go to the edge and lower myself into the water. A gasp escapes me when I first feel the shock of it, but I love the thrill. I go under, embracing the coldness until my body becomes accustomed to it.

There's something about being in water in the darkness that always makes it feel extra potent for me. All my senses tingle and come alive. When I resurface I look for Oliver, but there is only a pile of clothes where he was a minute ago. He must have come in while I was under. I feel arms circle my waist as he rises in the water behind me.

"You are determined to ruin me one way or another, aren't you?" he whispers, his breath warm against my ear. My whole body shivers then. I can never help how I react to him. I swipe my hands over my face as I turn in his arms to face him. He just looks at me, his eyes intense and his arms still holding me.

"Well, you have officially committed a crime. How does it feel?" I say quietly. Here in the dark, closed pool, it feels so quiet and abandoned. It's impossible to speak at a normal volume. He runs one large hand through his wet hair then.

"It feels fucking electrifying," he says at last. I feel myself swallow, and I can sense him watching my mouth.

"Truth or dare?" he asks then.

"Dare," I answer.

"Kiss me again, Grace, just once. We can make it part of the game and never talk about it again." I look into his eyes deeply and say nothing, I don't move either. Part of the game? How can I separate my feelings like that? He isn't playing fair. I push off his chest then and begin swimming away. "Only if you catch me," I throw over my shoulder.

He must be an amazing swimmer, because within seconds he's on me. I thought with my head start I stood a small chance of getting away, but that didn't happen. He pulls me against him again, laughing in his victory.

"You were saying?" he challenges me. I want to wipe that smug look off his face. So I wrap my arms around his neck and bring my lips right up to his but don't quite kiss him. There is barely a hairsbreadth of space between our mouths. The silence and stillness of the night around us is like a blanket.

"I was saying if there is something you want, you should be a man and take it," I whisper over his mouth. He surges forward, capturing my mouth with his then, bracing my back with his strong arms. His tongue plunges in and pillages me completely. We move through the water as he backs me toward the edge of the pool. I know I'm moaning, and he is too. Our sounds are so intertwined there is no way of differentiating them. He grips me tighter, and I hold onto him for dear life, drowning in this kiss.

Suddenly the darkness is broken with the bright beam of a flashlight shining on us.

"All right, you two. Out!" someone barks.

"Fuck," Oliver groans, lifting me to the edge and helping me out. "I'm coming, Officer. I just need a second," he says to the policeman standing there. He moves through the water toward the stairs as the officer chuckles to himself.

"Take your time, dude."

I quickly put my clothes on and begin trying to sweet-talk my way out of this mess. "Listen, please don't arrest us. This is all my fault, not his. I wanted to distract him because he's been depressed, so we played 'Truth or Dare'."

The policeman is young, and he is grinning mischievously, so I feel hopeful that we can somehow get away with this.

"I'm fairly certain you successfully distracted him," he says with a wink.

Oliver climbs out and moves to his clothes, rushing to get into them.

"When we got the call and came to investigate, I expected to find a couple of teenagers, not some grown-ups sucking face."

"I'm so sorry!" I plead again.

"We really didn't mean any harm, sir. It was just a game that got a bit out of hand." Oliver adds.

"Look, I don't want to arrest you two lovebirds. It would create a lot of paperwork and hassle. Besides, I have real criminals to worry about. Get in the back of that cruiser over there and tell me where to bring you so you don't freeze in these wet clothes." He points through the fence to his cop car, where his partner is waiting. We head over to it, thanking him profusely.

***

Oliver

When the cruiser drops us off in front of Grace's building, I don't know whether she's about to laugh or cry.

"There is never a dull moment with you, is there?" I look down at her.

"I'm so sorry. I could have gotten us arrested." She puts her hand over her mouth.

"No one was going to arrest your adorable ass." I give in and start laughing then.

"I just can't believe our quiet night on the couch turned into that."

"We never got our beer and snacks either."

We must look like a couple of drowned rats in our soaked clothes. "Come on, we should get dry." I take her hand and start toward her apartment. The look on her face tells me she is surprised I want to go back in, like she was expecting me to run away at the first opportunity I got.

Once inside she looks at me and says, "I don't have any clothes that will fit you. I can wash and dry those ones real quick if you want to shower and just wrap up in my bathrobe?"

"Yeah, I will do that. I think we should talk, so I don't want to go yet. Are you sure you don't mind?"

"Of course not. Here, I'll get you towels and the robe, and you just throw those wet clothes outside the bathroom door for me."

"Do you need to shower first?"

"No, I'll do that later. For now I'll just change into dry clothes."

The whole time I shower, my mind replays holding Grace in the pool, kissing her, and wanting her so badly it hurts. I smell her everywhere in the bathroom. The coconut shampoo and lavender body wash carry her scent, and I can't help but savor it. Her bathrobe is too small, no doubt oversized on her, but it just isn't going to work for me. The towels she has, however, are ginormous and thick, so I wrap one securely around my waist. Coming out, I find her curled up on the couch, changed into some sleep shorts and an oversized T-shirt, her still damp hair pulled up in a messy bun. She's got a mug of something that looks like hot chocolate, and the domestic coziness of the scene makes my heart ache a little.

"Sorry, the robe wouldn't fit," I say, clearing my throat a little and seating myself at the opposite end of the couch.

"Oh, sorry, I guess it wasn't as big as I thought." She looks me up and down, then quickly looks away.

"It's fine. Your towels are comically big."

"They're bath sheets, technically. I love wrapping all up in them after a shower or bath. Want a hot cocoa?"

"No, I'm OK. Thanks." I don't want her getting up; she looks so snug huddled in the corner.

"So you said that we should talk. I'm guessing it's about the kiss?"

I chuckle a little and feel my body relax at her words. "That's what I love about us: we just say things. No games or beating around the bush. Yeah, I want to explain something about my behavior."

"OK, just let me run into the bathroom first before you start. I have to take these contacts out really quick." When she returns wearing the cutest glasses I've ever seen, I have to swallow hard because I didn't really think Grace could be any more attractive, but I guess I was wrong.

"I didn't know you wore contacts," is all I manage to get out.

"Yeah, I'm pretty nearsighted."

"The glasses are a good look. You should wear them more often," I can't help but point out.

"I used to a lot more. They just got dirty all the time, and I was constantly cleaning them. Well, maybe not really. It was probably my OCD that made it seem like an issue more than anything. Anyway, the contacts helped me not obsess, so I switched."

I stay quiet for a minute, gathering my thoughts, then when I feel ready for what I want to say, I lean my elbows on my knees and rest my chin on my clasped fists. I stare at the wall in front of me and just dive in.

"I think I have been compartmentalizing things in my life lately. I have one box where I'm a husband who is still loyal to his dead wife. Then there's another one, one where I'm this guy who gets to have fun and flirt and enjoy the company of a gorgeous woman. The problem is neither of those are real life. I thought about it in the shower, and I realized I'm just trying to simplify something that isn't simple in the least. I'm scared, scared of being out of control with how I feel about you. I have stayed in control of how I mourn Ally for so long it became a way of life, almost. Then you burst into my life. I started doubting everything I thought I was sure of. Now I'm desperately trying to navigate what's happening but clearly doing a very shitty job. Even as I try to explain this, I know it makes no sense." I get up then, pacing in frustration.

"Who said emotions are going to make sense?" Grace says simply as she watches me. "Do you think what I'm dealing with makes any more sense? I understand everything you are dealing with. I want to respect it, and yet I can't stop myself from being drawn to you either. It isn't always fun for me, believe me. I was finally happy alone, finally getting my shit together. Then I met you, and suddenly being alone felt like a punishment. Not only that, now I can't even meet someone new because I compare them all to you. You, who I can't have anyway." She doesn't look at me as she speaks. Instead she is focused on the cushion in her lap, twisting the fringe of it around her fingers over and over.

"What should we do?" I ask, feeling no clearer than before.

"If I cared about you less, respected you less, I would know exactly what to do," is the only answer she gives.

I go back to sit next to her. "What would you do in that case?"

She just shakes her head from side to side, refusing to answer me.

"The same thing I would do if I cared less, probably, if I could say that you meant nothing to me. I could take you in that bedroom and do all the things my body is begging me to do, damn the consequences. If I didn't need to keep you in my life like I need to keep breathing, I could risk it all by just saying, 'Fuck it!' and having you in every way. But that's a risk I'm too terrified to take because if this isn't right yet, we could lose something irreplaceable." She just nods then, looking away from me.

A beeping sound indicates that the clothes dryer has stopped, and she gets up to retrieve my now clean and dry clothes.

"Go home, Oliver. All the talking in the world won't solve this," she says sadly as she hands them over. I take them and go change. When I return, I need to say one last thing before I leave.

"I will do anything not to lose you in my life. Please."

"I'm not going anywhere. I may be a fool, but I can't lose you either. Even if I only get to have a small part of you, I guess I'd rather have that than nothing."

"Thank you." It's all I can manage before I leave. If I stay a minute longer, all my resolve will be lost.

Closer

Grace

Managing to get things back on track is easier than I expected after our lapse. I suppose the chance that we might screw everything up beyond repair is enough of a warning to keep us from crossing the line again. Another two weeks go by, and normalcy is firmly back; being busy helps. I have been more active than ever. Besides taking my frustration out in the gym, I have started evening yoga classes, joined a weekly book club, and started visiting a shooting range in Manhattan. It's not my old, familiar Brooklyn one, but getting back into something I enjoy is good for me. Keeping myself so fully occupied leaves less time for hanging out with Oliver also. He asked what I'd be up to this weekend, but I have my parents coming into town for a visit, unfortunately, so I won't see him. That shouldn't feel as painful as it does. As much as I try to avoid him, we do manage to see each other almost every weekend one way or another, and I will miss it.

—That's nice you're seeing your parents.

—Is it though?

—Isn't it?

—My family isn't as nice as yours. Plus I haven't spent time with them for a long time, and I have some reservations…and questions. Questions I have no actual intention of asking, so that's fun. It will just be a big mental elephant in the apartment for two days.

It's OK. I'll survive.

—Sorry. Text me anytime. You can always run away and meet me for a quick drink and pep talk if need be.

—You're the best.

—Always here if you need me, night or day.

I don't answer that. Too many dirty responses flood my mind, and they need squashing, so yeah, no reply is best. Friday comes around, and my mother calls me at work to let me know they arrived and have settled into my apartment; she's going to have dinner ready for when I get home from work. I've been mentally prepping myself all week for the next two days. My parents aren't the worst people in the world. I just feel blocked off from them somehow. Like there are too many unspoken things between us that we can't overcome. They come from a generation that was expert at looking the other way, and I can't help but wonder if the abuse in my past is something either of them ever knew about. I'm not even close to ready for bringing that up with them. But it will still be in the back of my mind, and I hate having to feel like I'm being fake with anyone, especially the people who are supposed to be closest to you. At no point in my memory have we felt close, though, and I've never really understood why. My two older siblings tell me I'm crazy. They love our parents. They say they were the best parents we could have had. They claim our childhood was perfect, and maybe for them it was.

Obviously, something was different for me. I've always been the black sheep, the difficult one, the wild one, the one no one quite understands. That's why I moved from Connecticut to Brooklyn as soon as I could and haven't looked back once. Funny, but my parents never bothered visiting much before; it's like as they get older, they get more sentimental. Well great for them, but I'm not sentimental in the slightest, so no thanks.

"Hi, Mom." I give her the perfunctory expected kiss on the check. Physical contact with my parents is not my thing; hugs are not comfortable at all. Show me a handsome stranger, and I'll be ready for all sorts of touching almost immediately. Ask me to hug a family member, and I would rather eat dirt. Yes, I am aware that is insane. I can't help it, though. It's an involuntary reaction. I try to hide my discomfort the best that I can, but everyone in the family knows about this aversion and mocks it. Whatever.

"You get home pretty late, don't you?" Her first words to me, of course, feel negative, but I expect no less.

"Not really, it's the same time I always get home. No one is ever around to care though. Sorry."

"Well we made shepherd's pie and brought wine. Come relax."

"That sounds perfect, actually. Do you want to eat at the table, or should we watch some TV while we eat?" I get the feeling I'm not the only one who will struggle to carry on a conversation, and they might prefer not having to either.

My dad pipes up then: "I vote TV." He gives me a hug then. It feels slightly less awkward with him than anyone else, at least. There is something about a dad and daughter that is just that little bit extra special.

"Oh, fine, but no cop shows or autopsy shows," Mom concedes.

"I'll go get into something comfier while you two decide what we can watch." I run for my room and the much-needed pajamas waiting for me there. When I come back out, they are set up for dinner in the living room. I pour us all generous portions of wine and settle in.

"I want *Downton Abbey*, and your father wants *Peaky Blinders*. You have the tie-breaking vote, Grace."

"Well you know I'm going to choose Tommy Shelby. I mean, come on."

"Hmph, Branson is better."

"No, Mom, just no. Not even close!"

"I knew you'd side with me, kiddo. You have good tase." Dad is clearly triumphant.

This night isn't so bad after all. We don't have to talk about anything besides the gangs of Birmingham and how delicious the shepherd's pie is, and the wine is flowing. All in all, if I can keep the next two days on this level, I will be very happy. Here's hoping.

I insist on doing the dishes since Mom cooked, and she does sit and chat to me a little now. I feel my guard coming back up.

"So what's new with you?"

"Nothing much, just working, mostly. I try to have fun on the weekends, of course. Let's see…I got some new tattoos." That gets a *tsk* out of her, as I knew it would. I just laugh.

"You don't want to see them, then?"

"If they're anywhere decent, I will."

"Probably not, then."

"Figures. There must be something else happening. No new guy you're seeing or anything?"

"Nope, I'm not looking for a new relationship after Matt. Not till I work through some stuff. I told you that."

"Oh yes, your therapy." She says the last word like there are air quotes around it.

"Don't start, Mother."

"I'm just saying, in our day, everyone handled their own business in private. We didn't pay some stranger thousands of dollars to tell us what to think."

"Yeah, that's all they do: tell me what to think." My voice drips with sarcasm.

"Well what else have they done? Seriously!" she insists.

"I'm actually not prepared to get into this with you, but a lot, in fact. Let's talk about something else. How are you and Dad doing?"

"Oh he plays golf, and I babysit for your sisters. Same as every other retired couple in America. It gets monotonous, that's for sure. We are planning a trip to Ireland next summer, though, so that will be fun."

"I'm glad. You should get away more often."

"I agree, but your sisters are so dependent on me with the kids I feel like I can hardly ever leave."

"You need to put your foot down, Mom. You're the grandmother, not daycare."

"Well it's all part of what's expected. No one ever asks if I want to do these things; they just assume it's my duty."

"Duty? They chose to have kids. They should have made proper arrangements for their care. No way is that your problem! That always pisses me off."

"I am aware, and every time I talk to you about it, I go home feeling very rebellious. But alas, that doesn't last long. It's fine. You know I love doing it deep down."

"Sure you do, way deep down." I roll my eyes. We've had this conversation many times. I know nothing will ever change. I just can't manage to keep my mouth shut about it. Now it's Mom's turn to want a change of subject; good.

"Well your dad and I are tired. We'll say good night now. What's on the agenda for tomorrow?"

"Shopping, lunch, and then depending how we feel, maybe a stroll around Central Park, or we can do a museum."

"Sounds like the perfect New York day. Thanks, honey. You always treat us so well when we're here." If only she knew how heavily it all weighed on me, trying to maneuver through the waters of off-limit subjects and too-real feelings. I have to keep them busy and distracted. It's the only way we'll all survive it, I know. I always give them my room and sleep on the couch when they stay, so I go in and get what I need for the night. Fortunately I already made sure all the embarrassing things were put well away before today. Once they are snoring loud enough for me to need music on my headphones, I lie there and finally look at my phone. There's a text from Oliver from about an hour ago.

—How was the first night?

—Bearable because we watched *Peaky Blinders* and avoided any real talking, for the most part. Tommy Shelby makes everything better.

—Oh I see. So you like very bad men, then. Well he did marry Grace, so I guess it makes sense.

—Sigh, yes, that will forever make me happy. I get to hear Cillian Murphy declare his love for "Grace," most definitely a perk of my name.

—He smokes in real life.

I laugh out loud at that, remembering when I told Oliver that I hated the smell of cigarettes.

—He has to have at least one flaw.

—I'm sure he has more. I can do research and find out.

—Why are you determined to crush my dreams??

—I'm feeling irrationally annoyed with the man all of a sudden. No idea why. I'm sad. Don't ask me to make sense….just pity me.

—No, you can't play that card. I feel no pity. Who would be your number one celebrity crush?

—I have to think about this if I can only pick one. Give me a second…

—Take your time. It is an important decision.

—Elizabeth Taylor, the younger years.

—Are you for real? That's very classy but only proves yet again what an OLD MAN you are!!!

—You can't beat a classic. Her shape, her attitude, and her movies are just timeless.

—You will never cease to surprise me. I love old movies but would never in a million years have guessed that about you.

—You should come over, and we'll watch our favorite classics sometime. Mine is *Giant*: Elizabeth Taylor in her prime, James Dean, Rock Hudson. You can't beat it. Yours?

—Excellent choice. Picking only one favorite is very hard. I'll have to go with Camelot from the 60s. Richard Harris, Vanessa Redgrave, the songs, and the tragedy. Ugh, I love it.

—Now we definitely need to do it because I have never seen that.

—Well, then, it's going to happen. I hope you like musicals!

—Ally hated them, so we never watched a lot of them, but I'm down. The Knights of the Round Table is a great story. Now I'm excited to see it.

—It's a plan. So what are you up to tomorrow? I get to play tourist and guide all day. Yay.

—That's rough. I'll pray for you lol. I'm just going to visit my grandad at his care home and probably work out at the gym. That's my usual Saturday routine. When I'm not shark bait, jail bait, or otherwise doing crazy things with a certain someone, that is.

—I would rather be shark bait than parent bait.

—Well my offer stands. If you need to sneak away, I'll meet you for a drink.

—Don't be surprised when I take you up on that after a whole day with them. If I can even escape from them.

—I look forward to you needing rescuing, then.

I finally fall asleep with my music drowning out the parental snores. As I listen to songs and try to drift off, it's a little ridiculous how every song reminds me of Oliver. I had never been this sappy in my life. Not even when I had a longtime live-in boyfriend had I imagined every lyric I listened to was written just for my heart. Seriously need to put those walls up inside. Usually I did that without a thought, but with him it was the opposite. They came down and melted away without a thought. "Gotta work on that" was my last coherent thought before I drifted off.

***

By seven in the evening, I feel like we have covered the entire city. I've kept my parents moving at a breakneck speed. No lingering and getting all chummy; no way am I about to let that happen. On the way back to my apartment in Brooklyn, we stop at my local deli for sandwich things so we can stay in for dinner tonight but no one will have to cook a meal. I'm hoping I've worn them out enough that they will head to bed early. If not, maybe I can come up with some sort of excuse to duck out and meet Oliver for that drink. We all take turns showering the city off of us, which luckily takes up another hour. I'm almost through the weekend. I can do this, especially with the end in sight. Focus on the finish line, Grace.

"What wonderful agenda do you have in store for us tomorrow?" My mom interrupts my thoughts of finish lines.

"I think we should sleep in a bit, since today was long. I have us booked for brunch at ten at Sunny's, which is delicious. You'll love it. The mimosas are insane. So are the Bloody

Marys, actually. Then we can relax and do whatever really, until you have to leave. Anything else you wanted to do?"

"That all sounds great, but we never meet any of your friends. I wish just one time you'd take us out to a bar with a group of people or something."

"Mom, I work all week with Tara and Kyle, who you have met. I don't really want to hang out with them on my one weekend with you guys. I don't have a ton of other friends. Sometimes I do stuff with a few girls from yoga, but we aren't close."

"It seems so lonely, the way you live. In this big city surrounded by people and barely close to anyone."

"I know it seems that way to you, but it's exactly how I like things. I've always been a loner. You know that."

"I had hoped you would change, I guess." The disappointment is back.

"I'm sorry. I am thirty-four, you know. What you see is what you get at this point, I'm afraid."

I could tell her about Oliver, but no way is that happening. He's the one bright spot in my life right now, and I'm not about to have her find a way to ruin that.

"Why does it always feel like you're holding a part of yourself back from us, Grace?" Mom gives me a pitying look with that. Here we fucking go.

"Mom, don't. How many times have we done this? It never ends well. I try to explain; you get defensive and angry and shut down. It's a cycle, and we both know it. That's why I hold back."

"You have no legitimate reasons for your anger. I wish you would just stop."

"Really? No legitimate reason? Well I now know for a fact that isn't true, and it kind of pisses me off that you made me think I was crazy for so long by insisting that it was. But I'm going to choose to give you and Dad the benefit of the doubt and hope you really are in the dark about it all, and if that's the case, you would rather stay there. So please just drop it." I feel my blood turning to ice in my veins and get that feeling of a million ants crawling underneath my skin. The bile in my throat is rising, and I just need her to stop.

I see it in her face then. She hides it almost instantaneously, but it was there. She knows; she fucking knows what I am talking about and is denying it to my face. I don't say anything because I will truly lose it if I do. I simply stare at her. I let her know that she let the mask slip long enough to betray the truth for once.

"Fine. Have it your way. Be angry at nothing. We raised you perfectly well. You had a great childhood," she sniffs loudly and turns her back on me.

That's all I can take. I don't even think. I just need to flee. I grab my keys and say, "I have to go out for a bit. Something I forgot."

"Sure. We'll watch TV and relax," is all she says.

When I get to my car, I let out a guttural scream. I'm on the verge of hysteria but I get myself under control a minute later. I always thought she knew, but I couldn't imagine that a mother would just ignore or deny something like that. How is it even possible? How dare she claim to love me and act interested in my well-being all these years while pretending like that? I feel the vomit coming and quickly open my car door before it happens. Does my father know too? I can't handle these thoughts right now.

Instead I call Oliver.

"Hello?"

"Hey, I need that rescue badly." I can hear my voice trembling, and I hate my own weakness.

"Of course. How about you come over here to my place though? It's cheaper, cleaner, and quieter than meeting in a bar. I have most of what you would find in a bar to drink anyway."

"Sure, as long as there's alcohol, I don't mind where I am." I laugh without any humor at all.

"OK. You know the building. I'll text you the door code."

"See you soon."

As I exit my car, I realize I fled so quickly I didn't even think about what I was wearing. I'm in comfy wide-leg yoga pants and a camisole with a big sweater I usually only wear around the house. I took my contacts out earlier and have my glasses on. I feel like an old lady. Wow, this is embarrassing. Shaking my head, I make my way to his door because what I look like right now is honestly the least of my concerns.

When he opens the door to me, his first words are, "Grace, what on earth? You look like you've been crying." He steps forward and pulls me into a hug.

I remember then that I did cry as I drove. I was hardly aware of it, but I did. "It's my fucking mother. Maybe my father, too, who knows?" I sniff. "First I need to ask a favor: do you have a spare toothbrush? I threw up when I left my apartment, and I'd like to freshen up if I can."

"Of course, come on. Let me find what you need." He takes me to his bathroom and rummages in the medicine cabinet, producing a newly wrapped toothbrush for me.

"Thanks, you're a lifesaver."

"What else do you need?"

"This is good." I expect him to leave me then, but he seems reluctant to, so I just start brushing my teeth. He's looking at me with concern and so much compassion in his eyes it almost hurts. I've never even seen my own parents look at me like that.

He hands me a small plastic cup and some mouthwash afterward. "Here." This feeling of being taken care of is exactly what I need right now. How does he know what to do? I splash cold water on my face a few times, and he hands me a fresh towel.

"Better?"

"Much."

"Come on. Let's go have that drink now."

Oliver has scotch, and I have Irish whiskey. Neither of us bother with mixers or anything, because tonight is just not the night for fun drinking.

"You don't have to talk about it at all. Just tell me the best way to help you unwind, Grace."

I give a small snort at that. "How about the second-best way to help me unwind?"

"Naughty girl. Yeah, we'll go with the second best way." He smiles and shakes his head at me.

"I honestly don't even know. I just want to turn my brain off somehow. I'm so angry right now. How do I just relax and not think?"

"Well we can make some popcorn, put on a mindless action movie or a comedy. Either one is good in this situation. I watched a lot of them when Ally was first gone."

"Perfect! Popcorn and drinking, though; don't forget the drinking."

"Never. That's a huge part of turning the thoughts off." He leans over and pours us each another drink with a wink. "I say *Thor: Ragnarok*. It's got the action and the comedy, so it's basically perfect."

"It's got Chris and Tom, so yes, it is perfect. Not to mention Jeff Goldblum," I say.

Rolling his eyes at me, he groans. "As long as you're happy."

"I will be very happy, thank you."

He makes us homemade hand-popped popcorn, and it smells divine, all salty and drizzled in luscious butter. We settle into his couch as that Marvel intro music begins, and I feel a thousand times better already. He puts his arm around my back, pulling me close into his side, and I lay my head on his chest. It feels so normal and natural. The comfort is immense; it's exactly what I needed after that moment with my mother earlier.

***

Oliver

I've been holding Grace for a half hour and can barely concentrate on the movie. She has snuggled into me closer, and I am completely cradling her with my body now. She's nestled between my legs, my arms around her torso as she leans back into me with her small hands resting on my forearms, drawing lazy circles on my skin. My mind has to keep up a constant vigilance to keep my body from reacting to her in the way it wants, so it's fair to say I'm less relaxed than she is. I wouldn't be anywhere else on the planet, however. Whatever pain her parents caused her makes me furious. The anguish on her face when she arrived broke my heart. I won't push her to talk about it, but I have some ideas.

"This movie represents the three places I want to travel to most in the world," she says.

"Where's that?"

Holding up three fingers, she ticks them off as she names them. "New Zealand, represented by the director and lots of the actors. Scandinavia, represented when they go to Norway in the beginning. And Australia, represented by Hemsworth, of course."

"Why haven't you gone yet?"

"I don't know, really. Life just gets busy, and you keep putting your dreams on the back burner sometimes. Then I wasted almost three years with that loser Matt; he never wanted to go out of the country."

"You should go. Life is too short to have regrets." I say. "That's something I've thought about many times in the last couple of years."

"You're right. I should. I'm tired of just existing. I want to do more."

"Same," I agree. "Ready for a refill?" I ask.

"I have to decide if I'm going to drive my car home later before I do."

"You don't have to leave. You can stay tonight if you want."

She stays quiet for a while. I can feel her thinking. "I don't know. Last time was a bit of a disaster, wasn't it?"

"You'll get the bed to yourself, and I'll sleep on the couch this time." I promise. "I think you could use a break from your parents."

"I could. Let me text them and just let them know."

"Good." I squeeze her a little, glad she won't be going back there tonight where they caused her so much heartache. While she sends the text, I get us a refill of our whiskeys. We enjoy the rest of the movie in companionable silence. When it's over I stretch my arms out and yawn.

"How you feeling now? More relaxed?"

Turning to me, she says, "Much more. You are the best medicine I've ever tried."

Laughing, I pull her in for a hug. I say into her hair, "I wish I could fix everything."

"You do a pretty damn good job," she mumbles into my chest.

"If you ever want to talk about it, I'm here Murphy," I assure her.

"I just—I always had a feeling my mom, and maybe even my dad, knew I was sexually abused as a kid. They made me think I was crazy for years, but now I have confirmation of it all, and I hate them so much I just have no words for it. How can they think that pretending something didn't happen will make it all OK?"

"I can't imagine what that must feel like. Parents are supposed to be our safe place." It's useless, but it's all I can think to say.

"I had scars on my body I couldn't explain. I remember asking my mom about them when I was young, and she wouldn't even address it. She didn't even bother to make up a fake story. She just acted like unexplained scars and blanks in your memory were normal things. Hell, she isn't even a good liar."

I can tell she needs to just talk, so I don't say anything; I just hold her. I run my hands through her hair and hold her as she talks. "When I had sex for the first time, or what I thought was the first time, it was so strange. I had these uncanny flashbacks to vague things and this crazy feeling of having done it all before. There was no blood...I just knew something was off. I tried to talk to my mother about it afterward, but she completely shut me down. They probably know who did it. They probably have the answers I need, but they are such selfish assholes they'd rather pretend ignorance then help me."

All I can do is shake my head. "Hell, Grace. That's the most repugnant thing I've ever heard."

"If they hadn't insisted on this stupid weekend, I could have avoided all this crap. This is exactly why I left home as soon as I could. I cannot be around them. The fakeness and insincerity is sickening."

"After tomorrow you can put them out of your head again." I kiss her temple gently. Dumb idea, Oliver; her silky skin is warm and delicate. I want to taste more.

She takes in a deep breath and blows it out again. "One more day of faking it. I've booked a brunch at Sunny's for us, and then hopefully they will leave early to head back."

"Would it help if I tagged along for brunch? I can distract you or just hold your hand, metaphorically speaking."

"Why would you do that?"

"Because we're friends. I care about you."

"I'll think about it," is all she says.

"OK, well at least you don't have to deal with them tonight. You can get a good night's sleep."

"Yeah hopefully."

"You already have a toothbrush. I can get you a T-shirt or something to sleep in. Should I change the sheets for you?"

"No, don't go to any trouble. I'm sure it's fine. I just feel bad about taking your bed. Please let me sleep on the couch instead."

"No way. You need to rest, and I have an amazing mattress if I do say so myself. It's one thing I spend lots of money on. I want you to have a good night." I get up, pulling her with me.

After I make sure she has a big comfy T-shirt to sleep in and anything else she might need, I make myself comfortable on the couch, but sleep doesn't come. All I can think about is someone hurting Grace as a child and her fucking parents living in denial instead of dealing with it.

It's been about two hours when I hear whimpering and crying coming from my bedroom. Grace is tossing and turning, all twisted in the blanket. Her distress is palpable in the air, and I have to wake her. The sorrow coming from her is just more than I can stand.

"Grace, wake up. It's OK. you're safe." I shake her gently.

"Where am I?" Her eyes are huge and full of fear when they open. I gather her in my arms and rock her gently. She is sticky with sweat and panting.

"I've got you. You're with me."

"Oliver?"

"I'm here," I whisper.

"I'm sorry I woke you," she says, a little breathless.

"Don't be crazy. You never have to apologize to me."

"I had a feeling I might have bad dreams tonight." She's clinging to me so tightly.

"Want me to stay with you?" I ask.

"I thought we agreed not to share a bed again?"

"I think we can make an exception for tonight. You need to not be alone."

"OK, if you're sure. This is your bed, though, the one you shared with Ally. I don't want to upset you."

I just shake my head. "I'm fine." I keep stroking her hair. She is always thinking of me, always worried about my well-being even when she's falling apart. I lay us both back down, holding onto her tightly. As I soothe her to sleep, I wait for an inevitable feeling of shame or remorse to come at sharing my marriage bed with another woman. It never comes. For some strange reason I know deep down in my soul that Ally would understand what is happening here, much better than I do in fact. So for the second time, we fall asleep completely wrapped up together, and damn if it doesn't feel right.

***

Grace

The dream was a familiar one. A dark room that stinks of cigarettes, an overwhelming feeling of helplessness. Like when you sleep too deeply and can't wake up, feeling paralyzed in your tiredness. There's a man's voice there, always just a voice. Never a face.

"So pretty, little Grace." he tells me.

I try to get up and run but my body never works in these dreams. I can't move a muscle, I am stuck, incapacitated completely. I try to scream then, the next best thing to

running, but I have no voice, I just struggle to push air
out and no sound comes. The voice again, closer.
"*Don't worry Grace, it's all ok. Just keep our little secret*
and nothing bad will happen."
That must be when Oliver woke me up because it didn't get
further than that last night, Although I know what would
have come if it had, so it will play in my mind anyways.
But when he says he'll stay, and he holds me
close....it doesn't play in my mind all night.
Instead I focus on his hands, one stroking my hair
and the other rubbing my back, and somehow,
like a miracle I sleep and dream of nothing.

Waking up wrapped in powerful arms, surrounded by the smell of Oliver's cologne is probably the most incredible thing I've ever felt. He's still sleeping deeply. I can feel his chest rise and fall underneath my cheek. I don't move because this moment here makes everything I went through last night worth it.

"Good morning," a deep, gravelly voice rumbles under me eventually.

I smile to myself. "Morning." Neither of us move still. His hand rubs my back, and I just savor the sensation.

"What time is brunch?"

"Ten."

"Good, it's only eight thirty. Time for coffee," he says, glancing over at his bedside clock.

"We should probably get up, then," I point out.

"Eh, I guess, but this is pretty comfy."

We both chuckle. "It is."

"Five more minutes of cuddles, then," he declares.

"Cuddles?"

"Don't you like cuddles?"

"I never have before, but it's not so bad now."

After a moment of heavy silence, he says, "It's unsettling sometimes, how I feel with you. Like you have always been here, a part of my life. How is that even possible?"

I sit up then and lean on his chest, getting a better look at his face. "I know exactly what you mean. It's the same for me. I don't understand this connection I feel either. Usually I have these walls up with people, and I can't do anything about it, but with you I just say things. Things about myself I don't plan to say. But it feels so natural to be open with you for some reason."

He cups my face in his hands then. We don't say anything else. I see the moment he decides he needs space, the moment Ally enters his thoughts and his guilt rises. It's like reading a book as I watch it happen in his eyes. So I remove myself. Getting up, I go into the bathroom and shut the door. I take my time in there, knowing he needs time too.

When I emerge he's dressed and has coffee brewing. I'm back in my clothes from last night, and things have returned to more easy ground. He goes into the bathroom while I pour myself a cup of coffee and go to stand out on his balcony. There's a nice view, since his apartment is so high up. I love looking at the city like this.

"I always have my first cup out here too," a voice behind me says.

"I would for sure if I had a view like this."

"Ally picked this apartment because of the view. Her parents helped us with the down payment. We never could have afforded it otherwise. She was their only child, and they had some old family money. After she died they actually moved over to France for good, to a vacation home they own over there. I think it really broke them."

"The relationship between parents and children can vary so much from one family to another. I wonder if my parents wouldn't be relieved to have me gone sometimes."

"They don't deserve you."

"You maybe think too highly of me."

"No, I don't think so. I trust my judgment about people. You are very special, Grace. You just can't see it. Too many people have treated you like crap. I wish I could line them all up and do some damage back to them." He says it so very assuredly and with true vehemence behind the words.

I just look over at him. "I used to love the idea of a man wanting to defend me, even being violent on my behalf. How messed up is that? That was one of the things I thought Matt was like. Turns out his violent tendencies were geared more toward me than in defense of me. I definitely got him wrong."

"He doesn't still bother you, does he?"

"No, he found a new woman to torture, only she stupidly married him. I just hope they don't have kids. He would be an awful father."

"You really need to stay away from horrible people. I will gladly be your screener from now on. I have a good asshole radar."

I laugh at that. "Sounds good. That's a handy skill to have."

"So have you decided if I can come be your buffer at brunch?"

"I hate to put you through spending time with my parents."

"I will be glad to do it if it means they will behave with you."

"All right, let's do this. I need to go home to change and pick them up, so do you want to meet us there?"

"I'll go with you, keep you company. I'm already ready to go anyway."

***

Oliver

When we walk into Grace's place, her parents look thoroughly relieved to see a stranger with her, like they won't have to be alone with their own daughter and they are glad for it. My anger flares immediately.

"Hey, guys, this is my friend Oliver. I stayed over his place last night because we were drinking late and I didn't want to drive. He's going to join us for brunch. I'm just gonna go get ready real quick." I hate how empty and hurt her voice sounds even though I know she is trying to shut down all emotions with them.

"Oliver. How nice to actually find our daughter has friends," her mother says with sickening sweetness.

"Your daughter is an amazing woman. I feel very lucky to have met her."

Her father shakes my hand. "I'm Jack, and this is Maureen."

"Nice to meet you both." We stand around making small talk while we wait for Grace to return. We decide to walk to brunch since it's a beautiful day out and we have the time. Grace and I stay a few paces behind her parents. I feel the need to protect her from them, but clearly they seem determined to make as little effort to talk to her as possible. It pisses me the hell off.

Leaning down, I whisper, "I suppose if I held your hand in solidarity, that would give them too much to gossip about, wouldn't it?"

She scoffs, "Who cares what they think?"

So I do it, take her hand, and I squeeze it tight. She holds on like I'm a life raft in the ocean.

Sunny's is a great brunch spot, and we all have drinks, which helps. Grace's mother keeps up a steady stream of inane chatter that is grating on the nerves. I can't imagine having parents who refused to deal with your childhood trauma and even failed to protect you from it happening. I feel resentment on her behalf, and I'm so glad I came so she wouldn't have to do this on her own. Under the table I've held her hand on and off throughout the ordeal; I can't think of a better word for it.

Abruptly her father looks at me and says, "Oliver, are you my daughter's boyfriend? Because if you are, I think it's pretty shady that you don't just admit to it. You think we haven't seen how often you hold her hand?" His tone is strange, not hostile but clearly agitated.

"I'm a close friend who is here to offer support," I state matter-of-factly.

"Dad, seriously, what the hell?" Grace says sternly.

"I'm just doing my job as a father, sweetie."

That is the straw that breaks the camel's back; I see it in her eyes.

"Are you kidding me? You want to pretend to be protective, today of all days. Did Mom not enlighten you about why I left last night? I can't believe you. This farce of a happy family's weekend is almost done, and you go and say that." Her voice is cold, emotionless, and I take her hand again, determined to safeguard her in any way I can.

"Why do you think we deserve to be treated like this?" Her mother whines, clearly used to playing the victim. "And why does he think you need support? What lame sob story did you tell him, you liar?" She spits the last word out with venom. The sheer audacity of these people has got me at my limit.

I stand up then, ignoring them both. I look only at Grace, willing her to do the same and keep her eyes on me.

"Let's go, Grace. I think your parents can get the bill today." I hold out my hand and help her up. She is stunned but takes my hand and rises. Once I've got her on her feet, I turn to her father. "I'm going to take Grace for a lovely walk. Will one of you kindly text her once you've vacated her apartment and left town?"

The looks on their faces prove beyond any doubt that they are guilty of every single thing I've imagined. They know precisely what they have done, and they are stunned to be called out by a stranger. Pathetic. Her mother simply gapes, and her father merely nods without saying anything.

"Thank you." I say, my tone dripping with fake pleasantry in a mockery of how they act. I take Grace and get her the hell away from these two.

***

Grace

When we reach the sidewalk, I finally react to how Oliver just rescued me back there.

"That was the best thing I've ever seen," I say, absolutely gleefully.

"I couldn't take another second of it. I overstepped, but I'm not actually sorry for it. I understand now why you vomited on your way to my house last night."

"You literally are a hero. Do you realize that?"

"I'm not. I just have common decency."

"I don't think you understand the magnitude of someone standing up for me. It's never happened before. When Matt was my boyfriend, he acted like I was crazy and they were saints. And then when he was being abusive, my parents wouldn't even get involved, I told my dad about it, and he suggested that I try to be more understanding of Matt's issues as a solution. It gutted me."

"He did what?"

"Matt was ex-military, and my dad tried to say that his violent tendencies weren't his fault, that I needed to be more careful of how I acted so as not to make him upset ever. That was all he had to say. That's why when he acted like the dutiful father with you back there, I kind of lost it."

Oliver is just shaking his head in disbelief. "That's sickening," is all he says finally.

"I don't want to think about them anymore. I bet they won't ever ask for another weekend with me again. Thank god! Not now that they realize I remember the abuse they kept quiet about."

"Good. They don't deserve any space in that wonderful head of yours." He's stopped walking now, facing me, and he has my face in his hands again. People mumble, annoyed at us as they have to move around us on the sidewalk, but I don't notice anything but the way he looks at me like I really am worth something. I'm astonished at seeing myself through his eyes. It has done more for me than months of therapy, I swear. I may not be able to have this man as mine, but he has given me such a gift with his friendship. He shows me that I am valuable. I may be damaged, I may have been weak in the past, but in his eyes, I am worth so much more than everyone in my life has ever led me to believe.

"Thank you," I repeat.

"Come on. Let's go to the botanical gardens and look at beautiful things to cleanse our souls," he says.

"Yes, please."

"I can't believe I've never come here!" The New York Botanical Gardens in the Bronx are absolutely stunning. Oliver is apparently a member and has passes; such an unexpected thing to learn about him.

"It was one of Ally's favorite places. I just couldn't give up the membership. There were too many good memories here with her."

"I swear, the more I hear about her, the more I wish I had known her."

"She was special, like you. I can definitely imagine the two of you as friends. You're both so genuine."

"I may not have known her, but thinking about her death makes me sad. Is that weird?"

"I think it's sweet. You are very empathetic, you know."

"That's my INFJ showing."

"Your what?"

"INFJ. You know, the sixteen personalities? You take the test, and it helps explain why you are the way you are."

"I do not know. I have never heard of it." He laughs a little. So naturally for the next forty minutes as we walk around the beautiful grounds, I give Oliver the test and read him the results. We laugh and have fun analyzing everything. He gets ISFJ, which is no surprise at all.

"I'm glad you feel comfortable talking about Ally with me," I admit when we are in the cab after we leave the gardens.

"Me too. It doesn't hurt as much as it used to. For some reason, with you it's kind of cathartic. Maybe because you're so open about yourself. It makes me feel like being open back."

I get a text alert then from my father. I knew it would come from him. My mother will never get over the humiliation of being called out by a handsome stranger.

—We are gone.

That's all it says.

"Good, they're gone. I can go home now."

"Are you going to be OK tonight?" he asks, concern etched on his face.

"Yes, I want to clean my place and get to bed early with my book. I'm so mentally exhausted from all their mind games."

"Need help cleaning?"

I bite my lip then. I consider how to say what I need to without offending him. I am beyond grateful for everything he's done and how wonderful he is, but the more I'm with him, the harder I fall. I need to retreat back to protective mode now.

"No, I think it's better if I do it alone. I'm going to blast angry punk rock and indulge in a bitchy mood for a while. Best to do it alone," I simply say, instead of that I can't be

159

with him and not fall head over heels in love with him. That I need space if he expects me to stay in the friend zone where he wants me.

"I understand." He says, squeezing my hand.

Of course you do, I think to myself, you're perfect.

Denial

Oliver

J ess is chewing me out. I have gotten away with a lot since losing Ally because I got the widower pass, but apparently that's over now.

"Ollie, it's been weeks since we've seen you. It's a family dinner. Why on earth are you unsure if you can come? You don't do anything on weekends anyway. This is just ridiculous. We want to see you."

I don't want to explain that Grace has been fragile all week since her nightmarish parents left, and I don't want to be obligated in case she needs me on Saturday night. It wouldn't make any sense to her. I haven't mentioned to anyone in my family that we have grown close since running into each other at the Mexican restaurant that night. She is my own secret indulgence. I love having her all to myself.

"I just might be needed by a friend."

"Who?" Jess demands.

"Someone you don't know. They are dealing with some shit."

"And you may or may not be needed on Saturday evening at dinnertime? What are you, on call for them or something?" Her tone is incredulous, like I'm making it all up.

"Fine! I'll be there, whatever. But if I have to leave, I don't want to hear any crap from anyone." I decide giving in is the easier option. I can always bail if need be.

"You're being very weird. If I didn't know better, I'd think you had a girl you didn't want us to know about." How does she always do this? Is it a big sister superpower or something?

"I'm hanging up, Jess. I'm at work, and you're crazy. See you Saturday." Avoidance is key with her.

It has felt like Grace withdrew a bit since I left her at her place Sunday night. Not that she owes me any amount of contact or anything. I just wish I could see her. I want to know she's doing OK after dealing with those people. I asked her about doing our classic movie watching this week, but she said she was busy every evening. Yoga, therapy, dinner with friends, and some kind of book club thing. If I didn't know her to be a very open person, I would wonder if she was blowing me off. I shouldn't care so much, though, should I? It's not like we're dating. I just wish missing her didn't feel so potent. Like I'm having withdrawals from a drug I've become dependent on. By Thursday night I feel like I've been as patient as I can. I know she said she had book club, but how late can that run, really? I wait till 9 p.m. and then text her.

—This week has been so long. I feel like it's lasted a month. How's it been for you?

She is usually a quick responder, so when almost an hour has passes, I start to think of all the reasons she might be annoyed at me. I'm acting like some insecure teenager. Is she annoyed at how high-handed I acted with her parents now that she's had time to think about it all week? I decide to just chill and not stress about this. Yeah, like that's going to happen. I grab my iPad and head out to my balcony, having decided to write to Ally as a distraction.

Ally,

I miss you tonight, baby. My head is full of strange thoughts and even stranger insecurities. If you were here, we'd open a bottle of wine and sit on the balcony listening to the traffic of the city and just talk. I love hashing through messy thoughts with you. You were always much wiser than me and made things appear so much clearer. What would you tell me tonight, I wonder? Probably that I am expecting things from Grace that I have no right to expect. I tell her over and over again I can't do more than friendship right now. I talk about my dead wife all the time. And then I somehow expect her to want to talk to me every day and spend time with me every week. Yeah, it isn't quite fair, is it? She's a beautiful single girl. She should find someone who can give her a real future to spend her time on. So that decides it: if she is pulling back, I won't push her. I guess it would only make sense if that is what she decides to do, after all. Thanks for the "talk," baby. Even beyond the grave, your wisdom is still my savior.

I take out my phone again and look at my favorite pictures of my Ally. She was my world, and tonight I feel especially lonely and empty. Maybe because the one person who has been bringing me out of the pit isn't available to me. I play the song that is guaranteed to make me even more sad, "Fix You" by Coldplay, and I just wallow. As I listen, the words have such a different meaning this time though. Usually they all make me think of Ally, but tonight they mean something else altogether. Closing my eyes, the only face in my mind is Grace's. Everything is about Grace suddenly. My text alert goes off just then.

—Yeah, it's been a week for me too. I'm very glad tomorrow is Friday, not going to lie.

—Any fun plans for the weekend?

—Nothing big, just things I need to get done that I never seem to have the time for. Kyle and Tara want to check out an '80s and '90s music themed club on Saturday night, so that will be fun. You know my eclectic musical tastes.

—That does sound fun. You'll have to tell me how it is.

—Will do.

I let it end there. It's better if we have a small break from each other, I suppose. Maybe she'll meet some nice guy when she's out with her friends. Maybe Mark will show up again. Too bad the thought of that makes me want to crawl into a deep, dark hole.

***

Grace

Glory Days is, in truth, a very neat place. I wasn't expecting to like it as much as I do. Tara and I went all out with our '90s attire. I'm in stonewashed denim shorts with a wide black belt and a red plaid crop top with a black chocker necklace. Very Cher from *Clueless*. Tara went for more of a Spice Girls look, with army green parachute pants and a ripped Union Jack tank top and Doc Martens. Kyle is wearing a backward baseball cap, and his outfit is very "young Johnny Depp": baggy jeans, white wifebeater, and a black leather jacket that is way too big for the style these days. We have been having a great time dancing to all the throwbacks. Madonna, Springsteen, Michael Jackson, No Doubt, Nirvana, Bon Jovi, Green Day, Def Leppard, The Cranberries, Matchbox Twenty, Queen, Duran Duran, REO Speedwagon, Cyndi Lauper…I swear this place is like my dream concert. The cover charge wasn't cheap, but it's totally worth it. The drinks are priced well also, so that makes up for it. It's in a huge old warehouse in Brooklyn, and there are a few private booths in actual '80s and '90s cars parked throughout the space.

We are in an '80s Camaro convertible; it's orange and has been gutted and fitted out with leather couches and a table. Kyle knows the DJ here tonight and had the extra pull to get us this cool seating. For the first time in weeks, I'm having a truly good time that doesn't revolve around Oliver. It gives me a slight bit of hope. Maybe I'll meet someone else I can fall for, and then I can just enjoy being friends with him. I've danced with a couple of guys more than once tonight, but none of them have really drawn my interest. Right now I'm just putting my feet up for a while and enjoying a cold beer, listening to all the great songs. Idly I scroll through things on my phone, since Tara and Kyle are both still dancing. A text comes through from Oliver then. I'm surprised because it's almost midnight, and I would have imagined he'd be asleep by now.

—How was the club?

—It is actually awesome. We're still here. The music is amazing. So many good songs I haven't heard in forever. Why are you still up?

—Can't sleep. I had a big family dinner and didn't get home till eleven thirty, but I'm just not tired. That place sounds fun.

I snap a few pictures of the place, including a selfie of me holding my beer, and send them to show him how cool it looks inside.

—Are you sitting in a muscle car?

—Yes! I'm telling you, it's so cool here. I wasn't expecting to love it this much.

—I'm jealous. My night was not that fun. How much longer are you staying? I kind of feel like coming to check it out.

—They don't close till five, and I have nothing to do but sleep tomorrow, so I plan to get my money's worth tonight. The cover charge was high!

—You think I'd get in?

—Kyle knows the DJ. We can get you in.

—Send me the addresses.

—Seriously?

—Yes, I'm not a boring old man, no matter how often you call me that.

I find the location in my maps and send it to him, then I head to the dance floor to find Kyle and let him know we need to make sure he can get in. So much for my Oliver-free night. Not that I don't want to see him, but I'm hardly going to meet a new love interest with the one I really want coming to join me. Of course both Tara and Kyle try to make a big deal about the fact that he's on his way. I beg them not to embarrass me, remind them he is just a friend, and finally bribe them by buying the next round of drinks if they promise to behave. I decide I need to stay loose and distracted, so I continue dancing and make Kyle go wait by the entrance to get Oliver in. When I next return to our booth, he's there talking to Kyle, drinking a Stella Artois and looking better than I've ever seen him look. His hair is more slicked back than usual, and he's in all black. His black dress shirt is tight fitting and has the sleeves rolled up and the first few buttons undone. His slacks fit far too perfectly. He looks happy and is laughing at something with Kyle. My mouth has gone completely dry, and I can't seem to think of anything to say, so I grab for a glass of water and just gulp. Over the rim of the glass, his eyes meet mine, and there is a sparkle in them that reminds me of the time he caught me checking him out on the shark diving boat. Arrogant bastard is a good look on him, too, apparently.

"This place is incredible. Thanks for letting me crash your night," he leans in and tells me.

"Anytime," is all I can manage for the moment.

"Are you a dancer or just the listening and drinking type?" I ask a few minutes later.

"I haven't danced in years, but if the mood strikes, I am willing." he shrugs.

Tara returns then and greets Oliver. We all settle in with another round and start chatting. With the small interior of the booth, I end up sitting extremely close to Oliver, and he doesn't do anything to put space between us. I wish he would because I struggle to be the one doing it, and at the same time, one of us should. I hate that I am now overthinking everything and tense again.

I guess it doesn't go unnoticed that I'm feeling awkward because Kyle, ever the group leader, claps his hands together and announces, "OK, put your beers down, everyone. Time for 'Never Have I Ever.' Only allowed to drink when you have done the thing that someone says…you get the gist. Oliver, you go first because you're the oldest."

That gets a laugh from everyone, and Oliver shakes his head. Then he puts his hand up to his chin and appears to be pondering.

"Never have I ever gone on a blind date."

All three of the lame single people groan loudly and drink at that one, of course.

"Tara, you're up."

"OK, never have I ever kissed my best friend."

My eyes immediately go to Oliver's, and I find him looking straight back into mine. A slow and very saucy grin creeps onto his face as he lifts his beer and his eyebrow at me. I decide to drink also. That gets a giggle and gasp from the other two in our group.

"I'm offended!" Tara says, "I thought I was your best friend, but I know we've never kissed so I guess I'm wrong."

"I would say we want details, but I'm fairly certain Grace will yell at me. My turn," says Kyle. "Never have I ever had sex in a movie theater, because I think they are grungy, and it's disgusting," he laughs.

There's a moments pause, and I quietly lift my beer without looking at anyone. Oliver also drinks. I then realize how this looks and blurt out, "Not with him! It was Matt," at the same moment he says, "With my wife Ally!" Now we are all laughing at the awkwardness of this game and our stupid situation.

"But to be clear, the best friend kiss was the two of you together?"

Tara just has to bring that up.

"We drank too much and had to share a room in the Hamptons because everything else was booked. It was just a drunken mistake, that's all." I quickly explain.

"It was my fault," Oliver volunteers for some reason. Neither of us mention the "Truth or Dare" pool kiss. We had decided that one doesn't count since it was part of the game.

"Grace, your turn." Kyle gets us back on track.

"Never have I ever sent a naked picture of myself to someone." I look at Kyle for that one because I happen to know he has a very embarrassing story about this exact thing.

"Oh, you're so very funny, Grace. Fine." He takes a big drink. Tara also drinks, which I did not expect.

"You are both crazy. That shit is out there on the internet somewhere, you know," I laugh.

"Yes, Mom, thanks for the lecture. That's why my face isn't showing."

"Classy." I shake my head.

Just then someone shouts out from nearby, "Oliver?"

We all turn to look, and there's a young man coming toward us that I recognize as Oliver's younger brother that he was with at the Mexican restaurant.

"I couldn't believe my eyes. I thought, There's no way on god's green earth my old man of a brother is up past midnight and in a cool club in Brooklyn."

He claps Oliver on the shoulders and shakes him a bit. "Seriously, man, what the fuck?"

"Milo, nice to see you too…again," Oliver says dryly. "Everyone, this is my little brother Milo." Everyone greets him and introduces themselves. Milo jumps into our increasingly crowded Camaro booth and seats himself next to Tara with a flirty smile.

I instantly like him. He just exudes joy and fun.

"I have got to tell you guys, I had no idea my brother had cool friends. This is an exciting night for me." He is grinning from ear to ear. "I'm buying the next few rounds for everyone in celebration. I'm just so stoked right now."

"My little brother, the charmer." Oliver shakes his head some more. I place my hand on his knee and tease him a bit.

"Aw, don't let it bring you down, old man. We still think you're cool even if Milo is pretty amazing. We won't forget we loved you first."

"Hmph," is his only reply to that.

Milo has already started a quiet, clearly flirtatious conversation with Tara, and I think it's kind of cute how she is blushing at him. Kyle informs us he's going to go visit his DJ friend for a minute, squeezing his way out of the car. So things settle down a bit. Oliver and I just lean back and enjoy the nostalgic music. When "Creep" by Radiohead comes on next, I say, "Ugh, this song! I love it so much. It's like my theme song."

He turns his head toward me with an incredulous look. "This? This is your theme song. Really? You are not a creep... you should have a much better theme song."

"Nope, this is perfect. Even when I was young, I felt like I didn't belong anywhere. My family felt off, I was different and didn't know why. I felt dirty and didn't understand it. I had all these unexplained perceptions of things. It's hard to explain to someone who hasn't experienced it."

He takes my hand then. Holding it tight, he brings it up to his chest and holds it over his heart. My song plays loudly, pounding through my soul as we just look into each other's eyes.

"You are so fucking special Grace," he finally pronounces.

I give him a weak smile and remove my hand from his grip. I'm feeling far too much at this moment and need a change of subject as soon as possible!

"What would your theme song be?" I ask then.

"Lately I don't know anymore. My life keeps changing so much. There is a Paul McCartney song I've been relating to a lot."

He stops speaking abruptly, as if he said more than he wanted to. Then he looks at me and asks, "Want to dance to the next slow song? I'm not a good fast dancer, but I can just about stand there and sway."

"Sure, I can do that. I need to run to the bathroom first." I get up and head for the restroom hallway, knowing it will take me past the DJ booth. I make a stop and tell Kyle to see if he can get his friend to play a slow song sometime soon. I probably shouldn't. Being held in Oliver's arms is the last thing I need, in all honesty, but I just can't seem to help myself.

After I return to the booth I find only Oliver there. Tara and Milo are apparently dancing.

"They seem to have hit it off," I note.

"Milo is such a flirt."

"Tara too; she can handle him."

A slow song starts playing a few minutes later, and Oliver gets to his feet, holding out his hand to me. "Time to fulfill your promise, Murphy. Let's go."

I smile and get to my feet. We head out to the dance floor, and I'm trying to identify the song. "What song is this?"

"It's Bonnie Raitt, 'I Can't Make You Love Me.' I only know that because my mother loves her and this song, I swear."

I laugh. "Sure, that's why." His arms go around my waist, and I bring mine up around his neck. My head naturally goes against his chest, and we begin a slow sway to the music. Talking is superfluous right now. Just being this close to him, feeling the hard curves of his muscles, inhaling the scent of his cologne, and feeling his hands against the bare skin of my waist is all so perfect. Too perfect, really. He rests his head on top of mine, and I can feel him take in a deep breath. It's dark on the dance floor, and we could be the only two people in here at this moment. The majority of dancers went to get drinks when the slow song came on.

Bonnie Raitt sings out, straight into my slowly cracking heart. If I let myself fall much deeper for this man, the wreckage will be catastrophic. He pulls back a little then, looking down at me.

"Why do you feel so perfect in my arms?" he murmurs quietly, almost like he's asking himself.

"You have to stop doing this to me," I say at last, closing my eyes tightly to stop the tears.

"Can you give me some more time, Grace?"

"I can't deny you anything, even when I should." We don't talk anymore. We just dance.

I decide I need to call it a night soon. There really is only so much I can take. Unless he's willing to move on from Ally and actually do something about this spark growing between us, I need to step back from the flames. I can't be the one who ends up burnt to a crisp.

When the song ends, we separate our bodies and walk unspeaking back to the group. I pull my phone from my back pocket and make a show of checking the time, then produce a large yawn.

"I hate to be the first to succumb, guys, but I think I'm ready for bed. I'm going to order an Uber and get going." I open the app and order my ride home.

"You can't get in an Uber alone at almost two in the morning," Oliver states.

"I'll be fine. It wouldn't be the first time," I say. "Anyway, I don't live far."

"I don't care. I'm coming with you. I will make sure you arrive home safely. No arguments, Grace."

I roll my eyes at him. "Yes, Dad."

Milo bursts out laughing at that. "You are good for him, Grace. Keep him young for me, will you?"

"I'll try." I wink at him, then make my goodbyes for the night and head for the exit, needing to grab my coat first.

I stay quiet as we ride to my place. My head is full of a million thoughts but can't put any of them into words.

"Is everything OK?" he asks, breaking the silence.

"Yeah, I'm just tired," I lie.

"I got the feeling you were maybe avoiding me a little this week."

I stay quiet for a few minutes. Of course he noticed. "I think I kind of was," I finally admit.

"Did I do something to upset you?"

"No, you didn't do anything. It's because I need some space if I'm going to keep respecting your situation, that's all. I need to think about damage control for myself sometimes, you know." I expel a deep breath.

"I'm sorry." He is looking at me, I can feel it, so I turn to look back at him. There is a lot going on in his eyes, so I just wait for what else he has to say to me. The car comes to a stop, and I realize we are at my building.

"Can I walk you up?"

"If you do, will you stay?" I decide to ask because I need to know. He looks down, and I can sense his hesitation.

Finally he says, "I can't. I just want to make sure you are safe."

I just shake my head, knowing I can't keep letting this go on. The pain is overtaking me.

"No, I just need to be alone now, but thanks for seeing me home. Goodbye, Oliver."

Something's Gotta Give

Grace

I feel like after that dance and those words sung out by Bonnie Raitt, I need to give myself a wake-up call. You can't make a person love you, no matter how right it may seem. We only get one heart. If he gave his to Ally, it just may be impossible for him to ever move on. I haven't wanted to face up to that, but I need to. How much longer will I torture myself before giving up the fight? Besides, I am reaching a breaking point physically. The sexual frustration has consumed me to the point where I can think of almost nothing else. It's unhealthy, for goodness sake. I have been trying so hard to be understanding about his situation. I can accept all the reasons he isn't in the right place in his life for a relationship now. I won't try to change his mind. I also need to do the right thing for myself, and my vibrators are no longer enough; it's that simple. The fact of the matter is I'm not anyone's girlfriend. I am a totally single woman who is free to do what I need to do. In an ideal world, I would get to be with the person I want to be with, the one who makes my heart and body sing. But this is the real world. In the real world, we don't always get what we want.

Usually when this kind of thing happens, I have a one-night thing, I'm not necessarily proud of it, but I'm honest with myself. I have always been a very sexual person, and I know my limits, and I am beyond my freaking limits. I have a friend with benefits; like me, he is honest about his needs, and we have been open about our views with one another. Neither of us is interested in a relationship with the other. We do, however, have amazing chemistry and have happily used each other without complications.

Lately I can't help but think that I need to call him and see if he is available to spend the night soon. I need to relieve this incredible tension before I explode. It is a last resort because I'm not naive, and I understand that even with no strings attached, sex can have unintended consequences. I simply need to be as careful as possible. After considering it for days, I finally bite the bullet and text Anthony. He is about as physically opposite from Oliver as you can get, and, in all likelihood, that is a good thing. Half-black and half-Cuban he is without question handsome. Dark and sensual, but not as tall as Oliver and slimmer. We met a few years back and got along well, completely incompatible as a couple, but that was never an issue since neither of us wanted it from the other.

Anthony responds to my text almost instantly, understanding exactly what's going on. We make a plan for him to come over Friday night, bringing dinner and then staying over. I avoid talking to Oliver all week. He is the one I want to be planning a sexy rendezvous with. That, however, is not possible, so I need to keep him out of my head and heart as much as possible for now. That hasn't stopped him from texting me though; today he sent me info about a cool little international pop-up market happening this weekend, saying we should check it out. I don't want to blow him off, but I also can't mentally think about spending time with Oliver at the same time as I'm trying to plan a night with Anthony either. I try to go with a noncommittal but pleasant response.

—That does look cool...I haven't been feeling great
all week, though, so I want to wait and see if I feel up
to it. If I'm better, we can check it out.

Not feeling great is no lie either; I am like an overtightened guitar string ready to snap. Maybe by Saturday afternoon, I can get my shit together enough to relax in Oliver's presence. If Anthony does a good job, I should be thoroughly relaxed, I think to myself wryly.

The time has come, and I feel strangely ready and not all at the same time. On my way home from work, I go by the liquor store for a bottle of my favorite expensive vodka, knowing I need to somehow unwind tonight. Back at my apartment I shower, making sure I'm shaved and prepared for my body to be fully on display for the first time in quite a while. After that I go around lighting my favorite scented candles and play my music, gradually loosening up more and more. Pouring my first drink of the evening, I'm finally feeling genuinely serene for the first time since setting up this booty call—because let's be honest, that's what it is. When my phone buzzes with a text, I figure it's most likely Anthony with an ETA or something. It's not; it's Oliver.

—How are you feeling? Do you need anything... chicken soup? Medicine? Company?

My eyes shut involuntary. I feel the sting of tears rising up, and the tightness in my chest is almost unbearable. *No!* my brain screams. I can't do this tonight. I can't have him ruin this for me. A woman can only take so much. I want this man with every fiber of my being, and I have no way of having him. It's time to nip this crap in the bud for the evening. No way will I be conversing with him throughout the night. So I answer quickly while my resolve is strong.

—No thank you. I'm going to head to bed now, actually. I think I just need extra rest more than anything.

With that I down the rest of my drink, get up, and making sure my phone is silenced, I place it facedown on the mantle, where I'm determined it will remain. No more thinking about him tonight, period. I will take this time for myself. Mentally shaking myself, I decide to do a final check of how I look. There are most definitely advantages to hooking up with someone familiar; you don't have to overthink your seduction methods, you don't have to worry if they want you, and you know exactly where things are going. However, I still like to make sure I look cute. He always looks incredible, so it's only fair. I'm wearing a sexy little pajama set of booty shorts and a cami. It's made of olive-green silk and trimmed with black lace along my ass cheeks and bust line. My hair is soft and slightly curled at the ends, hanging loose on my shoulders. No need for coyness with Anthony, so I went straight for the lingerie, and it also has the benefit of being comfy after a long week. I decide to also spritz some of my perfume on all the right spots. The knock on my door startles me, but I feel ready. I take one last deep breath and clear my mind.

Anthony looks just as attractive as I expected, and as he envelopes me in a hug, his spicy cologne smells heavenly.

"Looking beautiful, Irish," he says in his deep voice, placing a kiss on my forehead. I had forgotten about his little nickname for me, and it brings a smile to my lips.

"Not so bad yourself," I add, taking him in fully. "Can I get you a drink?"

"Nah, I'm good for now. It's been so long since we've been together I kinda want to take you all in without distractions for a bit." He smirks, running an appreciative glance up and down my body.

"Such a flirt." I shake my head with a smile. I'm secretly pleased he's so good at breaking the ice quickly though. We head toward the kitchen, and I ask about the bag of takeout he's got,

"What did you bring us for dinner?"

"I grabbed some sushi from that place you like down the street. Is that good?"

"Perfect." To be honest, food is the last thing I care about right now, and I doubt I'll want more than a bite, but I love that he remembers these things about me. I pull out two plates and start opening the containers.

"So to what do I owe the pleasure of this booty call?" Anthony asks, leaning on the counter with his arms crossed over his chest, a sexy smirk on his face.

"You don't even want to know," I laugh sardonically.

Arching an eyebrow, he says, "Really? Interesting, very interesting. I think that I actually do want to know."

"That isn't really part of what we do, though, is it?"

"Maybe not, but I honestly didn't expect this from you right now. I saw some stuff on Instagram lately, and you just seemed really happy and busy. I actually thought you were seeing someone on the down low. Guess I was wrong." He shrugs.

"Oh." I clear my throat, realizing that it probably does look like that from an outsider's point of view. While I try to decide how I'm going to answer this, I hand him his plate, and we head toward the couch, settling in to eat a relaxing dinner.

"OK look, while we eat we can catch each other up briefly, but after that can we please just turn it all off? That, more than anything, is what I need tonight."

"Of course. You don't have to tell me anything. You know I just want to make sure everything is OK with you."

"In some ways I'm genuinely good and happy. It's just that, well, the person that makes me happy isn't interested in a relationship. Long story short, he's a widower and isn't over his dead wife. I can't lie: I've fallen for him; it just can't be plain and simple. So as happy as I have been these past few weeks, I am also incredibly miserable and horny at the same time."

After a minute of thought, Anthony says, "Oh shit, that is something. Well, I'm glad you told me. The timing makes more sense now. I can usually tell when we're going to have one of our nights, but this time caught me off guard. Not that I wasn't happy about it though." He rubs my thigh in a familiar and comfortable gesture.

"How about you? No romance in your life still?"

"No, you know me. I don't have the time for romance these days. My business is still new and has taken off like crazy, so that occupies all my time. I'm lucky if I have time to see to myself most days. That's why I made the time for you tonight when I got your text. It's been far too long." Now his expression is downright sinful, and he rubs the back of my neck with the hand he has draped across the back of the couch. I lean my head back and close my eyes, trying to relax into his touch. I hate that we ended up talking about Oliver, but at the same time I am glad I told him the truth about what's going on.

"I think I'll make another drink," I say, getting up.

"Grace." Anthony stands up too. "Are you completely sure about tonight? I've never seen you on edge like this."

Stepping into him, I decide that it's time to make myself clear. I run my hands under the hem of his tight T-shirt, feeling his warm skin. I slowly slide it up and over his head, throwing it to the side. Leaning into his chest, I place a soft kiss right in the center and whisper, "I need this Ant, please. It's been hell. It's not just falling for a guy I can't have; there's been other stuff too. But I don't want to talk anymore. I am on edge, and I'm tense. I need you to help me fix that. Do you mind?"

I bring my eyes up to his, and I know they are pleading with him also. He takes my face in his hands and runs a thumb along my bottom lip slowly.

"All right, baby girl, here's what we're gonna do. This isn't going to be like our other times. I think you need me to do the work tonight, and it would be my fucking privilege. I'm going to take care of you." With that he scoops me into his arms and carries me into the bedroom. I guess I don't need another drink after all, maybe just a man who isn't afraid to give me what I need.

Revelation

Oliver

I can't stop thinking about Grace being sick. She lives alone here in the city, and it worries me for some reason. It shouldn't, because she's an adult and can certainly take care of herself, but after she said good night so abruptly last night, I had a strange feeling. With Ally being a paramedic for so long, I heard too many bad stories for my own good. My mind keeps conjuring up ridiculous images of her passed out in her apartment and no one knowing. Maybe losing someone unexpectedly turns you into an overworrier for the rest of your life. I am being ludicrous, I'm sure, but I don't actually care as I head to her place Saturday morning without telling her. I just need to see her with my own two eyes and be sure she's OK. I'm bringing a bag of bagels for her. I wanted to buy a bouquet of flowers, but I thought it might not be best.

I knock a couple of times and start to feel alarmed when she still hasn't come to the door. I saw her car outside on the street, so I lean my ear against the door to see if I can hear anything. That's right when it opens, and I practically fall into her green silk-covered cleavage.

"Crap! Oliver, what are you doing?" Grace reaches out to steady me and keep me from face-planting in her boobs. Smooth, very smooth.

I clear my throat and feel a flush coming to my cheeks when I just give in and start laughing. "Um, checking your breathing?"

She laughs and looks down with a blush at her skimpy outfit. "Wait a minute while I grab my robe." And then she heads back to the bedroom. I try really hard not to watch her walk away, but who am I kidding. Damn, those pajamas are not fair. The black lace skimming her plump ass cheeks are doing all kinds of things to my brain, and I suddenly feel the need to sit down. I walk over to her couch, trying to clear my head of all the inappropriate thoughts flooding it.

Setting the bag of bagels down on the coffee table, I notice suddenly that there are a large pair of men's shoes kicked off to the side in a corner. Looking around, I see a T-shirt flung off on a side chair. I also hear Grace talking to someone in the bedroom and a man's voice answering her.

Fuck, fuck, fuck! I need to go now. This is not good. I get up and head to the door, not even worrying that I'm about to leave with no explanation. Before I can get there, though, Grace is coming out of the bedroom followed by an extremely good-looking guy.

"Look, I'm sorry. I shouldn't have shown up unannounced. I was just worried because you've been not feeling well and wanted to check how you were doing. It was stupid of me. I'll go," I ramble.

Grace reaches out and puts a small hand on my arm. "Oliver, calm down. We're all adults. It's OK. Thank you for coming by and checking on me. That's really sweet of you.

There's no need for you to leave." I realize that for someone who has insisted that we're not involved, I'm acting pretty senseless. So I take a deep breath and then decide to man up and handle the situation like I actually have a pair of balls.

I reach my hand out and smile at the man that I really want to punch in the gut. "Hey, man, I'm Oliver. Sorry for barging in."

"Anthony. No problem, man, don't worry about it. I was actually about to get going, so you're fine." He goes and retrieves his shoes and shirt and sits down at the kitchen table to put them on.

Grace has started making coffee in the kitchen. "Do you want some coffee before you head out, Ant?" she asks. Why does the fact that she has a nickname for this guy hurt like a sore throat?

"Nah, baby girl, I'm good. I gotta head into the office anyway, and we have fancy-ass espresso machines there. No offense to your little percolator." The smirk on his face and the way he says it makes it sound like it has a dirty double meaning. Grace throws him a look over her shoulder.

"Snob."

He goes up behind her and hugs her. "I'll see you later, Irish." I have to look away, but I can hear a loud kissing sound, like he kissed the top of her head. When I realize I'm grinding my teeth, I try to relax my jaw before turning back to the scene in the kitchen.

"Nice to meet you, man." Anthony extends his hand to me with a broad grin. I try not to consider all of the reasons he has for such a relaxed, happy look on his face this morning.

"You too, man," I lie through my teeth and give my best impression of a grin.

It's just me and Grace left alone in the apartment now. She brings two cups of black coffee into the living room, handing me one. "You brought me bagels?" She eyes the bag of bagels I left on the coffee table.

"Yeah, I thought if you still weren't feeling well, I could make you breakfast, but I guess you weren't really sick, huh?" I hate that my voice has an edge to it. I have zero right to be mad at her, but I feel like there's a fire burning in my bones right now.

"Listen, Ollie, I'm sorry if you think I lied to you. I was trying not to; really, I was. I was not doing great this week. It was just in a different way than you thought I meant. And I did go to bed early last night, just not how it sounded." That makes me grunt in anger. But her voice sounds so small and defeated, and now I feel like a jerk.

"Grace, I don't know why you didn't just tell me you had a date," I sigh.

"It's not like that." She sips her coffee and looks anywhere but at me.

Now I'm really confused. "What? Not a date? So…what, then?"

"Anthony is just an old friend. We get together sometimes. It's just…" Obviously flustered, she's blushing and playing with the tie of her bathrobe. Now I get it.

"Oh, I see. I'm an idiot. He's a fuck buddy." I sound harsh, I know, but this pisses me off. "No wonder he didn't mind leaving you here with another guy. Boy, I sure am naive."

Suddenly she looks up and stares straight into my eyes. After how she was a few minutes ago, I'm surprised at the fury I see in her face. "What exactly is it you object to about me having sex? Is it because I'm a woman, and we shouldn't need sex as much as men do? Do you think this is what I want? Do you think I wouldn't prefer a real, loving relationship?"

I get up and start pacing. "Grace, I asked for a little more time, why couldn't you have given it to me?" I'm practically yelling at her now.

"I tried! For months I've waited and been patient, Ollie. There is never any end in sight! I thought I could keep going, but I just reached my breaking point. This wasn't anything more than sex. I had to do this for myself. If you hadn't come here this morning, you would never have known about it."

"Is that supposed to make me feel better?" I scoff.

"No, because I'm not trying to make you feel better, not today. I do that all the time, and for once I'm doing something for me, not you. You have no idea how hard this has been on me. All the times you touch me, when you kiss me and hold me, and then to watch you shut down and pull back every single time." She is standing now, too, her robe falling open, and all I want to do is rip it off her and claim her as mine. Then he enters my mind, and I can't keep looking at her, imagining them together all night. Running my fingers through my hair, I wish I could somehow make sense of all that's going on inside of me at this moment.

Never have Grace and I fought like this. The level of emotion in the room is so high at the moment that it feels like the calm before the storm.

"I just thought you were different." I see the blow land. Her eyes show the pain even if she refuses to show it anywhere else. In this moment I am so hurt I want to hurt her back, but when I see that I've succeeded, it feels like I may actually vomit.

"I'm messed up. I told you that. I guess you just didn't understand me." Her voice is cold and full of something I can't quite put my finger on. Regret floods in, overwhelming me. I reach for her, grabbing her arms.

"Look at me. I'm sorry. I didn't mean that. I have no right to judge you. I've been a fucking coward who couldn't claim what he wanted."

"And now?" she challenges, not moving from my firm grasp.

"Now I'm getting a rude awakening to what the real world is like. If I can't figure out how to be the man you need, I'm going to lose you. I've been so selfish. What the hell is wrong with me?"

She brings her hands up to cup my face, gently holding me. "You lost the woman you loved. No one knows what amount of time is enough to get over something like that. Maybe if I were a stronger person, I wouldn't need to turn to someone else while you work through that."

I shake my head because that isn't fair. "I never gave you any guarantees. Now I'm jealous, and it's so unfair. All I know is when I saw him come out of your bedroom, my heart wanted to explode. You don't deserve that. You deserve to be able to do whatever you want with whoever you want."

Grace shakes her head sadly. "Don't you get it? All I wanted all night was for it to be you." Slowly, a tear falls down one cheek and then the other.

Seeing her cry undoes me. I drop my head into my hands. "Shit. Why didn't you talk to me about this? We can talk about anything, you and I."

"What, tell you that if you didn't have sex with me, I would lose my mind? Put pressure on you to just get over your grief and pain? How could I? I would've been disrespecting your love for your wife. I would never do that."

"My late wife," I correct. It's been two years, and this is the first time I've been the person saying it: "my late wife." So many things I've been fighting and denying are suddenly coming into sharp focus.

"I have to think, but listen to me…this isn't like all the other times I've been an idiot. I won't leave you hanging anymore, Grace. Please give me one last chance?"

Her eyes search mine. They are so full of pain and uncertainty, and I hate that I'm the one that has put them there. "What are you saying?"

"I'm saying that I need to fix my stupid head today. No more waiting. Just give me this day, and after that I will prove to you that I can be the man you deserve."

Thinking Out Loud

Oliver

Leaving Grace's apartment is nearly impossible, but I need to clear my head badly. I've been in denial about too many things for too long, and it's all biting me in the ass right now. Having been married for fifteen years, I got used to having someone to discuss everything with. I wasn't always the best communicator, but Ally was amazing at it, and she really taught me the benefits of just talking through your thoughts. It's one of the things I miss the most, one of the biggest voids in my life. Lately I've talked to Grace about many things, mundane and ordinary things mostly, but it's felt so wonderful. Now I need someone to talk to about this. My thoughts are all jumbled, and I just can't handle them all alone. I can usually count on my big sister, Jess, for a good old therapy session, but this isn't the kind of thing I want to go over with either of my siblings.

As I walk and think, I just wish I could find a kind stranger with wise words to unload all my crap on. I decide to get more coffee because of course, more caffeine is always a good idea, and head into the next corner café I come across. In the line in front of me is none other than Grace's handsome fuck buddy, Anthony…great, that's all I need.

"I thought you wanted the fancy coffee at work," I say to his back sardonically. I just can't help myself.

He turns around, and a grin breaks out on his face that I really wish I could hate, but it's really very genuine.

"Oh, hey. Yeah, no, I just said that because I thought the two of you might appreciate a little privacy, actually. I don't have to be at work for a couple of hours."

"Well that's very understanding for a man who just spent the night with her." I know my tone is bitter, but really, what else can be expected? As Anthony steps up to the cashier to place his coffee order, he says, "Also, whatever he's getting," pointing to me. He's buying my coffee? Like hell!

"No, thank you, but I'll get my own."

"Just place your order, dude. You're going to hold up the line, and caffeine-deprived New Yorkers will start to riot." He winks at me. Whatever, fine, let him buy my coffee. I'm not in the mood to deal with this.

As we move over to the waiting area, I remember to have some manners. "Thanks. Sorry if I'm acting like a jackass. It's been a trying morning." I run my hand over my jaw, shaking my head in despair.

"It's fine. I don't expect you to like me. But honestly, you have zero reason to be worried about me when it comes to Grace. You're the whole reason behind why I was there, actually."

"What?"

"Look, I don't really know all that's going on between you two, and I don't want to stick my nose in where it doesn't belong, but from my perspective, it's pretty obvious what's up."

He gives me a knowing, man-to-man kind of look. Despite everything I actually like this guy; he has an easy, straightforward manner, and it's obvious why Grace is friends with him.

Shit, I'm probably going to regret this, but it's already been a screwed-up day, so why not?

"I know you don't know me, but I actually could really use someone to talk to right now. You might be the worst possible choice, but what do you say?" I just put it out there.

"I thought you'd never ask, Oliver," Anthony says in a mock flirtatious manner that makes me bark out a laugh. We find a table with our coffees, and I realize I have no idea where to begin, so I just sit there thinking across from the man who screwed Grace all night, like an idiot.

"OK, let me give you some background info," Anthony says at last, leaning back in his chair, getting comfy and stretching his legs. "Grace is a great girl. We've always gotten along like a house on fire, but neither of us is under any illusions that we would be a good couple. I am a very busy man. I run my own real estate business, and it takes all my time and attention, even on nights and weekends. I'm not trying to settle down anytime soon. Grace is not like most women…I'm sure I don't have to tell you that. She has been through some stuff. I don't know details, honestly, but I know it's shaped her into who she is. She has a hardness to her; she guards herself tightly. But she also knows herself pretty damn well, knows what she wants and needs. And she isn't afraid to go for it like a lot of people are. It's an interesting combination. When we first met, we recognized a mutual attraction and decided we could both benefit from it. That's it. There's nothing more to it: friends with benefits in the purest sense. I don't mean to upset you with my bluntness, I'm just explaining how it is."

I nod tightly. It's not easy to hear, honestly, but at the same time, I'm glad to know.

"I don't have experience with this kind of thing," I start slowly, leaning forward with my elbows on my knees. "I got married young, and I've never been with anyone else. This whole hookup culture is a foreign concept to me if I'm being honest. It makes me uncomfortable, but I get it. I know that's what people do."

"What you had is something unique and special. Not many people of our generation get to have that experience. You should be proud."

"I am, don't get me wrong. I wouldn't ever change a thing about it. But now with Ally gone, I'm like a fish out of water. I have no clue how to handle any of the things I've come across lately. When I met Grace, I was not looking for a new girl. I was just drawn to her. I couldn't help myself. She was the first person I think I even noticed in two years. I told her I only wanted to be friends because I'm scared to move on from Ally."

"Yeah, she told me that. I haven't been with her in about eight months, and when she texted me this week, I was surprised. She seemed so happy lately; I actually thought she had met someone and was dating. But then I get a text from her, I go over, and she's so tense I think she's about to snap in half. She said there was someone she wanted badly, and he had made it clear that wasn't an option. Suddenly the timing made sense. Then guess who shows up the next morning?" He smirks at me knowingly.

"It wasn't fun. I wanted to punch your face in when you walked out of her bedroom."

He bursts out laughing. "Oh man, I'm sorry, it's not funny. But damn, you two really need to get your shit together!"

"Yeah, well, I most definitely do." I shake my head. "I'm trying. It's just been so hard admitting to myself that I'm falling for someone else. I was never supposed to lose my wife, never should have had to move on from her. But that's not how life worked out. I guess I just need to wrap my head around the fact that my heart is moving on. Don't get me started on my body; that bastard is a fucking mess."

"Yeah, well, that's because you're still alive, Oliver. It may not always be ideal, but it's a fact. You were one unit with your wife, then half of it left, and now the other half, you, is realizing that life goes on, even in a romantic way, maybe."

I sigh heavily. "I write to Ally, you know. I've never told anyone that, which makes it ridiculous for me to tell you, because we're strangers."

"Sometimes a stranger is exactly who you need to tell things to. You write her letters?"

"Yeah, I have a file on my iPad. They're kind of like diary entries. At the end of the day sometimes, I just tell her about all the stuff that happened or what I'm thinking, you know."

He's nodding with a look on his face like he's thinking about that. "It helps?"

"It did for a long time. It made me feel less alone. But lately I think it's not been such a good idea." I'm surprised I said this out loud. It's something that's been in the back of my head for a while now, I realize. Putting it out there into words is making it clearer though. "I think it's stopping me from letting her go. It makes me feel guilty for having feelings for Grace because I'm still talking to Ally. I think I need to stop.

That's the only way I'm going to be able to move forward. I need to really, truly let her go."

"Grace deserves someone who will give her everything, fully and completely. I know I'm not that guy. I've never pretended I was. But I will tell you this: I care about her as a friend, and I can tell she has deep feelings for you. You have the potential to hurt her a lot, man. You need to think about that seriously also. I know she seems tough and wild, but inside, she's soft and so loving. When she gives her heart to someone, he's going to be one lucky son of a bitch, and he needs to not hurt her."

"I agree. I would rather die than hurt her."

"Good to hear."

"I just have to say this is the weirdest day ever. I thought I hated you this morning, but you aren't half bad. I just wish you were a girl or gay or something." I wave my hand in his general direction.

"Yes, sorry about that. Listen, I highly doubt Grace will be calling on me anytime again now. You are the one she wants; that's clear to me. And not just for a night—she wants everything with you. I really hope you and I can be friends, though, because she's a good friend. It's not like that'll be easy. I get that because of my history with her, but it never meant anything more than sex. I hope you understand that."

"Fuck, that is bad enough. I'd actually prefer it if I could hate you, but I don't have the right to be mad about men from her past. I just need to ask that you never touch her again. Seriously."

"If you are in her life and with her, that's a guarantee. I don't mess with taken women. But just so we're clear, if you hurt her and she needs someone to pick up the pieces, she won't be alone. I may not ever be a relationship option for her, but I will always be there for her, however she needs or wants me."

"You know the saying, 'Keep your friends close and your enemies closer'? I think you and I should be close."

He laughs, "I think you and I would make better friends than enemies, but I understand how you feel."

"I can always use another friend." I put my hand out and shake his. It's a tentative truce, and we both know it, but I feel much better than I did before. Leaving the coffee shop, I decide that a little self-torture is in order because that's the mood I'm in. So I pull out my AirPods and select a song that's been in the back of my mind ever since seeing Grace with another man earlier, "Mr. Brightside" by The Killers. I let the pain and anger flow through me as I listen to the song on repeat walking through my city. Time to open up my eager eyes, Mr. Brightside.

When I get back to my apartment, instead of going in, I head to my car. I've decided there's one more person I need to talk to today. My grandfather has always been the one I could confide in the most about Ally's death. The only other widower I know, he's the one I look to as a perfect example of what to do after losing the love of your life. When my grandmother died, he never even considered remarriage. I don't know how many women he's dated or been with, but I think it's time I ask him more about that. I wonder if watching him stay faithful to her memory hasn't affected me and made me think I had to do the same and never move on from my first love.

Driving to the care home he lives in, I think as honestly as I can of all the things I've been too afraid to face up to. I worry because how can I already have fallen so hard for someone I only met a few months ago? Isn't that the height of folly and disloyalty? Grace is so different from Ally: she is damaged, wild, and a little crazy. When I first met her, I thought she was sweet and innocent. I was right and wrong simultaneously. She is a living contradiction, uninhibited and fragile all at the same time. When I look at her, I see someone that has been broken but refused to stay broken. Someone who is scared of nothing and yet afraid of being hurt somehow—I know that makes no sense. Grace makes no sense. I don't think any other person on this planet could have made me stop hurting the way she has, and that scares the shit out of me. I feel more alive with her than I can ever remember feeling. Therein lies more guilt. Will I love her more than I loved Ally? That wasn't supposed to be possible. I'm like a man demented, screaming inside my head while I look like the same old boring Oliver on the outside. She has set my soul on fire, and I have been fighting the flames, but if I let them consume me, I have a feeling it could be the most amazing thing I've ever felt.

The care home my grandfather lives at is idyllic, sur-rounded by lovely grounds containing rose bushes and benches scattered throughout. I decide I'll go get him from his room and bring him outside for a chat.

"Oliver, my boy, it's good to see you."

"You too, Gramps. You feel up for a walk on the grounds today?"

"Of course. I'm always up for a chat with you."

I call it a walk, but he's really in a wheelchair while I push him around. If it weren't for the last stroke he had, he would still be living on his own. But the level of care he needed went up drastically after that. Still, I have to be grateful he didn't lose his ability to talk, because these conversations mean more to me than I can say.

"So spit it out. I can tell there's something on your mind." We've barely made it out the door before he's interrogating me.

"That's what I love about you, Gramps. You always get down to the dirt right away. No beating around the bush."

"When you get to my age, you learn you're going to run out of time and you need to deal with everything as it comes. Not waiting for people to feel like they're up to it."

"All right, here goes. I want to talk about you and Grandma and after she died. Why did you never remarry?"

He thinks for a minute, then says, "I never remarried because I didn't find anyone like your grandmother ever again. But listen to me, Oliver. That doesn't mean I was a monk the rest of my life, if that's what you're really asking. She was my only wife, it's true, and I'm glad about that, but I was still a man. Eventually I had other romantic interests. They just never came close to meaning what she did."

"What if you had found someone who meant a lot to you? Would you have considered another serious relationship?"

"I suppose maybe I would have. Thing is, I really didn't want to, but that's just my stubborn old self. I don't want you to think that means you should be the same as me though. We were older when I lost your grandmother. I had my kids and my grandkids. I didn't feel like I was missing a whole lot in my life. I told you I wrote to her, so I kept her close to me even when she was gone. I had my whole family, I had her in my heart, and I didn't want anything else."

"I remember you telling me about the letters. It inspired me, you know. I've been writing to Ally. A little differently, with an iPad, so more modern tech, but same idea. The thing is, it was good at first. But now I'm afraid it's stopping me from moving on. I met someone, someone I really connected to, but because I still write to Ally, I feel like I'm being unfaithful. I think I wanted to copy how you handled losing Grandma. With the fact that you never seemed to have someone else after her, maybe somehow I thought I shouldn't either."

"You know, for a smart young man, you can be awfully dumb. Whoever told you I was an ideal widower? Nobody knows what they're doing in these situations, and nobody does it perfectly. Besides the fact that you only saw things from a grandson's point of view, I bet you thought your grandma and I had a perfect marriage, too, didn't you?"

"Well, pretty close to one."

"There's no such thing. We loved each other. We worked through hard times, and we fought for each other. But we most certainly did not have a perfect marriage. That doesn't take away from the whole of what it was, and it doesn't negate how much I loved her at all. At the end of the day, I chose to stay single after losing her, but I wasn't always alone. If I had wanted to remarry, I don't think she would've held that against me. Ally wouldn't hold it against you either, Ollie. You are still young with so much life in front of you. You need to be happy. You were gutted after losing that woman, but these last few weeks, the whole family has noticed a difference, and if that's because of this someone that you've met, then I know deep down, Ally would be glad about that. Loving someone once in your life doesn't stop you from ever being allowed to love again, you know. You won't in any way diminish what you and Ally shared all those years by opening up your heart again to someone new now."

I come to a stop by our usual bench and sit down next to him. He reaches out and grips my hand. "Also, I hate to tell you something, but it's not up to you to let her go. She's already gone. She's gone, and she isn't coming back. The only question is, Are you going to let yourself go with her, or you going to stay here and learn to live a new life?"

"I've already started. I just couldn't admit it to myself. And it's getting screwed up now because of that. I need to do something to make sure I don't lose another woman that I love. Because I do love her: Grace."

"Is that her name? Grace. That's pretty. I'd like to meet her."

"I'd like you to meet her too. She's something else. A little wild, but she makes me feel so alive."

"Your eyes light up when you talk about her. I don't even need to ask you if it's real; I can tell. I'm sorry if my example held you back at all. Seems like you've been trying to live like an old man, haven't you?"

That makes me laugh. "That's what Grace tells me, that I'm acting like an old man all the time. She says she'll make me feel younger the more I stay with her, and she's right."

"So when do I get to meet her?"

"First I have to make sure I haven't lost her. I haven't been fair with her, so I have a little bit of making up to do there. She deserves to be happy, and I want to be the one to make her happy. I think I'm ready to start now."

Bye-Bye Baby

Oliver

I need to do this. My heart has already decided. My body is one hundred percent settled on Grace, and now it's time to get my brain on board. I've been pacing around the apartment without even realizing it. I stop pacing, pour myself a whiskey, and set up my iPad for my final letter. I take a deep breath and begin. It's time.

Ally,

Well, the time has come, baby. I'm ending this thing we have going on. It has been one-sided, so I guess that makes it less of a thing, but still, it meant a lot to me. When you first left, it was so unexpected, so unfair; I just couldn't accept it. I never knew that last time I saw you that I should have held you tight and told you how much I loved you. Things would've gone very differently if I had known that was our final goodbye. I think I've changed a lot since you left, Ally, and I honestly have no idea where you are or if you still see me or not. If you do, I'm pretty sure you've laughed your beautiful ass off at how long it's taken me to realize I needed to move on. I remember times we talked about how if one of us died, we would want the other to be happy and find someone else. Of course, we never really thought it would actually happen. We were too arrogant in our happiness to imagine tragedy could really tear us apart like it did. But I know deep down in my soul, you would want me to move on and be happy. That's the kind of person you were: unselfish. I thought I wouldn't ever want that for myself at first, but I've come to realize that I can't stop living. I want to be the man you once loved, joyful and alive. I owe that to you and your memory. Life is a precious gift, and I don't want to waste mine anymore. I think a life without love is no life at all, and that's something you taught me. So I'm letting love back in, but in order to do that, I need to say goodbye to you. It wouldn't be fair to Grace if I didn't. I hope you would approve of her, but I also kind of hope you'd be crazy jealous and want to kill me. I'm a twisted bastard like that. Either way, we always decided everything together, and I feel like it's still that way, so I'm going to assume that I have your blessing. I'm ready now. I will always love you, baby, but I'm done holding onto you. You have my broken heart; you keep that one. I think I've grown a new one. That's how I choose to see it. My heart is like a phoenix. It burned up when you left, and now it's been reborn. So with this goodbye, I will spread my new wings and try to fly. Wish me luck, baby.

Whatever We Are

I finish typing my final goodbye to the Ally I've been talking to in my head for the past two years. I thought this moment would be more painful, but I feel a strange sense of peace. One last thing to do. I look at my gold wedding band on the third finger of my left hand. I will keep it in the same place where I have Ally's rings stored. It's a beautiful hand-carved wooden box my grandfather made, and it means the world to me. It's the perfect resting place for our wedding rings.

Taking the Leap

Oliver

The freedom and exhilaration I feel having finally made this decision fully is indescribable. It's like a festering wound that I was trying to ignore is finally healed, and the new skin is clear and healthy. I'm energized, excited, and can't wait to see Grace. I only pray she still wants me and I haven't fucked up so many times she's decided I'm not worth the trouble. It's late Saturday night, but I don't think I can wait another second before I have some sort of plan in action, so despite the time, I send her a text.

—Can we meet tomorrow, please? It's important.

I hope she isn't asleep because if I have to go all night without an answer, I may have to go back to her place and barge in again. It takes only a few minutes for a reply to come through.

—Yes, of course.

I've thought this through, and I hope my idea is a good one. I want to make her smile more than anything. The thought of waiting till noon the next day is difficult, but that's when the tattoo parlor opens, and I want to do this the way I've planned out. I'll spend the morning working out to distract my mind and burn off energy.

—Meet me at Dragonflame Tattoo at noon?

—OK sure, see you then.

***

Grace

I can't for the life of me figure out why Oliver wants me to meet him at a tattoo parlor today. I mean, don't get me wrong, it sounds fun. I love those places, and he's inked, of course. It is just not what I was expecting when he asked to see me. I could barely sleep all night. Between what went down with Anthony and then Oliver showing up, I've been so keyed up. I never wanted him to know about my little arrangement. It was always supposed to be private, secret: a one-time thing to clear my mind, and I could get back to focusing on enjoying time with Oliver. Instead, I had to see that look on his face when he realized I was no sweet, innocent thing like he had imagined. I can't help but wonder if he's decided I'm not who he thought I was, not worth his time and affection. Despite his parting words to me, my mind is determined to throw all my doubts around and make me crazy with them.

I walk around the park all morning to try and clear my head. Staying in my apartment and sulking is just pointless. After showering and putting on a pair of ripped jeans, a plain white tee, and my favorite green jacket I decide to take a cab to the parlor. I always dress according to mood, and today I have not got a clue what to feel. I think my clothes are showing that appropriately. The shop is in Midtown, in an old brick building up on the third floor. As I head up the stairs, I admire all the beautiful artwork showcased on the large brick wall. It's a cool space, with floor-to-ceiling windows on one whole side, and I see Oliver is already talking to a heavily tatted, bearded man.

When he sees me, he calls me over to them. "Grace, this is Elvis. He's done all of my tattoos, and Ally's, too, actually."

"Hi, nice to meet you, Elvis. Your work is beautiful."

"Thank you. It's good to see Oliver smiling again, and now I can see why." He gives me a flirtatious wink.

Oliver takes my hand and pulls me closer to him. Slipping his arm around my waist, he whispers in my ear, "Can I talk to you for a second?" I simply nod, unsure if I can even speak yet.

"Give us a second, Elvis?"

"Sure, let me know when you're ready." Elvis heads to the back of the shop, and Oliver leads me toward a leather couch by one of the large windows. Nervous, I sit down, even though I know I have nothing to fear when I'm with him. Oliver sits so close our legs are practically entwined. He's still holding my hand in one of his, and he puts the other across the back of the couch, bringing our bodies as close as humanly possible.

"What's going on, Oliver?" I finally blurt out because I can't take it anymore. I feel like I may explode any second if I don't have some clarity.

"What's going on is I'm finally awake, Grace. I'm done fighting this. If I'm not too late and I haven't been too stupid, I want to know if you will be with me? Completely with me, no one else. No more Anthony. I want to be the only one you look to for all your needs and desires. I want to be your everything; god knows you're already my everything. No matter how hard I tried to fight it, it happened. It was inevitable, me falling for you. I should have known that from the first minute I looked into those gorgeous green eyes. I was a goner."

I search his face. I need to see if he's still holding back. If there is still that fear, hesitancy, guilt, and regret. But there's nothing but passion and honesty. I've never seen him look at me so openly, so full of hope. The pain that's always in his eyes has cleared. Instead, they burn with something else.

"You're sure? We've been close to this before, and it never worked. You won't regret this?"

"The only thing I might regret is if I spend one more second in denial. I'm sure. I took the time yesterday to make certain, but I hardly needed it. I just needed to get out of my own way."

I look down for his wedding band, and it's gone. "I took it off, Grace. I put it away with Ally's rings. That's my past now. You are my future, and I want it to start today. Please."

"Yes." It's all I can say, but I put all the conviction that my entire soul and being feels about this man into that one word as I look into his gorgeous cobalt eyes. He doesn't say another word. He just takes my face in both his hands and brings his mouth to mine.

The whole world disappears in that moment because this is what I've been waiting for. He's finally giving himself to me completely, without holding any parts back. My lips part as his tongue searches for entry into my mouth, and our kiss becomes fiercer. I hear myself moan but can't really be bothered to care that we're sitting in a public place because I've been starving for this.

A loud clang sounds somewhere behind us, and Elvis says, "Sorry, dropped something. Don't mind me. I'm not watching…if I was, I'd say it's hot though. But I'm not."

We both laugh, slightly embarrassed, and move apart a few inches.

"Why did you want to meet here?" I ask, finally remembering where we are.

"I want to add something to my chest, and I wanted your opinion." He stands up, pulling me with him, and we head toward Elvis.

I see then that there's a drawing with the tattoo that is on the left side of Oliver's chest, the words of the Coldplay song he had done for Ally: "Lights Will Guide You Home." But now underneath is also another line in the same script. It says, "And Ignite Your Bones."

I look up at him, my brow slightly furrowed. "From the same song, right?"

"Yes, but this line is about you. That's what you did to me, Grace. You set my whole soul on fire. It brought me back to life. I want to mark it on my heart. It means so much to me. I'll never be the same man since meeting you."

"Ollie, that's…I have no words." I can feel tears in my eyes, and I don't want to cry, but this man is melting my heart, and I don't know what to do about it.

"You're sure?" I ask yet again.

"Very," is all he says. And he slowly starts lifting the hem of his shirt.

"So you ready?" Elvis's voice breaks through the moment of intensity. I have a moment of panic then, my mind spinning.

"Wait! What if this doesn't work out and you hate me one day? You'll regret this. I don't want you to do something and have remorse down the road."

Holding both of my hands, he kisses them sweetly. "Baby, it's OK, I've thought this through. It's not a name or anything. It's symbolic of how you've changed my life, and that is never going to change. I'm not going to pretend to know what the future holds. But I'm also not going to be afraid to live for a single second more. I want this. My eyes are open fully with you, and I am not scared. I want to mark you on my body. For better or for worse, you have already marked my heart and soul."

"Oh my god, Oliver, could you please stop being so perfect?" He kisses me again then, crushing my body against his passionately.

When he pulls back just a fraction, his next words are spoken over my mouth, barely a whisper. "Tonight, I want to show you how perfect I think you are."

"If you think you can handle it, old man." I decide it's time to tease him because Ollie has no idea what I want to do to him, and I hope he's prepared.

Growling, he retorts, "I'm going to prove once and for all how wrong you are about that nickname. Be prepared, wild girl."

The whole time he is getting his tattoo, my heart goes a mile a minute. Not only because his body is beautiful and I am sitting practically in his lap, but also because of the shift in our relationship. We touch the entire time in one way or another. It is like if our skin isn't in contact, we might die.

"What about you, Grace? You want some ink today? I'll give you one on the house," Elvis looks up at me at one point and asks.

"Wow, that's nice. Why would you do that?"

"Because I like Oliver and I liked Ally. I never thought he'd look this happy again. I think the girl who made that happen deserves a reward."

I look at Oliver, wondering if talk of Ally will bring sadness back to his eyes, but he's grinning up at me like a lovestruck fool. "You want something?"

"I might. I've been wanting something on the back of my shoulder for a while. I just haven't fully decided what."

"Tell me any ideas you've had," Elvis says.

"I wanted to get my favorite flower maybe: red poppies. Do you know if they have a meaning?"

"They have a few different meanings, actually. Remembrance is the most common meaning. The red ones often represent passion and love though too. Also the poppy itself is interesting because of all the things made from the flower: opium, heroine, and medical pain killers…so make of that what you will." He chuckles.

I think about the for a few minutes. "I like that a lot. I don't do drugs, but I'm a bit of an adrenaline junkie. I have definitely used that to mask pain, almost like a drug. And I've always been passionate."

Oliver squeezes my hand, and I look down at him again. "I think that would look stunning on you."

"OK, I would like that. Thank you," I tell Elvis.

"Happy to do it."

By the time we leave, I have three delicate watercolor style red poppies on the back of my left shoulder. The work

Elvis did is truly exquisite. While I was lying on my stomach getting it done, Oliver was tracing my other tattoos idly with his finger, sending shivers all through my body. The bow and arrow are low on the right side of my lower back, almost at my ass. The large flaming phoenix under my left boob especially got his attention. He spent a while examining that one. It has the words "Find Your Fire" with it, and I explained it was to represent finding ways to rise above things that are meant to break you and letting them remake you instead. I got it done after my breakup with my abusive ex, determined to never let my past bring me down. After, when I sat up, I showed him the final one he hadn't seen: "Obscurum" written low on my pelvis, just below my hip bone on the left side. It means "darkness" in Latin, I explained. I got it to remind myself of my dark side. It's a hard one to explain fully without getting into deeper territory than I was prepared to venture into in a public place, but Oliver just nodded like he understood there was more to it.

***

Oliver

The hours spent in the tattoo parlor have me so worked up and horny I wonder if I will be able to make it back to my apartment with Grace before I attack her. As we head out and to my car, I think about that phoenix tattoo on her side.

"I told Ally that my heart was like a phoenix when I wrote my goodbye letter to her yesterday," I say suddenly. "I couldn't believe it when I saw your tattoo. It was like a sign of some kind."

"You wrote her a goodbye letter?"

"I did. I wanted to make sure I had nothing left hanging on when I started being with you." I squeeze her hand. "That's why the phoenix; I'm starting over new as of now with you."

"I didn't think it would ever happen," she admits.

We've reached my car, and I can't take it anymore. Grabbing her by the waist, I push her back against the side of it, kissing her deeply while my hands explore her body yet again.

"God, Oliver, I want you so bad," she pants in my ear while I devour her neck.

"Come back to my place with me?" I say.

"Yes, please."

The drive back is sheer torture. I can't stop touching her the entire time. I rub her leg; I hold her hand. At every red light, I devour her mouth again and palm her perfect breasts through that tight white tee she's wearing. I'm harder than a rock, ready to burst out of my stupid jeans, when she leans over into my lap and strokes my cock through them.

"You're going to make me come in my fucking pants, Grace," I growl, holding her wrist to prevent that from actually happening.

"Not yet, baby," she says over my lips, then slowly runs her tongue over them.

"Shit!" I hiss. Horns honk around us as the light turns green. I give her a warning look. "You stay in that seat, or we will be fucking in this car, and that's not how I want our first time to go."

"Yes, sir." She gives me a sultry smirk and moves away. We don't touch again after that, and we don't say anything either. There's an electric charge in the air around us, and it's intoxicating.

In my building we enter the elevator, and there's a woman and her young son in there with us. Good thing, too, or I'd be all over her again. Instead, she leans back against the wall across from me and stares straight into my eyes, eye-fucking me silently all the way up. I lean back, too, and enjoy the heat that consumes me; the not-touching is almost more erotic than groping each other in this moment. The woman in the elevator must feel the sexual tension, because she clears her throat loudly and starts chatting to her son about some nonsense. I just grin wickedly at my wild girl, undressing her already with my eyes. Once inside my apartment, the time for waiting is over.

I scoop Grace up into my arms, holding onto her ass while her legs wrap around my waist and our mouths meld together. Her back lands against the nearest wall, and I brace my arms on each side of her, caging her in.

"You're mine now, no one else's. No more fuck buddies, right, Grace?"

I stare into her eyes.

"Always. I'm so sorry about yesterday." Her fingers are tracing my lips as she speaks, holding my face with her small, sexy hands.

"You don't owe me an apology for that. I was the idiot who insisted we could only be friends. I was such a fool. I could have lost this." I kiss her again, drinking her in. "Never going to give you up." I pepper kisses all over her face and neck. "It's all in the past now. I plan to make you forget every other man who's ever touched you."

"You already have. I have never wanted anyone like I want you." She takes my lower lip in between her teeth and pulls on it as she grinds her hips against me.

"Fuck, no more talking. I'm going to devour you whole now." I grab her again and make my way to the couch because it's closer than the bed.

Laying her down, I kneel over her and peel off my shirt. Grace reaches up and undoes my belt, her eyes never leaving mine. I reach for her shirt, and in a dance of limbs and desire, we strip each other down to nothing but skin. Finally having her bared to me is pure bliss. I take in every inch of her. She's doing the same, her emerald eyes radiant with mischief and lust. Slowly her hands run down my chest, over my abs, and lower. I'm barely breathing as she takes me in her hand at last. Her other hand goes behind my neck, bringing our mouths together. As I kiss her I explore her body, kneading her breasts, teasing the taut little nipples, drawing a moan out of her. I kiss my way down till I take one of those luscious peaks into my mouth, and my hand goes between her legs, delving into her heat.

"Oh god, yes please." Grace moans. My thumb finds her clit, and I press on it while I slide a finger into her soaked pussy, sucking her breast and holding her up with my other arm as I continue pumping my finger deeper inside of her.

"I'm gonna come, Oliver!" Her incoherent moans turn into a declaration.

"Yes, baby, come on my hand," I pant against her neck, then raise my head because I need to watch her face as she unravels in my arms. It's ecstasy stronger than I've ever felt.

When the tremors of her orgasm subside, I can't wait any longer. "Let me get the condoms." I get up and head for the box of condoms I made sure to buy in preparation for tonight.

Coming back, I prepare to open one, but she stops me. "Wait, can I taste you first? Before you put it on."

"Fuck, baby, you never have to ask twice," I moan. She places a hand on my chest and settles me back onto the couch in a seated position while she kneels between my legs. The sight of her licking her lips as she stares at my dick practically undoes me before she's even touched me.

"You're so gorgeous all over," she tells me as she grips my cock with one hand and massages my balls gently with the other. Her pert tits are standing at attention, and I'm literally about to lose my mind with craving for this woman.

"Baby, you keep looking at me like that, and this will end quicker than we want," I warn her.

She giggles and says, "Fine, I'll just have to get to work, then." Leaning down, she doesn't immediately take me into her mouth, though, or even kiss me. She does something else I never expected. She deliberately runs her face along the side of my dick, inhaling deeply, taking in the smell of me, and she whispers, her voice a slight tickle against my cock, "You smell unbelievably amazing, I knew you would."

I involuntarily let out an exclamation, "Shiiittt…that's so fucking sexy!" I can't hold back. I grip her head, wrapping her hair around my fingers to try and maintain some semblance of control. Just then she takes me into her soft hot mouth, drawing me down deep. It's the most mind-blowing thing I've ever felt. My head falls back, and I groan loudly.

"Grace!"

Her head is bobbing, and she sucks me hard. I know I can't take much more.

"Baby, you have to stop, or I'm going to come. I want to be inside you." I'm practically begging for mercy.

She gets up and reaches for the condom, opening it and rolling it down with her delicate little fingers as I watch her.

"Sit on me, baby." I bring her into my lap to straddle my dick, and when she lowers down onto me, we both moan in unison. Her fingers grip my hair, and our eyes lock as she begins riding me. There are no words. It's a connection deeper than I ever expected to find again. The intensity of this moment is almost more than I can take. We build closer to our release. I grip her hips hard and pound up into her. Then I move one hand to her center and circle her clit, her head falls back, and I lean forward to taste her gorgeous breasts again.

"Yes, yes, so good," Her words sound strangled. I feel her pussy tighten around my cock as she comes, and in another second, I've grabbed her hips and thrown her down beneath me. I pound into her with all my might as I come so hard I feel like I could black out.

"Fuck Grace, yessss," I'm moaning into her ear.

I stay there holding her, still inside of her for a minute while we both catch our breath. Afterward we are entwined and fully relaxed when I ask, "Do you remember at Glory Days when you asked what my theme song would be?"

She shifts up onto her elbows on my chest to look at me better. "Yes, you wouldn't tell me. You just said it was a Paul McCartney song."

I trace her lips with my finger slowly, soaking in being able to touch her all I want. "'Maybe I'm Amazed' is the song. I guess I already knew on some level that you had captured me completely. It's exactly how I feel about you, every single word of that song."

***

Grace

After that first time on the couch, we both realized we had barely eaten all day from nerves and anticipation. So while Oliver places an order to have some Chinese food delivered, I get up and try to put myself somewhat back together again. I find my panties and wrap one of the throw blankets around me for the time being. Then I decide now is a good time for a bathroom break before we go again, because I have no doubt we will go again. I'm standing in the bathroom in only the panties, washing my hands, when he knocks lightly.

"Come in."

He's holding a large T-shirt that's obviously his. Walking up behind me, he slips it over my head.

Cradling me in his arms, he bends down to whisper in my ear, "I want you in my clothes. I want to mark you all over as mine, every inch of you."

I look in the mirror at the shirt. It's a faded black AC/DC band tee, and it's divinely soft. "You have good taste in shirts," I point out.

"I have good taste in girls," he counters. Turning in his arms, I take him in. He's now wearing a pair of low-slung, well-fitting black sweatpants and nothing else. It's almost sexier than when he's naked because of how manly it looks.

"You aren't so bad yourself," I say in appreciation.

"Will you stay with me all night?" he asks, leaning his forehead against mine.

"Yes. I'll go into work late tomorrow since I'll have to go home in the morning, but I don't care. I don't want to leave you."

"I'll go in late too. I can take you to your place in the morning and then to work."

At that moment it's like we can't wait one second longer without kissing again. Our lips come together simultaneously, and our tongues dance in an erotic battle for dominance. He grips my hips and hoists me up onto the counter as my legs once again wrap around his waist. His hard length stirs my desire, and I'm ready all over again, feeling my panties soak through. His hand finds out the same thing a moment later, and I feel him smile against my lips.

"So ready for me, baby."

"I've been this way for weeks if you want to know the truth."

He groans deeply then. "God, do you have any idea how many times I jerked off thinking of you?"

"You could have had me at any moment."

"I won't ever waste time with you again," he vows. Just then the doorbell rings, unfortunately, and we have to take a break to collect the food delivery.

I tell myself that taking a dinner break is important because we need the fuel, but I'd rather eat Oliver again. The way he's looking at me tells me he is of the same mind. He opens a bottle of white wine to go with our dinner, and we eat on the couch. Me in just his big T-shirt, him in only his sexy sweatpants.

I can't help but stare at the new tattoo he got today in my honor. It's got the clear bandage over it, but it is still fully visible. I lean forward and place a kiss next to it on his hard pectoral. "I'm still a little in awe that you did this."

"My heart has room for you, just like there was room here for the words that capture how you make me feel. I used to think I would never feel this way again after Ally was gone. I had no idea someone like you would come along and turn my world upside down in a glorious way."

"For a while after Matt, I thought I would never let anyone close again. But then I trusted you right away. I didn't even know why. I just had this feeling that you were someone I could let in."

He threads his fingers through mine, kissing the tip of each one slowly. I swallow audibly and then say, "You know, we haven't known each other that long. Is there anything you want to ask me? I worry that one day you'll discover something you don't like, and I'll be broken."

We have both forgotten about the food now, completely engrossed in one another. He pulls me onto his lap until I am straddling him yet again. "First of all, I will never break you. I want to hold you together and fight anyone who tries to hurt you ever again. Second, I know everything I need to because I know this." He places one hand over my heart.

I look down and tease, "You know my boob?"

"Smartass, I know your heart." He leans forward to bite at my bottom lip as punishment for my teasing, his other hand squeezing one ass cheek. After a moment he says, "I do have a question, actually."

"What?" He lifts up the shirt and finds the tattoo low on my hip bone, the one that says "Obscurum."

"Will you tell me more of the story behind this one?" He slowly traces it, causing goosebumps to rise all over my skin and a shiver to run through me at the touch.

I inhale deeply, closing my eyes to prepare myself to share this. Exhaling, I look at him, and I feel so safe and cared for I know I can share this part of myself. "I have a scar there. You can't tell now because the word is covering it. I always had a strange feeling about that scar. I couldn't remember how I got it, but it filled me with shame and horror whenever I looked at it, even at a young age. I asked my mother about it when I was around eight, I think, and she told me she had no idea what I had done to myself. I thought that was so odd; how could she not know?"

I feel my voice trembling. Oliver is holding onto me tightly like he can help hold me together if need be.

"When I was in therapy and my repressed memories came back, the ones of the abuse...I had one where I was fighting against a man, a big man. I can't remember who still. I just know he was so much bigger than me, and he smelled strongly of cigarettes. He wanted me to be quiet, and I wouldn't, so he took his cigarette and he held it against my skin. He did it over and over until I finally agreed to just shut up. When I finally had the answer of where that scar had come from, I wanted to erase it. I was so angry and disgusted. I chose the Latin word for darkness because it reminds me of my dark side, the same way the song 'Creep' reminds me how I've never fit in anywhere, even in my own life."

We both stay silent for a long time. He's thinking, and I feel his anger on my behalf. At last he breaks the silence. "That is something abominable that some disgusting person did to you. *You are not dark, Grace.* You are my incredible, strong, and beautiful girl. You covered over those scars and overcame that pain to shine bright, because when I met you, I was dazzled. And I've just been more and more blown away by you every single day since. I know somewhere you fit in; you fit right here in my arms."

The time for talking is over. I am drained from all I have told him, and now I need him to make love to me again.

"Oliver, I need you. I want you inside me again…" I kiss him savagely, begging for him to make me forget everything except him tonight.

"Gladly. Let's go to bed." He lifts me up in his strong arms and carries me into his room.

Walls Closing In

Grace

"Kyle, can you check out this phone number for me?" I ask after the third call and voicemail from this same number.

"What do you think it is?"

"I think it's some sort of scam. They keep calling and saying they need to get in touch with me about some inheritance. Sounds like complete bullshit to me. No one would leave me anything. I just don't get why they're so persistent."

"Have you gotten any mail about it?"

"I don't know. Most of the mail I get is junk. I hardly open any of it. It's in a big pile at the moment. If I had received something, I wouldn't even know."

"OK, give me a few minutes. I should be able to tell if it's a scammer."

"Thanks." Once he can confirm there's no truth to the messages, I can block the number and stop being bothered. It won't stop nagging at the back of my mind. I guess every time things are good in my life, I worry when something is going to come along and ruin it. My happiness with Oliver feels like it must have some kind of expiration date. It feels literally too good to be true, and I keep waiting for the other shoe to drop.

About twenty minutes later, Kyle comes back to my desk and leans on it.

"They are legitimate lawyers Grace, in a small town in Connecticut." He looks down at his notes. "Chester. Do you know anyone who lives there?"

"Chester...no. My family all live in Bridgeport. I don't even know where Chester is. This makes no sense." I sigh, my uneasy feeling growing stronger by the second.

"Well next time they call, you should answer or give them a call back. Also, check your mail when you get home. I bet they've tried getting in touch with you that way too."

"Yeah, I will. Thanks."

I want to wait till I get home to deal with this, but as the day goes on, I know I won't be able to accomplish anything until I handle this. I take a break and head outside to call the lawyers back. It's a very brief conversation. They can only tell me that I have inherited my uncle's estate. He died of a heart attack a few weeks ago and left everything to me. I need to go into a meeting with them, and then they can give me more information at that time. Agreeing to come in on Saturday at noon, I hang up more distressed than before. My father's only brother, Ronan, is not a close relative. There is only one reason I can think of that I am the beneficiary of his will: my mind keeps telling me that it's him. He's the faceless person who I can't quite remember. I try to remain calm and be rational. That isn't the only explanation. Maybe he just feels bad because I never got married, and he thinks I need the money? I start feeling shooting pains in my stomach as my mind spins out of control. Returning to my office, I tell my boss that I am sick and need to head home. No way can I keep working with all of the turmoil that's going on inside of me right now. As soon as I enter my apartment, I tear through the pile of unopened mail. Sure enough there's a letter from the same lawyer's office. It doesn't provide any additional information, however, and I feel no closer to answers.

My phone rings, and it's Oliver.

"Hello?"

"Baby, are you OK? I came to your office to surprise you with an afternoon coffee and danish and they said you went home sick. I'm on my way now. What's wrong?"

"I'll explain it when you get here, then. I'm not sick, really, just shook up. How close are you?"

"Just crossing the bridge."

"OK, well, don't worry. It might be nothing. I'm glad you're coming though. Thank you."

"All right, I'll be there as soon as I can."

While I wait for him to arrive, I take a scorching-hot shower, trying to wash away all my bad thoughts and feelings somehow. Getting into comfortable clothes always makes things better, and I feel somewhat calmer when I open the door to the man that means the world to me.

He takes me into his arms immediately. "What happened?"

I give him the letter from the lawyer and explain the phone call and that I have an appointment for Saturday to find out more.

"Were you close to him? Is that why you're upset?" he asks, unsure still of what it all means.

I simply shake my head. "No, I haven't seen him since I was a child. I don't know what happened, but he and my father had some kind of falling out, and then he was just gone from our lives. It's not that I'm sad. It's that I'm scared. I just have this awful premonition that I know why he left me everything he had."

Understanding dawns on his face, and I see the anger come. "Son of a bitch," he murmurs.

"I might be wrong. I just can't shake the thought."

"You might very well be right, too, Grace. I know your parents know what happened to you. I saw it in their faces that day. If they had a falling out when you were young, that would fit, and now this." He holds up the lawyer's letter. I wrap my arms tight around me and sink down onto the couch.

"I don't think I can do this, I don't want anything from him if this is true."

He sits down taking me in his arms, "I know, baby, I know."

We just sit there. I don't know when I started crying, but the tears are streaming down now as he wipes them away, murmuring words of love and comfort. "Listen, if you don't want to deal with this, we can figure out a way to make it go away. I can get in touch with some of the lawyers I know for advice."

"If this gives me answers and closure, though, I think I should find out one way or another, now that I think about it."

"OK, listen then." He takes my face in his hands, kissing me gently to make sure he has my full attention. "On Saturday if you still feel that way, we go and do this together. We get the answer if it's available. I will be with you every step of the way, and I will handle anything that feels like too much for you." I nod in agreement. With him by my side, I can do anything, no matter how horrific.

"I love you." I say the words I have felt for so long, because I may be scared of the future, but I have no doubts about that one thing at least.

"Grace, I have loved you for a long time. I just didn't want to scare you away saying it too soon. I love you more than I ever thought possible." He peppers my face with kisses, ending with my mouth in the most passionate kiss we've ever shared. I grip him tightly, needing more, needing everything.

In one way or another, I survive the next two days of work. Each night Oliver holds me tight and uses all sorts of sweet diversions to keep me from overthinking about Saturday as it looms. We finally watch our favorite classic movies together. He cooks us a special meal one night and orders my favorite takeout the next. I don't have a clue what I ever did to deserve a man like this in my life.

Saturday morning we get into Oliver's black Range Rover and start the two-and-a-half-hour drive to Chester, Connecticut. The drive is scenically beautiful, and it's a crisp fall day. If only my stomach wasn't twisted in agony and fear, I could actually enjoy this excursion. I don't want to talk, so I just quietly sing along to music and look out of the window. I know he gets it because he doesn't try to force conversation. He just holds my hand tightly.

We don't bother trying to eat, only getting coffee before heading to the lawyer's office. My stomach can't handle food right now. The big colonial style house that they are located in gives off an air of old New England money. We get settled into the leather wingback chairs, prepared for whatever may come now.

"Miss Murphy, good to meet you at last. We represent your late uncle, Ronan Murphy's estate. He was very clear that everything, with no exceptions, is to be yours. We will get more into what that includes in a bit. Firstly, though, he wanted us to give you this letter. We don't know its contents, but he was adamant that you read it before we proceed." The lawyer is much younger than I expected, and I am disconcerted. He looks expectantly at me as he holds out the envelope. I take it and hand it to Oliver immediately.

"I can't read this," is all I say.

Oliver nods and begins opening it. I can tell the lawyer wants to object to this, so I stop him. "My boyfriend is here to help me. I need him to tell me what I might find in that letter. You have no idea what is going on here, so please don't get involved right now." My voice leaves no room for arguments. I grip Oliver's thigh, holding on for dear life as he reads the three-page letter in silence. I can sense the fury rolling off of him, and I know I was right.

Finally, he turns to me and just gives me a slight nod. Mr. Too-Young-to-Be-a-Lawyer is completely flustered and clearly unsure how to proceed. Oliver addresses him then. "Can you give us a few moments alone, please?"

"Sure, I'll do that." He gets up and heads out with a look of relief on his face.

"Tell me," I say, my voice cold and much calmer than I expected.

"He confesses. He begs for your forgiveness. He says he saved all his money and planned his whole life to give you everything he could when he died to try and make amends." He scrubs a hand down his face and lets out a whoosh of air. "Grace, the confession is...it's not good. He gives details. He says he thought you might need answers. He also explains that your parents know. I can't with these people. I want to kill someone right now, violently." He clenches his jaw firmly, and his fists are tightly curled.

I just sit there, frozen. I am numb to a degree I have never experienced before. After all this time I have the answer; the faceless monster of my nightmares has an identity. There is proof that I'm not insane. I didn't imagine this, didn't make it all up for attention, as my mother would have me believe.

I know this coldness and numbness is a protective mechanism, so I decide to use it. I need it to get through the rest of today, anyway, so I embrace it. "OK then, I have my answer. Let's finish up here and go home."

"Are you OK?"

"I am. I will not be at some point, but for now I am," I reassure him. "I won't give him the satisfaction of reading his words, though. That's him seeking closure, and he doesn't deserve it. I just needed to know the answer. Thank you for taking that blow for me."

"Good, I don't want you to ever read this. We can burn it." He places it in the inside pocket of his jacket. We call the lawyer back in, and he begins explaining all that I have inherited from the man who took my innocence from me. Apparently he lived a miser's life, never married or had children, thank god. He made wise investments as well, so in total I have about $4.5 million from him, and that doesn't include the house or vehicles. I shake my head in disbelief. How this man thinks money makes up for all his sins is beyond me. I sign a few papers that are presented to me, and then the lawyer tells us he wants to take us to the property that I now own. We follow behind the lawyer's car as he drives a little out of the center of town, pulling up in front of a modest-sized Cape Cod–style bungalow with a large garage building in the back. Getting out, he hands me a ring of keys, explaining that I have also acquired three cars that can be found in the garage. Apparently cars were Ronan's one indulgence.

"I'll leave you now. Feel free to let us help you with anything you need as far as how you'd like to proceed. If you're interested in selling the property, I can get you in touch with a great local realtor." He gives me his business card, adding, "Call with any questions, please. We're here to help."

"Thank you."

When it's just me and Oliver at last, he says, "We don't have to go inside. I can make arrangements to have it cleared out and put on the market. I don't want you even touching anything he touched." He stands behind me, my back tight against his chest, and holds both my hands.

"OK. I don't need to see anything inside. Maybe just the cars? Then we can go." We find the key that opens the garage and inside discover a classic Corvette in mint condition, a vintage Jeep Wagoneer with wood sides, and a Toyota Tacoma that was clearly his everyday vehicle.

"I don't understand how he had so much money." I confess in confusion.

"It's all he lived for, I guess."

"And he thinks this means I will just forgive him?"

"He was clearly a twisted, deranged man. This is the best he could come up with."

I stand in the middle of the cars, and I feel nothing.

"I'm scared Oliver. This numbness, I've felt it before, and it's not good. It makes me reckless and crazy. Don't let go of me no matter what happens, promise me?"

"I will never let go of you, Grace. Nothing would make that happen! This time you aren't dealing with it alone;

remember that, baby. Come on, let's go back to the city." He leads me out and locks the garage behind us.

As we are headed back, I see a sign for Bridgeport, and I think about confronting my parents.

"Can we make a detour?"

"Of course, we can do anything you want." I punch my parents' address into his GPS and explain that I need to tell them I have all the confirmation and proof I need.

"I just need them to know that they can't gaslight me anymore, and also that I never want to see or hear from them again."

He nods in agreement. "I will gladly take you there for that."

Being in the driveway of my childhood home is as far as I will go, going back inside where other bad memories can come up is not an option. Oliver goes to the door and asks that my parents come outside to talk. They are mostly silent the entire time I explain the undeniable proof I now have of the things I only suspected before. It is a confrontation with the people who caused my birth, not a chat with parents. My father won't make eye contact with either Oliver or me, and my mother cries, trying to make herself a victim still somehow. The excuses are pathetic and useless.

"I want nothing from you. Don't even try to explain how you handled this. I just need you to understand that you can't hide any longer. We are done. I don't care if one of you needs a kidney and mine is the only option; do not contact me. You will never see me again, and I'm quite sure you'll be fine with that. I was always just a reminder of your failure as parents, anyway, wasn't I?"

"Grace, he manipulated us too," my mother whines.

"Stop!" Oliver practically roars at her. "You don't get to talk now. You only get to listen."

I continue, "Tell yourself whatever you need to face yourself in the mirror each day. I won't listen to it any longer though."

I look to my father then, hoping against hope to feel any trace of the protector I always craved him to be for me. Instead, he is blank. I shouldn't be surprised, it is exactly what I knew I would find but I can't help the last shred of hope that extinguishes from hurting still. Somewhere deep inside I knew this about them all along and yet their mind games and pretense messed with my head so badly I wondered if I had imagined this coldness.

"I have all the answers I need now, this is the end of our relationship."

With that, we take our leave.

***

Oliver

Grace is barely reacting to everything that has been heaped on her today, and I worry the protective walls she has around her emotions will come crashing down soon.

"Should you make an appointment with your therapist?" I venture. She has reduced the amount of times she goes in to talk to her, and now I fear that is going to be a bad idea.

"Maybe. I'll think about it. I don't really know that there is much that can be done. I have the final piece of the puzzle now, at least."

I keep driving, desperately thinking of how I can fix this. Logically I know I can't, but the man in me needs to do something.

"We should do something fun," she says out of the blue. Her voice is high and excited.

"Like what?"

"Have you ever been rock climbing? I love that. Or we could do something like skydiving or bungee jumping."

I glance over at her. "You need an adrenaline hit, don't you?"

"Yes. I really do."

"I'll do anything that makes you happy, but go easy on me. I'm not quite as adventurous as you." I give her my best flirty smile and squeeze her hand.

"OK, old man, let me think about what you can handle."

"No sharks this time, please." That gets a laugh out of her.

She starts looking on her phone, no doubt finding some crazy activity that will make me want to pass out in fear. It doesn't matter; I'll do whatever this woman wants or needs.

About ten minutes later, she looks up. "I have two options for you: we pass a zip-lining course on our way back to the city in Purchase, New York. Or we can go to the trapeze school at Pier 40 in Manhattan. Both mild choices."

I lift one eyebrow as I glare at her. "Why does everything have to include me being so high up off the ground?"

"Are you afraid of heights?"

"Not necessarily. I also don't feel the need to taunt gravity for fun, either, though."

"Hmmm, so you need two feet on the ground?"

"I'll do it if it will make you happy. I just can't guarantee I won't scream like a girl," I laugh.

"We could always have sex in public and get another tattoo," she states matter-of-factly.

I almost swerve off the road. "What!"

"I'm just listing some of the other options." She shrugs, giving me a seductive smile.

I feel worry rising in my chest at the mood she is in. "No unplanned tattoos, OK? That's the kind of thing that leads to regret."

"You're right," she sighs. "I'm sorry, you probably think I'm insane. I told you I go a little crazy sometimes."

"Hey, look at me." I make sure she sees how sincere I am when I tell her, "I am not judging how you handle this shit. I love your wild side, and I never want to try and change you. I just need to try and keep up sometimes, that's all; be patient with me. I choose zip-lining, by the way." I wink. "And depending on your definition of 'public,' I'm down for the sex."

There's a glint in her eyes as she turns in her seat and reaches over, palming me through the crotch of my jeans. "I'd say a highway is pretty public. Do you think you can stay in control of the car if I decide to have a little snack?"

"Fucking hell, Grace!" I hiss out at the thought and the mental image I get along with it, her gorgeous mouth on me as I drive. "I don't know if we'd survive that," I admit honestly. "You give the best head in the world, and I always lose control."

She slowly unzips my pants and takes me into her hand. "Then just a little hand action? I'm craving you so badly right now, I can't help myself."

I lean back in my seat, groaning and trying desperately to keep my eyes on the road and not look down. "You will be the death of me, baby," I grit out finally. Her delicate, soft hand pumps me hard, and I want nothing more than to find a rest area as soon as possible. I need to touch her too. The universe is on my side, as a sign shows that one is coming up in half a mile.

"Good thing I got the darkest tinting I could on these windows. I'm about to take you right here on the side of the highway, baby."

"Yes, please. I need you," she murmurs. I pull onto the exit and find a parking spot far away from all the other cars. Before I can even get my seat all the way back she has her glorious lips wrapped around my cock.

"Shit, baby, that's so good." I stroke her head in my lap. Reaching down into the front of her pants, I find her clit and stroke it. Her moans reverberate around my dick, increasing the mind-blowing sensations. "Baby, I'm gonna come if you don't stop," I tell her. She just nods, however, letting me know that's exactly what she wants. I hold onto her head with both hands now and stroke deep into her hot little mouth. The spasm of my release is so intense I wonder if I am going to hurt her. I try to hold back, but it is impossible.

"Did I hurt you?" I immediately ask as she sits up.

"No, that was incredible. Just what I wanted." Her lips are swollen and red, and she has never looked sexier.

"I need to taste you now," I practically growl. "Get in the back," I instruct. Climbing into the back seat, she slips off her pants, and I can finally touch her freely. I follow her onto the back seat, devouring that delectable mouth first while my fingers pump in and out of her heat.

"Is this what you want, Grace?" My voice is low and gravelly as I kiss her neck.

"I want you to eat me and then fuck me," she moans. "I need everything."

Without another word, I grip her hips and hitch her farther up the seat till my face is nestled in between her legs. Holding her down, I drive her to the edge with my mouth, then I add my fingers to push her over. Her cries of pleasure are loud, and it's a wonder no one has called the police on us yet. Her grip on my hair is so strong it borders on painful, but I love it, love when I make her lose her mind with ecstasy.

I move on top of her and position myself at her entrance.

"Look at me baby," I instruct. She opens those stunning emerald eyes, and I see the tears shining in them. I kiss her with all the love in my heart.

"I love you so much."

"I love you too," she whispers as one tear trickles down. I kiss that away too as I slowly enter her. I grip each side of her head as I move in and out. She digs her nails into my back under my shirt, and I relish the pain.

"You want me to come inside you bare?" I know she is on birth control, but I need to make sure she is OK with this also.

"Yes, I want to feel it," she moans deeply, and I can feel her walls grip my dick even tighter. Her legs are wrapped around my waist, holding onto me, and I want her to just hold onto me forever. As I thrust into her, I imagine driving away all the hurt and anguish in her life. I wish I could take all her pain away like this. We come together soon in a breathless climax. I stay there, holding her tightly under me while we just breathe, and my mind wonders how it's possible that I love her so much.

"You know, I used to worry I would love you more than I loved Ally. That's one of the reasons I fought this so hard,

I think. Now I know it's true. Does that make me an awful man?" I ask as I sit up and fix my jeans. Giving her my deepest, darkest confession in that moment.

She pauses in her adjusting and looks at me. "How is that even possible? I'm such a fucking mess. You are so pure and clean and bright. I'm all the opposite things. Dark and dirty and defiled. Ally was better than me in every way, I'm sure."

Tears start running down her face again. Gathering her into my arms, I hold her as tightly as I can. "You aren't those things. Those kind of things have been done to you. There is a difference," I say firmly.

"I have been promiscuous and crazy, too, though. You don't know everything I've ever done."

"I don't need to either." I kiss her on the temple, then the cheek, and then the mouth.

"Of course there were effects from how you were treated. I don't blame you for any of it. You are here now, with me. We found each other."

"Let's go home, Oliver. I don't need to do anything crazy or fun; I just need you."

"You have me, always."

Expecto Patronum

Grace

We lie in Oliver's king-size bed that night, *Harry Potter and the Half-Blood Prince* is playing on the TV, and he cradles me in his strong arms. Somehow, I haven't lost my mind yet from everything that happened today. Holding onto this man is like being grounded, sheltered underneath a solid oak tree that protects you with its large branches. I have never felt so safe in my entire life. If I had a Patronus it would look like him, I think to myself with a small chuckle.

"What's so funny?" he asks me.

"I just had a ridiculous thought that my Patronus would be you," I admit.

He clutches me tighter to him then. "I promise to chase away all dementors that try to come near you," he vows solemnly. I shake my head, loving that he has silly conversations with me even when the world feels like it could crush us at any moment.

"Hey, do you think you can take some time off of work soon?" he asks as he threads his fingers through mine.

"Like how much time?"

"I want to take you somewhere for a long weekend, so if you could take from a Thursday to a Monday, say."

"We are almost done with a big campaign, and then I could do that in another week, probably. Where do you want to take me?"

"That is for me to know and you to find out." He taps the tip of my nose. "Do you trust me?"

"Of course I do."

"All right then, you get the dates off and let me know when it's for sure, and I'll handle the rest."

"What about this inheritance business? Don't I need to handle that soon?" I worry my lip and feel bad for bringing it up, but it won't just disappear, no matter how much I would like it to.

"That is something we'll handle when you feel ready. No one can rush you," he reassures me.

"OK."

I get the days off that I need for our long weekend, and Oliver instructs me to pack for warm weather. I try to guess what he's planning, but he refuses to even give me a hint. Milo drives us to the airport on Wednesday after work, and he seems to know where we're going even though I still don't.

"Milo, just give me one clue," I cajole.

"Nope. My brother can be very mean to me when he wants, and I have been warned not to break under your interrogation. No matter how cute you look." He winks at me flirtatiously.

"Watch it, Milo." Oliver slaps him in the back of the head.

"See, mean! I told you."

"Don't flirt with my girlfriend."

"Why? Afraid she'll realize I'm the better catch?"

I laugh out loud. "I thought you were talking to Tara."

"She's nice. We text. I don't think it is anything serious though."

"You never have anything serious," Oliver points out.

"I'm too young and studly to be tied down."

"Is studly even a real word?" I question him.

"Should be. Look it up and there should be a picture of me."

At least this vacation is starting off with some entertainment. I always enjoy being with Milo; he better not break Tara's heart though.

"Just make sure she knows it isn't serious."

"Don't worry, Grace, I'm good at handling women. If you ever get tired of this old man, I can show you what I mean."

"Stop antagonizing him!" I shove him a little.

"OK, you two are physically abusive, and I'm doing you a favor here," he mocks effrontery.

"Thank god we have arrived," Oliver groans as we pull up to the curb of the airport. "Thanks for the ride, little brother, and the comedy show."

Once we enter the airport, I finally get to know that we are flying to Orlando. "Oh my god, Oliver, please tell me this means what I think it means," I squeal happily.

"Yes, Grace, we're going to Hogwarts." His grin is wide and triumphant.

I jump into his arms with a gleeful shout. "I have always wanted to go! I never had anyone to go with, and it would be so sad to go alone, so I never did."

He spins me around and kisses me. "You have someone now, for everything you want to do."

"I don't deserve you."

"Bullshit, you deserve the entire world. I am going to give you everything I can and more. When will you realize what a treasure you are?"

"I spent my whole life being told I was crazy and treated like an annoyance by my family. Then when I was in a committed relationship, I was treated like dirt under his feet and thought I deserved it for some reason. You don't understand that until you, I thought I wasn't worthy of anyone's love. I still don't feel worthy, but I do feel loved."

"Baby, it absolutely kills me to know that your mind can make you feel so worthless. Those pieces-of-shit people who twisted your thinking like that should pay. I wish I could be the one to make them all pay." He's holding my face between his hands. I bring my hands up to cover his and turn to place a kiss on his palm.

"Let's just live for us and forget them."

"Yes, let's do that." And with that determination in our hearts, we head off to my dream weekend.

***

Oliver

I know I'm going to marry Grace. There is no question in my mind. I just want to find the perfect time to ask her. I considered doing it in Florida, but I want to have all the inheritance crap behind us when I do it. Besides, I am designing a ring, and it won't be ready for a while. It has a round-cut emerald in the center surrounded by small diamonds. It reminds me of her eyes.

If someone had told me I'd be ready to ask another woman to marry me this time a year ago, I would have sworn they were insane. I never imagined loving again. Now I can't imagine a version of me that doesn't love Grace. Watching her light up as we go through the parks is pure joy. I wanted to find a way to get her mind off all the problems that need sorting through, and taking her to Universal Studios and Islands of Adventure seems to have done the trick. She adores the rides and all the magical things we explore together. I got us a suite at one of Universal's nicest hotels, and I make love to her daily. By the time we get back, we will both be thoroughly exhausted.

On the plane home she is quiet, and I wonder if the reality of what's waiting for us back in New York is weighing on her.

"You all right?"

"Yeah, I'm going to miss it, that's all. It was all so wonderful. I really can't thank you enough."

"That was nothing," I tell her. "I haven't forgotten your top three travel destinations. Which one do you want to go to first?"

"You can't spoil me like this! It's too much."

"That's where you are wrong: I can and I will." I bring our entwined hands up and kiss her knuckles.

"I'm nervous," she admits suddenly. "Nothing in my life ever stays this good for long. I keep wondering what is going to happen to ruin us."

"I understand what you mean. but maybe nothing will. We haven't exactly had an easy time of things, and we still have plenty of crap we have to face."

"That's true."

"Just don't pull away from me in fear, Grace. Whatever we have to face, we'll face it together. Promise me?"

"I'll try my absolute hardest. I want to be worthy of you." She kisses me roughly then, and my mind starts to wander to other things as she practically climbs into my lap.

"You are trouble, wild girl," I mutter over her mouth, unable to hold back the wide grin that she always brings out.

* * *

Back to our daily routine of work and life, I can see the tension returning to her eyes. I had arranged for a clearance company to sell everything they could in her uncle's house and dispose of the rest while we were away. The place is empty now and can be sold whenever she feels ready. I know she has put the money from him in a separate account and hasn't touched a penny of it. I don't blame her; it feels like blood money. I have to fight my own anger with my entire being daily at how people have hurt the woman I love. The desire for vengeance is strong. I felt this way when Ally died too—only the man responsible then was dead, and nothing further could be done. Grace's uncle may be dead, but her parents aren't, and in my eyes they are equally as guilty as him.

It scares me when she talks about feeling unworthy and polluted. I worry she thinks she doesn't belong with me. Every time I kiss her body all over I can't help but linger on her tattoo that covers the scar he put on her. She thinks he made her dark; I think she shines like a diamond. All the trials and turmoil life has put her through only make her more brilliant and beautiful than ever. If only she could see herself through my eyes.

I have told my family about Grace, and I want to find a time for them all to meet her. I just need to make sure she feels ready for that. She has so much weighing on her at the moment; I can't add anything else that might stress her. Milo often hangs out with us, so at least I know she is comfortable with him. Lately we alternate between spending time at my place and hers, never wanting to be apart. Tonight we will be at my apartment, so I plan on cooking some pasta and having wine ready when she gets here from work.

I made sure I got home early and cleaned up a bit. I light some candles and put on my music while I get started on dinner. I work on making the pasta carbonara as perfectly as I can, all the while pondering all the things I want to talk about with Grace tonight. I won't push the subject of selling her uncle's place. It can sit there and rot for all I care. Until she feels ready to deal with it all, I will just wait. The only reason I want it taken care of at all is to have it out of her life for good. I've made some discreet inquiries so that I will be ready when and if she needs help selling the house and the vehicles. Beyond that, I can't do anything more to prepare.

I think of Ally for a minute and wonder what her reaction would be to all the awful things Grace has been through. I've always gotten the feeling the two of them would have been friends, and Ally was fiercely protective of her friends. I can imagine her joking how we could easily murder Grace's awful parents since she has access to real drugs through work. She used to watch crime shows and say if anyone crossed her, she knew how to hide a body. I laugh to myself at the memory. It still shocks me how now that I have Grace in my life, the thoughts and memories of Ally are not painful like they used to be. I am completely transformed, remade by her love.

"Something smells amazing." Her voice breaks through my reverie.

"I made your favorite pasta." I call out as she enters the kitchen. Her arms come around my waist, and I feel her place a gentle kiss in the center of my back.

"That is exactly what I need. Well that, and some serious loving later."

"Both are guaranteed," I assure her, turning to pull her fully into my arms.

"Hi, you," I say in between kisses.

"Hello, handsome."

"It's almost ready. You want to change into something more comfortable?" I slap her on the ass playfully.

"Good idea." She starts unbuttoning her blouse and throws it off behind her, then sensually slides her skirt down to reveal a very sexy black lace thong and matching bra.

"Grace Alice Murphy, I am going to burn our dinner because of you." Gripping her ass in one hand, I bury my face in her cleavage and moan. "You really don't play fair." She smells so goddamn amazing. I love her perfume, but its more than that. It's her natural scent; I wish I could bottle it and get drunk on it forever.

"I have been craving you all day, Oliver Dean Bekker," she moans in my ear.

Turning the stove off, I quickly undo my pants. I grip her waist and spin her around. Bending her over the counter, I lean down to whisper in her ear, "All right, wild girl, I'm going to fuck you hard and fast. Then I'm going to wine and dine you and make love to you slowly for hours." I know this is what she wants. Sometimes Grace craves the rough fucking more than the gentle lovemaking.

She breathes heavily and moans, "Take me." I lick a trail up the side of her neck, biting along the way. As I move her thong aside and push into her, she is already soaked and ready for me.

"Mmmm, you have been thinking dirty thoughts, haven't you?" I say as I thrust hard and bite her earlobe just how I know she likes it.

"So dirty you have no idea, baby," she grits out between moans. With one hand I grip her wrists, locking them above her head, and with the other I release a perfect breast from the bra holding it. I roll her nipple hard, squeezing the tip while I palm her soft mound and nibble on the sweet spot between her shoulder and neck.

"Fuck, you are so good at this!" she yells out. My neighbors can doubtless hear, but I couldn't care less. I pump harder, moving to hold her hips in place. One hand goes around, and I rub her clit knowing this will push her over the edge, I'm ready, and I want us to come together.

"Fuuuuccckkk!" I grunt as I lose myself in the orgasm we share.

"Yesssss!" I hear her cry out at the same time.

I fall forward, heaving in breaths as I hold her and pepper kisses along her spine. "You make me so crazy, my wild girl."

"Good, you fuck me so good when you're crazy." I hear the satisfaction in her voice and can't help feeling a little bit smug about it.

Losing Ground

Grace

The fast kitchen sex was exactly what I needed. These days I want him constantly, and I couldn't wait until after dinner. Not that I haven't always wanted Oliver constantly, but lately it's like when he isn't inside of me, the emptiness is overwhelming and it hurts somehow. I crave sex like a madwoman. I can't help but worry that he will grow tired of my voracious appetite, but so far there are no signs of it. The dinner he made me is heavenly, and I am fully relaxed now. We have moved to the couch with more wine, and my head is in Oliver's lap as I just lie there with my eyes closed, soaking in the pleasantness of being with the man I love. He plays idly with my hair and leans back, equally relaxed as we listen to music and sip our wine.

Looking down at me and smiling, he says, "I want to get you together with my family soon. They are dying to meet you. I think Milo has been making them all jealous that he knows you and they don't."

I chuckle at that. "I am not at all surprised. Your brother is so mischievous. He's definitely the Loki to your Thor."

"Did you just liken me to Thor?" His look of surprise makes me burst out in laughter then.

"You're a superhero to me, babe. I wish you knew how incredibly sexy and heroic I find you."

Shaking his head in disbelief, he just says, "I'm flattered."

"Do you think your family will like me?" I try not to let all my doubts show, but I have never felt worthy of this man, and I can't help but compare my family to his, and I definitely come up short when I do.

"No, I think they will *love* you, just like I do," he insists. That does nothing to calm the raging storm inside my head, but I don't let him see it.

He clears his throat. "I also think we should talk about moving in together." He says it a bit nervously.

That makes me sit up. "Really?"

"Yes, really. We already spend almost every night together at one of our apartments, and it would eliminate wasted time traveling. Besides, I want to share a bed. When we can't, I hate it."

"I do too."

"So why wouldn't we?"

"I don't know. Where would we live? Here or at my place?"

"Either works for me. I just want you; that's what matters to me."

"But this was your home with Ally. You can't seriously be considering leaving it."

"Yes, actually, I can. I'm thinking about the future, not the past. That is wherever you are."

My nerves are growing with each second. He seems so sure, but I can't help but fear that something is going to ruin this.

"Hey, Grace, talk to me. What are you thinking? You look panicked."

"It's just a lot in one night: plans for meeting your whole family and moving in together. I need some time to think about it all. I'm sorry."

I see his disappointment even though he tries to hide it. "It's OK. There is no rush. I just think we should consider it."

Letting out a deep breath, I nod. "OK."

"I won't push anything you aren't ready for. I just needed you to know what I'm ready for."

"Yeah, I get it. I want this too, I do…I am just scared, you know? I never want you to have regrets about me."

He can't possibly comprehend how much I'm freaking out inside right now. It's not from a lack of love for him or trust in him. The doubt and fear is all about me. How does he not see that he is a million times better than me? One day when he wakes up and comes to that realization, will he feel trapped?

"You aren't just my girlfriend, Grace. You are my world. That is the reality, whether you see it or not." I see the frustration brewing in his eyes.

"I feel the same. I do. I just have a lot going on, you know that. Give me some time, OK?"

His eyes clear immediately. "Of course, baby. I'm so sorry. I'm being selfish."

"You are never selfish. I promise I will get all of this resolved soon."

I bring his face to mine then. Running my lips over his, I pour everything I am into kissing him. I want to lose myself in him again. I want to stop thinking again. I will worry about everything else tomorrow.

***

Oliver

Like a fool, I never see it coming. I don't even get an inkling when we say goodbye in the morning and each go to work that I won't see her again after that. The first time I text around eleven, I don't think anything about not hearing back until it's past one. It never takes her that long to get back to me, so I text again. Then I call. Then I call her office. That's when the real panic starts setting in. Grace took the rest of the week off and didn't say more than that she needed personal leave. I ask for Tara then to see if she knows anything more, but she is as clueless as I am. She asks Kyle, and his answer is the same. I believe them because they both seem worried.

"Fuck!" I yell out.

It's a good thing my office door is closed, because I can't contain my emotions when I finally recognize what's happening. She is running from me. I saw the panic in her face last night. I felt her distracting me with more sex instead of opening up about her apprehension, but I let it go. I figured eventually we would work through it together, like we always do. I knew all this shit with her past had been building up, getting on top of her, and I stupidly assumed there was still time for me to fix it with her. I should have known she was on the verge of something drastic. I immediately let my bosses know I have a family emergency and head over to her apartment. All I can do is pray that she is there, hiding out while she works through her emotions and thoughts. Not bothering with knocking, I use the key she gave me and go straight in. It doesn't take long to see that she isn't there, and as I look around, I think she has taken a few things with her also.

My terror-stricken heart is beating out of my chest as I try to remain calm. Where the hell is she? How could she just disappear without leaving a note or texting me, at least? I try calling her again, and when I hear her phone ringing in the apartment, I really start to lose it. Without it she is untraceable. Anger, despair, and panic are all warring inside of me.

I need to think; she has to be somewhere. I look down at her phone in my hand. I decide to try one thing that I truly hope doesn't work. Looking in her contacts, I find the name Anthony. I punch his phone number into my own cell and call it.

"Anthony Ortiz," he answers.

"Anthony, this is Grace's boyfriend, Oliver."

"Oliver, good to hear from you. How are you two lovebirds doing?"

"Listen, I won't waste time: Grace is missing. If you know anything about her whereabouts, I need to know." I don't bother to shield the alarm in my voice.

"What the hell? No, I haven't got a clue! What do you need? Let me come help you."

Rubbing my forehead, I just mutter, "I don't know what to do. I'm at my wit's end."

"Oliver, where are you?"

"I'm in her apartment. She left her phone, so it's not even like the police could trace it."

"Listen, give me half an hour, and I'll be there. My brother is NYPD. I'm going to have him meet me there."

"She is gone of her own volition, Anthony. It's a long story. She is very upset about something she found out, something deeply personal I can't disclose to just anyone. I don't think I can involve the police."

"OK, well, then I'll come alone for now, but at least let me help you."

"OK, yeah, thank you. I can't really think straight right now, so help would be good." I hang up, wondering if I've lost my last brain cell turning to Anthony of all people for help.

The problem is I can't handle this alone. I keep flashing back to the day I lost Ally. I remember every detail so clearly. That feeling of wishing I could have known when it was going to be my final goodbye. What if I have had my final goodbye with Grace and didn't know it? Is it happening all over again? I won't be able to survive this twice; I just know it. My mind starts replaying all the awful memories. When the police came to my work to tell me. When I had to go to the morgue and identify her body. I fall back against the wall, overcome with the feelings of anguish flooding me along with the dreadful recollections. I slide down until I hit the floor, and I feel my chest caving in as I fight to keep breathing. I can't lose Grace. I don't care where she is, just let her be safe.

Losing all concept of time, I just focus on breathing until I hear a voice.

"Oliver? Are you OK?" I raise my head, and Anthony is kneeling in front of me, unease written all over his face.

"The door was wide open, and I thought you were passed out or something."

"I'm losing it, man. I can't do this again," I admit to this virtual stranger.

"I know. It's going to be OK. Can you start by explaining what in the fuck is going on so we can make a plan?" He gives me a hand and pulls me to my feet.

"Yeah, OK. Last night we talked about moving in together and her meeting my family, and I know she was worried—I just had no idea she would bolt like this." Running my hands through my hair, I yank on it, trying to pull the answers out of my brain. "She hasn't been great since finding out about her uncle and the inheritance and cutting off her horrible family. I didn't think she would push me away though."

"I got about half of that, but honestly it's probably not all my business. What matters right now is thinking straight. I need you to breathe. Clam down and try to think, Oliver. Where might she have gone?"

I pace around, listening to what he says and knowing he's right. What matters is what we do next.

"OK, well, she might have gone to the property in Chester, of course. Maybe she just wants to handle that without interruption? But why wouldn't she just tell me that?"

"She wouldn't go to her parents?"

"No way, but we can always call them just to be one hundred percent sure."

"All right, first step, then. I will call her parents and just ask very quickly if they have seen her. You keep thinking. Let me have their numbers."

Anthony's calm and collected manner is doing a good job of bringing me back from the edge. He is taking control of the situation, for which I am truly grateful. I find her parents' numbers in Grace's phone for him and then go to get a large glass of water while I try to stay calm.

After talking on the phone in the other room for a few minutes, Anthony comes into the kitchen. "No luck. They haven't seen or heard from her. They didn't seem to care much either."

"Yeah they are real pieces of shit, believe me." I just shake my head. I don't have time or energy to waste on getting angry at them again. Tapping his hand on the counter, it's clear he's trying to think about what is the next best step.

"How far away is the property you talked about?"

"Two and a half hours." I answer him.

"We shouldn't both go, in case she is still here in the city. Do you want to stay here or go there?"

"I think I need to go there. It's the most likely place that she will be." I can't really imagine anywhere else she could be.

"OK. I can stay here, and if I find out anything, I'll call you immediately. I don't think you should go alone though. Who can you take with you for help and support?"

"Milo." I clarify for Anthony, "My brother, he will help me."

Milo arrives quicker than I ever expected. His look of distress is also a surprise. I never see my unflappably cool younger brother upset like this.

"What do you mean Grace is missing?" are the first words out of his mouth as he slams his car door and heads toward me, where I've been waiting on the sidewalk in front of her building.

"Look, I will explain on the way. We need to drive to Connecticut *now*." I open the passenger door and get in without delay. He just shakes his head in disbelief and annoyance and starts the engine.

"Explain," he insists.

I try to explain things the best I can without divulging too many sordid personal details about Grace's past. It is obvious I'm leaving stuff out, but Milo can just deal with it.

"I don't even know what to say. She is always so happy and fun. I had no idea she had all this shit going on."

"I know. She doesn't usually let it get the better of her." I scrub my hands over my face. "This is my fault. I kept trying to move things along when she wasn't ready. I should have been more patient."

"I apparently don't know half of what goes on between you two, but from the outside looking in…you are crazy about each other. Whatever this is about, it's not you; it's her inner demons. She has to fight them in her own way, maybe."

"Without telling me, just disappearing?"

"It seems like she panicked, man. I know you are worried, especially after losing Ally. I get it, but that isn't this. Grace is probably just clearing her head and will be back soon to explain everything."

"I can't just sit back and do nothing, Milo. I can't wait for another visit from the cops with bad news. I have to find her."

"We will." He reaches out and takes a hold of my shoulder, squeezing to reassure me.

Fire and Rain

Grace

After Oliver fell asleep, I couldn't stop my brain from spinning out of control. All I could think is I have to find a way to be clean and worthy of this man. He doesn't see the darkness of my soul, all the stains and scars that aren't visible. How can I let him tie his life to mine? I make a plan to purge myself of all the demons haunting me, but I have to do it alone. I can't let him see everything. I need to protect him from it. This is why being alone was so much easier: no one to disappoint, no one to let down, and no one to worry over.

We say goodbye in the morning. Instead of going to work, I head back to my apartment. I call work and explain that I have to handle some personal business and need a leave of absence. I guess knowing I have a bank account with $4.5 million makes blowing off work feel less worrisome. I never want to touch that money, but it's impossible to forget that I have it. I grab a backpack and throw a few things in. I look around hoping I'm not forgetting anything important; my state of mind is far from clear. The determination I feel keeps driving me on. Double-checking I have all the keys for the Chester property, I quickly head out.

The first place I'm going isn't Connecticut, however. I find a florist shop that has beautiful blooms spread out on display in the windows. A tinkling bell sings out cheerfully as I enter.

"Welcome!" A middle-aged woman comes out from the back, her arms full of sunflowers and a bright smile on her face.

"Hello, I need some help creating a bouquet," I explain as I approach her.

"You have come to the right place then, dear. I love nothing more!"

"Do you know the meanings behind flowers?"

"Yes, that's something I specialize in. Tell me, who is the bouquet for?"

"My boyfriend's late wife's grave, actually," I say a bit hesitantly. Saying it out loud sounds odd.

"I haven't encountered that one before, I have to say. It's a lovely thought though."

"I don't care so much about the appearance of it. It is more important that it has the right meaning for me," I try to explain my jumbled feelings.

"I understand. I will make it look beautiful no matter what, but we will get the meaning right, don't worry."

"OK, thank you."

"If you were going to tell her something with this gift, what would that be?" She gives me an encouraging look.

I take a deep breath and think about that.

"I want to tell her that I love her husband deeply, but I never want to disrespect her memory. I want her to be cherished in his memory forever. More than anything, though, I want to be worthy of him. I hope that she would think I'm good enough for him. I think they had a beautiful, pure relationship, and I can only hope to bring him the same."

She reaches across the counter and takes my hand. "That is very lovely. I know just what we need. We will pick out the perfect blooms, OK?"

"OK."

She hands me a galvanized steel bucket to hold, and we begin walking around the fragrant shop. She seeks out the specific flowers she wants and explains the meaning of each one as she adds them to the bucket.

"I want to start with a pink camellia. It means 'My destiny is your hands.' Two of those to represent two hands. Next I think purple irises for respect. And then lily of the valley—that's for purity."

The delicate white bell-shaped blossoms are so beautiful. I touch them gently.

"Purity, yes, I like that. Can you add a little more?"

"Of course!" She thinks for a moment after that, then heads to some delicate little blue flowers. "Forget-me-nots, to keep someone in your memory. Yellow lilies mean gratitude; do you like that?"

"Very much so, yes."

"And also pink zinnias: they mean 'Never forget the absent ones'. Lastly, for you I want to put daffodils; they mean new beginnings."

"My favorite flowers are red poppies. I know one of their meanings is remembrance. Do you have any of those?"

"I do. Let me get you some." Gathering a large handful of beautiful red poppies, she adds them to my bucket. I look down at all the wonderful colors and sniff the glorious scents. Tears spring into my eyes, and I close them.

"Thank you, it's perfect," I whisper.

"Come, I'll put them together for you now." Thinking of them being for a grave she finds the appropriate vase.

When it's all arranged, I get my wallet out to pay. She stops me. "No, this is on me. I insist. My husband died not long ago. I understand what you're going through more than you know."

I have no words, so instead I hug her. Her kindness feels like the best start to the day I could have had.

Having already found out where Ally's grave is, I head to it next. She is buried in a beautiful spot, right near a large oak tree that casts its shade over her plot. I sit down on the ground and place the flowers in front of her gravestone.

Allyssa Anne Bekker

née Harper

Beloved Wife and Daughter

June 12, 1982–November 3, 2019

"Until we meet again."

I trace the words with my finger as I think of everything I know about Ally. I would have liked her; I have no doubt. There is no way to think about what life would have been like if I had met her and Oliver as a married couple. I can't imagine not loving him. Things only happened the way they did, and nothing can ever change that. Clearing my throat, I start talking quietly.

"Hi, Ally, I'm Grace. I don't know if you're up there watching or if you're really completely gone. I do know that I wish I could ask you if you think I'm good enough for Ollie. You know him better than any other person. Do you think I'm the one he needs?"

I play with the grass and lean against the cool stone.

"I love him. I'm sure that's something you can understand. I tried not to. I really did. For his sake and yours. It just didn't work. But I worry. I don't think he understands what a mess I am inside. My soul is damaged. I didn't have the nice family he and you did. What if I fail him somehow? He doesn't deserve to be hurt ever again. The sadness I used to see in his eyes when he talked about you, it broke my heart. I can't bring sadness back to his life. What if he's better off with someone else? Someone clean and pure. Unsullied."

The weight of all these worries has been crushing me, and talking about it releases something inside. It makes no sense, but I begin to fall asleep. Sitting on the ground, leaning against cold, hard stone, it's hardly comfortable, but my exhaustion is unbearable all of a sudden.

I have no idea how long I have been asleep when the raindrops start falling, and I wake up. I go to reach in my back pocket where I always keep my phone to check the time, but it isn't there. I must have left it in the car. The rain is cool and refreshing, and I don't immediately move. I turn my head up to the sky and watch the big drops fall. They feel cleansing, and I let them wash away all the invisible dirt I constantly feel covering my skin. My tears start to fall and mix with the rain. I'm not sure if I believe in signs, but if I did, I might think this was one from Ally. I feel like I'm being gently washed clean, made new. I stay there for a long time, letting the rain soak through me. I lean against Ally and feel like she is supporting me.

When I return to my car hours later, I reach over to the other flower the kind florist gave me: a single white lotus blossom. She said it was for me especially because it signifies a pure, new beginning. It is a symbol of hope, strength, and resilience, she explained. Lotus flowers bloom from muddy water and yet they come up clean and beautiful, therefore the symbolism of regeneration. Even with roots in the dirtiest water, the flower is perfect. I hold the delicate thing in my palms and think of the metaphor. My roots are, without a doubt, filthy, but I don't have to let that shape who I am, do I? Can I, too, rise from the dark depths of murky waters to sit in the sun and be cleansed? Hope surges through me that I can have a future in the light. I don't have to punish myself anymore for others' sins. I need to bury the rest of my past now so I can begin anew.

***

Oliver

We finally arrive at Grace's uncle's house. Her car isn't in sight, but I jump out before Milo has even come to a full stop. Running to the door, I pound on it, yelling for her.

"Grace! Where are you, damn it!"

"Ollie, calm down. Her car isn't here." Milo is behind me. His face shows I am scaring him.

"I don't care!" I scream. "I'm out of options. You don't fucking get it. I can't do this again." I don't know when I started crying, but the tears are flowing now.

"OK, OK. It's all right. She is OK. This isn't the same thing." He takes me into his arms and holds me tight.

"You don't know that!" I sob.

"Let's look around, give it time too. We got here pretty fast. If she stopped somewhere else, it's possible we beat her here." His soothing tone is helping me, and I let myself breathe deeply.

"OK, let's check everywhere."

We do, twice. I feel on the verge of collapse when the sound of a car pulling up breaks through my crazed mind.

"Milo, it's her car!" I grab his arm, desperate to know that he sees it too, that I'm not just seeing what I want.

"It is. Oh, thank god it's her. She's OK." He hugs me again. I tear myself away from him and make for my girl.

"Oliver? Milo? I don't understand. What are you doing here?" Grace is exiting her car like my world hasn't been ripped apart for hours, like everything is normal.

"Are you fucking kidding me, Grace?" I grab her and hold her tight against me, drinking in the scent of her, running my hands over every part of her, making sure she is OK.

Milo speaks up then. "He's been beyond frantic. He didn't know where you were, and you left your phone, Grace. It was too much for him after what happened with Ally. He was losing his mind." His tone has reproach in it, and I turn to him.

"It doesn't matter now. She's safe. That is all that matters."

There are tears in her eyes as she pulls my face to her. "Oh my god, baby, I'm so sorry. I forgot my phone. I didn't notice till I was almost here. I had some things I needed to do alone, just to clear my brain. I wasn't thinking straight, I know. I should have talked to you. I just wanted to disappear for a bit till I felt OK again."

"I know I pushed you. I will give you time. Just never do this to me again. I can't feel this pain again. I can't lose you too." I kiss her frantically, willing her to understand what she means to me. If words won't convince her, maybe my caresses can.

"You won't lose me. I figured out how I can be worthy of you. I visited Ally. It helped me."

"What?" I ask, confused.

"That's why you asked where her grave is?" Milo puts in then.

I look at him then back at Grace. "We have a lot to talk about, don't we?"

"We do, but I need to deal with this place first." She gestures at the house behind us. There's a firmness in her voice, and she turns and walks to the trunk of her car, opening it. I see three large red gasoline containers inside it.

"What are those for?" I say cautiously.

"Oh, shit," I hear Milo whisper behind me.

"I need to do this. I don't care about right or wrong. It's the only way I can get past it. You guys should go back to the city though." She reaches for one of the containers. I grab her hand.

"No way. This is not the answer, Grace!"

Milo interjects then also. "Um, I love that you're a little crazy and wild, don't get me wrong. I mean, it's actually hella sexy, but I have to agree with Ollie. I know I dropped out of law school, but I can tell you that this doesn't end well. Arson is serious shit." He pushes between Grace and the trunk, physically moving her away.

"I won't hurt anyone. I need to do something to this place though. It's a mockery. He thinks he can buy my forgiveness?

It makes me sick. It was all just to make himself feel better! I hate everything about it." Her desperation grows with every word. "You weren't supposed to be here anyway. Just go!"

"Thank god we are here! I understand why you want to do it, baby, I do. Listen to me: we will find another solution. I promise."

"I want to see it burn to the fucking ground, the way he burned my skin with his cigarettes when I was too little to fight back." She chokes out a sob, and I gather her into my arms.

"I know, I wish we could get justice, but if you end up in prison, he wins again." I just hold her and let her cry. My eyes meet Milo's and his distress is palpable. He paces around, clenching and unclenching his fists.

"Son of a bitch," he mumbles, his face red with rage. I just nod.

"I have an idea," he says after a while. Grace sniffs loudly. My shirt is soaked through with her tears, but I don't care.

"What idea?" I ask him.

"We donate the house to the fire department for one of those controlled fires they use to train new firefighters. We watch it burn, but no one goes to jail. Then we sell the empty land and never come near this cursed place again."

***

Grace

"I still want to light something now." I sound petulant, I know, but I felt so sure that I would do this. I had made up my mind, repercussions be damned. I wanted this one act of vengeance. Both of them laugh at me, and Oliver embraces me even harder.

"How about a bonfire in the back? I have something we can burn."

"You do?" I sniff again and look up at him.

"I have the perfect thing." He leans down and kisses me gently. Then he takes an envelope out of his jacket pocket; I know what it is instantly. He's wearing the same jacket he wore the day we came here to see the lawyer. It's Ronan's letter.

While Milo and I gather kindling from the wooded area behind the house, Oliver searches the large garage for rakes. The crisp fall air is so fresh and clean that I truly begin enjoying myself. We have cleared a large circle and built a pyre big enough to burn for a few hours. I pour a little of the gasoline I bought earlier on everything and light the match. It's dark now and the light flares up, beautifully bright. As everything catches, the heat sears in all its hot, cleansing glory.

Oliver takes my hand in his. We hold Ronan's letter to the flames together, watching it catch. We hold it as long as we can, then drop in it the inferno. Milo goes and gets us some food and drinks in town. When he returns, he backs up his Toyota 4Runner till it is close to the fire. Opening up the hatchback, we sit in the back and feast on fried seafood and drink local craft beer. Milo plays music through his speakers, and right now it feels more like a party than a revenge ceremony. Facing the woods, you can't see the house, the garage, or any sign of the man who took my childhood and twisted it into something grotesque. All we see is a glorious fire, the stars, and the brightly colored fall leaves on the trees.

Leaning on Oliver, I tell him about the flowers I brought to Ally. I won't tell him what I said when I was there because that was just for her and me.

He kisses the top of my head. "I can't believe you were just fine, calmly doing your own thing all day, while I lost my mind. I imagined a million different horrible scenarios, even one where you were choosing to end it all." His voice is low and sad.

I sit up then, turning to him. "You mean suicide?"

"Yes."

I climb into his lap, straddling him and holding his face, ensuring he hears every word I tell him.

"Listen to me. I have survived so many appalling things, and I have finally found love. I am not going to leave that behind. If Ronan didn't drive me to it, or even Matt or my own family, for fuck's sake, how can you possibly think that silly fears about my future with you would?"

"I wasn't being rational," he admits. "I was out of my mind, Grace, the whole day. You can't imagine the way my whole world felt like it would just crumble if I didn't find you and see for myself that you were OK."

Just then he jumps up, placing me on my feet. He groans loudly. "Anthony. Crap, I need to call him."

"Anthony? What does he have to do with anything?" I am completely lost.

"I called him looking for you, and he came to help me. He's probably still at your apartment waiting." Pulling out his phone, he curses again. "Two missed calls from him. He must be trying to check on me. I was so relieved to find you I completely forgot."

I have to laugh at the thought of my old hookup and my new boyfriend working together and acting like friends, but deep down it makes me happy. Eavesdropping a little, I smile as I listen to their phone conversation. They even joke and laugh together. Never would have seen that coming, but then there's a lot in my life right now I didn't see coming.

Milo is sitting on my other side, and he has been unusually quiet since we started the fire.

"Thank you for keeping me out of prison," I nudge him with my shoulder. He gives me a crooked smile.

"Someone has to."

"I guess so. I didn't think about it enough, I suppose. I was just determined to take action."

He takes my hand and holds it tightly. "I don't blame you. I can't imagine what you've been through."

"It's all in the past now. I won't let it bring me down anymore." We both stare into the flames until I remember something he said earlier and decide to ask about it.

"I didn't know you were in law school."

"I didn't last long, I'm not cut out for the corporate life. I need independence, freedom, and creativity. It would have killed me, trying to fit into that suit-up, nine-to-five daily grind."

"I know exactly how you feel. My job has a creative side, and that is the only thing that saves my sanity. Sometimes I think about giving it up and just following a passion, something that makes me feel alive."

"You could now, couldn't you? If you used the money?"

"Maybe, but I'd have to wrap my head around where the money came from and why first." An involuntary shiver runs down my spine.

"What are you passionate about?" he asks me, tilting his head a little.

"Honestly, books. I would love to have a bookstore or even write my own book. But besides that, I have been considering something else these past few days. I want to help other people who have been abused. I know there are organizations and foundations out there for that, but I want to do something myself. It's an experience you can't possibly understand if you haven't lived it. Maybe I could help someone else heal one day. Not that I'm even in the right place yet myself, but eventually I could be."

He grunts in thought. "Wouldn't that be a way to use the bastard's money? Helping others who have been hurt by cockroaches like him."

I nod slowly. "It would." The thought appeals to me, and I file it away for further consideration at a later time.

"I want you to know I'm your friend too, Grace. I like you a lot, and not just because of Oliver. If you ever need me, I'm here."

"Same." I lay my head on his shoulder. "And thank you."

After a few moments of silence, he perks up and turns to me. "Want to dance?" The music is still playing, and the night is peaceful all around.

"Yeah, that sounds nice." I say and get up. Together we sway in front of the bonfire, the shadows dancing along with us. "I'll Stand by You" by The Pretenders is playing, and it's a priceless moment that I know I won't forget. I lean back, looking up to the sky where stars sparkle bright and let the breeze move over me as we spin. Milo grins, spinning me out with one hand, and I find myself landing in Oliver's strong arms. It feels like home.

Lotus Blooming

Oliver

Eventually the fire burns low enough that I can smother it with dirt. It's late. I had no concept of time most of the day as I went mad. Checking the time, I see it's almost three in the morning. Grace is sitting curled up, hugging her legs to her chest, leaning her head on Milo's shoulder as they chat quietly, and I smile to myself, loving how well the two of them get along. She has two older sisters, but they aren't a part of her life. They have treated her like a leper for the majority of her existence and always sided with her awful parents. I want her to know that my family is nothing like her horrible one. They will love her and have her back. It will take time for her to trust it, I know, but she already has a bond with Milo, and that's something.

I join them, pulling her into me. "We need to decide if we find a place to stay over or drive back. I'd say we could try to sleep in the cars, but yours is toy sized." I grin at Grace, giving her the usual shit about her Mini.

"My seats all lie down," Milo volunteers. "Should we have a cuddlefest?" He wiggles his eyebrows.

"Not going to happen," I say flatly.

Grace just laughs. "I actually took a long nap on Ally's grave earlier, so I could drive home. At least there won't be any traffic right now."

"Wait a minute, back up. You took a nap on your boyfriend's dead wife's grave?" Milo is looking at her like she has lost her mind.

"OK, well when you say it like that, it sounds worse. I was just overly exhausted, and I sat down for a while. It happened...I don't know. I guess it is crazy." She buries her face in her hands in embarrassment. "Why did I open my big mouth?"

"Only you." He laughs.

"Actually, I need to stay in town to make some arrangements. I better see if I can find a hotel room," Grace points out.

"I would like to stay and help with it all, if you don't mind," I say with some trepidation. I know she wanted to handle this on her own. However she might be in jail right now, had Milo and I not been here this afternoon.

"You didn't expect to be staying. You have no clothes or anything."

"I'm fairly certain there are stores here."

Milo pipes up then with his two cents, of course. "I can stay, too, not that anyone invited me. But I haven't had this much adventure in years."

"Don't you work at all?" I ask him, mockingly stern.

"I'm basically my own boss. Don't be jealous, big brother."

"What do you say, Grace? Will you let us help you and possibly keep you from committing any felonies?" I try to sound light and playful, but I really have no intention of leaving her. I will stay in town and follow her around in the shadows if need be.

"Stay." She holds my face in her hands, resting her forehead against mine for a second before placing a gentle kiss on my lips. "Always," she adds with a wink.

"Yes ma'am." I give a mock salute before scooping her up into my arms and kissing her longer and harder.

"OK, well now you guys are just being rude." Milo sounds sulky even though I know he's happy for us.

"You can stay too, Milo." Grace is back on her feet now, and she goes to him, planting a sisterly kiss on his cheek.

"Thank you. I do like feeling needed. Besides, I don't want to have to remind you it was my idea to let the fire department burn this place down. It's obvious that I'm the brains here."

"Clearly. What would we do without you?" I give my little brother a playful shove.

* * *

Grace

We spend the next few days in Chester. The lawyer helps us find buyers for the two classic cars. Even I don't want to burn those, as long as I never have to touch them. The fire department agrees with our plans. They will use the house, garage, and Tacoma truck as live training exercises. The date when it will happen is set, and after that a local realtor is planning to list the cleared land for sale. I don't plan to return for the burning. Our bonfire was more personal and intimate. It gave me all the closure I needed. The rest is just business.

Milo wasn't really needed, but the comic relief he provided was perfect. He makes everything more fun with his presence alone. I secretly hope he and Tara really do become something; they would be a good match.

One night in the hotel, the three of us are sitting around, enjoying each other's company and drinking tequila at Milo's insistence. The more we drink, the looser we naturally get. Eventually we start playing a round of "Never Have I Ever." Milo hadn't been there the last time Oliver and I had played this game, and he claims it will be a good way for us to discover more about each other. He just can't help his little brother tendencies, always trying to stir the pot.

Starting us off, he begins with, "Never have I ever been arrested."

I have to drink at that and find I am already regretting allowing Milo to have a say in how we spend the evening.

When two sets of blue eyes stare at me expectantly, waiting for the story I simply say, "I went through a phase in my teenage years where I sought thrills constantly. One day I got caught driving my boyfriend's dad's car without permission or a license. His dad happened to be a cop, and he and his buddies thought I needed to be scared straight. I wasn't very smart back then." They both chuckle at that but don't seem too surprised.

I take my turn next. "Never have I ever gotten a lap dance." I raise my eyebrows in challenge at the two men. Milo immediately takes a shot. Oliver is slower to react but eventually also does. He avoids eye contact with me for a minute, and his flushed face is actually adorable.

"Oh, do tell." I keep staring at him and prop my chin in my hands, waiting for the story with an impish grin on my face.

He clears his throat uncomfortably and says, "It was at my bachelor party. My stupid college friends thought it would be funny even though I told them not to hire dancers or strippers. Ally wanted to murder them and me when she found out. I didn't blame her!"

Milo is laughing more than ever. "I remember that night! That was my first real taste of debauchery, back when I was still a teenager. I loved that party and didn't understand why you were such a sourpuss about it all."

"Because you didn't have to deal with Ally!" Oliver huffs. I just laugh at them.

"Oh, poor baby. I'm sure deep down somewhere you enjoyed it a little." I give him a wink.

"Anyway, my turn. Never have I ever had a threesome." He looks pointedly at his brother. Milo grins proudly and takes a shot.

"I have and I will forever be proud, so don't think you're shaming me, big brother."

I really hope no one notices as I discreetly take a very swift shot. No such luck. They both gape at me, one of them a bit more amused than the other.

"I'm not explaining it," I say.

Milo refills all our glasses to the brim with a fresh round of tequila. "Oh, but you must. That, my dear Gracie, is the whole point of this exercise. Oliver would never have known this about his wild girlfriend if not for my brilliant idea to play the game. Now we get to the good part: details. First we will all do a shot together to make this easier for everyone to hear." He motions for us to lift our glasses as he is doing.

Showing no emotions whatsoever, Oliver stands up and heads to the door of our room instead, opening it. I hold my breath, terrified that he's leaving in anger or that he wants me to leave. But he simply looks at his brother and motions for him to leave with his head. "Time for you to go to your room, Mi."

"What? No, come on, man, it's just getting interesting!" Milo protests.

"Out!" Oliver simply states.

Once we are alone, I wait for his real reaction. His eyes are glued to mine as he slowly returns to where I am seated. They smolder with an intensity I have never seen before. He says nothing, just lifts his glass and takes the shot, still staring.

I can't take the wait any longer.

"Are you upset?" I ask with trepidation.

Wiping the back of his hand along his mouth, he simply shakes his head no and leans down over my chair, caging my body in with his.

When he finally speaks, his voice is low and full of desire. "No, Grace, what I am is very curious. And so fucking turned on right now that I don't know what the hell is wrong with me. I can't decide if I want the details or not. I can't think straight at this moment. All I know is no one is going to hear this story but me. Especially not my little brother who would find it far too fascinating."

I lick my lips. His intensity has me feeling so many things in this moment, and suddenly my mouth has gone dry. I go to reach for my shot, and he grabs my wrist, stopping me.

"I want you to drink that off of me." His eyes are burning into me.

"What, like a body shot?" I say, getting more turned on by the second. I want to lick every inch of him now. "Yes, please," I say, practically salivating for him.

"If you want to do that, I think I want to hear your story first." He has me by both my wrists now. He knows exactly how much I like it when he takes control during sex, and he is fully aware what he's doing to me right now. I can tell that he's getting off on the idea of hearing about my threesome, so decide I will tell him about it. I want him as worked up as he has me right now.

"OK, but you have to promise not to judge me. It's in the past, and I love you now. I was a different person back then."

He pulls me up then. "I think for story time we should be less...clothed." He begins stripping off his T-shirt and unbuttoning his jeans. My eyes never leave his body as I slip out of my shirt and leggings. In just his boxer briefs, which do little to contain his straining erection, he settles back onto the bed. In my lace bra and panties, I climb onto him to straddle his lap. We both breathe heavily as we take each other in. No matter how many times we have each other, it feels so raw and electric every single time.

"I have always been very sexual," I begin, as I trace his abs with featherlight touches. "So when a guy I was dating once wanted to know a fantasy of mine he could fulfill, I told him I always wanted to have two guys at the same time."

He sucks in a breath then and briefly closes his eyes. I can't help but notice his already rock-hard cock twitch and grow even more engorged.

I trail my fingers lower down his abdomen. "He asked me which one of his friends I wanted. So I picked one, and he told his friend that he was going to be his gift to me." He grips my hips then, pulling me hard against him.

"When?" he grits out as if trying to maintain control.

"I was twenty-six, so eight years ago now."

"Tell me how they took you."

"Are you sure?" I bite my lip nervously, unsure he really wants details.

"Very," is all he can manage to get out, hoarsely.

I lean into him, lowering my voice. "They took me many times, in a lot of different ways. My favorite, though, was when I was on my hands and knees, with one pounding me from behind while the other took my mouth. It was incredible." I take his mouth with mine then and kiss him deeply, ensuring that he understands I only ever want him to pleasure me from now on.

Whatever control he had snaps at that moment as he completely takes over. Before I even know what's happening, I'm on my back, my mouth being completely devoured. Then he moves down to my neck and then my breasts.

I pant, "Did I earn my body shot?"

He lifts his head and the dazed, desire-drunk look in his eyes clears for a moment.

"Baby, you earned anything you want." He lies down flat on the bed, putting his perfectly chiseled abs on display. I slide my body over his deliberately as I reach for the shot glass and bring it over him. Slowly I dribble it into the valley between his ab muscles, and leaning down I lick my way downward. When I reach his waistband, I pull it down with my teeth until his dick springs free. He has his arms behind his head as he watches every move I make, barely breathing. Poised right over his cock, I pour the remainder of the shot into my mouth but don't swallow it. Instead I take him in my mouth while it's full of the tequila.

"Fucking hell, Grace!" I hear him hiss as I suck him hard with the added sensation of the warm liquid all around him. His hands land on my head then, and he holds on as I continue my ministrations. It isn't long before he explodes, and I swallow all of his delicious cum along with the tequila. His grunting is so intense I know the people in the rooms around us must hear, but I can't help but feel pleased to have brought him such intense pleasure.

His head falls back as he catches his breath and pulls me up along his body. "That was the most intense thing I've ever felt," he says at last, kissing my temple.

"I was so scared you were angry when you got up to tell your brother to leave," I admit to him as he holds me.

"I don't hold anything in your past against you, Grace." Cupping my face in his hands, he brings my gaze to meet his. "I only need to be concerned with your future. You are mine now. But I'm not going to pretend that you were a nun before me. In fact, I thank fuck you weren't. Sex with you is the most mind-blowing, amazing thing I can imagine. I sometimes feel unworthy of it because I was only ever with Ally. I hope I can please you…satisfy you as much as you do me."

I kiss him hard and deeply at that.

"I have never felt anything like what I feel with you. With you it's like you make love to my body, my soul, and my mind all at once. I didn't even know such a sensation was possible. Back when you wouldn't sleep with me, I was so insane for your touch I thought it might actually kill me. Now that I get to have you, it's never enough. Every time I think, that was the best I've ever had. Until the next time. Then I think it all over again."

He takes me then, giving me so much pleasure I want to cry. Afterward we talk more about our pasts, discovering things about each other that we don't know yet. What started out as a silly drinking game turned into one of our most intense nights ever. We grow closer than I ever thought I would with someone. Wisely Milo never brought up the question of my threesome story again. It seems he could tell when his brother meant business about our privacy.

As we drive back home, I bring up the things that used to scare me so much. "I want to get together with your family soon. I feel ready."

"They will be so happy, especially Gramps. He hasn't stopped asking when he's going to meet you. You saw Jess once, but she is dying to get to know you." He gives me a warm smile, his eyes shining with joy. Loving Oliver has given me so much more than I ever expected. For the first time, I think maybe it will give me a family too. Will I finally know what a real, loving family feels like?

"We should decide where we want to live also." I give him a half smile, hoping he understands I'm apologizing again for my freak-out that scared him so badly.

"I've had some ideas about that too."

"You have?"

"I have. I heard you talking to Milo about how you consider a change in work sometimes. Do you ever think about living somewhere else also?"

"Yeah, of course. I have always thought I'd like to see where life could take me. I haven't had any specific ideas really, though. Have you?"

"Well not before you I didn't, but now that's changed. I feel like this is a new start, and I want it to be a real new beginning, like somewhere else altogether. I have made some inquiries about other countries where my job is in demand. Guess what one of them is?"

"Another country? England? They need you to keep London Bridge from falling down?"

Laughing he says, "No, New Zealand. Civil engineering is in high demand there, with all the new infrastructure they are working on. I am pretty certain I could get a job there for a few years at least, if not permanently. Their immigration policies are fairly straightforward. I've been in contact just to make sure it was a real possibility before I got your hopes up."

My jaw is hanging open as I stare at him, I'm sure of it. "You're serious, aren't you?"

"Yes, completely."

"You would move across the world with me, leave everyone and everything behind?"

"I don't need anyone or anything else, Grace. One day maybe you'll understand that." He brings our entwined hands up to his mouth to kiss my knuckles.

"I'm speechless. I don't even know what to say. You are the most ridiculously amazing man in the world."

"If we did this, you might not be able to work right away. Only certain jobs can go to foreigners, but I was thinking that would give you the perfect opportunity to write. And we could travel around exploring the country. You know they love extreme sports there." He gives me a knowing look, adding,

"This way we won't have to choose which of our apartments to live in. We can have a new place in a new city."

I think on it, really, seriously consider the possibility, then look at him.

"It's a big thing, but I love it. I only want this if you can make me believe you are a thousand percent sure, Oliver. I can leave my family behind without a backward glance, if they all died while I was gone and I never saw them again, I don't even know if I would mourn. You and your family are different though. You have to consider how far away you'd be in case of an emergency with one of them. There are many factors. It isn't something to rush into."

"True. I tell you what: let's start a pros and cons list when we get home. We don't need to rush this. We'll take our time, and when we are sure, we will make the call. OK?"

"OK. In the meantime, though, I was thinking I can sublet my apartment and move in with you. I don't ever want you leaving the home you shared with Ally."

"That would make me the happiest man in New York."

New Beginnings

We are back at Dragonflame Tattoo. Grace is leaning back, watching as Elvis inks the small white lotus flower on her inner wrist. When she was explaining the meaning behind the flower to me and how it had helped her that day, her face was so serene and happy I suggested it be her next tattoo. We planned it out together, choosing to have it done in all-white ink so it almost looks like it's made of lace, feminine and delicate. I am getting one done next; she just doesn't know it yet. I'm sitting on her left side since the lotus is going on her right wrist.

Reaching into my pocket, I finger the emerald-and-diamond ring I designed for her. She isn't really paying any attention to me as I slide it on the third finger of her left hand. When she glances over at what I'm doing, her eyes go as wide as a deer in headlights. I hear her gasp, and I smile.

"Marry me?" I whisper.

She looks up at me, grinning from ear to ear and exclaims, "I am going to marry the shit out of you!"

Elvis barks out a laugh at that, as do I. Shaking my head, I lean in to claim this very special kiss, the first one from my fiancé.

"Good thing you accepted, because the tattoo I'm planning to get wouldn't have worked out so well if you had said no."

"Dude, if she had said no, I wouldn't have given it to you," Elvis informs me.

"What are you planning?" Grace asks me as she holds up her hand, examining the ring I designed for her.

"You have to wait and see." I kiss her on the cheek. "Do you like it?"

"No, I absolutely *love* it! It's the most beautiful ring I've ever seen."

"I had it made especially for you. I was inspired by your eyes. I made the jeweler find me the exact right emerald, with just as much depth and sparkle as these." Leaning forward, I place a kiss next to her stunning green eyes. They have tears in them now, making them sparkle just that bit more.

I get my tattoo done next. "Grace" is inked around my ring finger on my left hand. I always thought it was dumb how women wore engagement rings but men don't. I want to be marked as taken just as clearly as her, and I want it to be permanent. Every time we take a step closer together in our lives, it only feels more right than the last, and today is no exception.

At first Grace planned to sublet her apartment, but that quickly changed to her leaving it behind completely because she realized she didn't need a backup plan or safety net to fall back on. With me she doesn't need to fear the future. As her colorful and eclectic things moved into my apartment, it became better and better until it now feels like she has always lived there. We have a giant pad of paper on one wall in the kitchen where we keep our "New Zealand Move" pros and cons list going. Every time Milo comes over, he writes his name in the cons column. I never knew my little brother was so sentimental. Although I wonder if it's me or Grace he would miss more. They have grown closer and have the sweetest sibling-type relationship ever since the day of the bonfire.

Tomorrow night my parents, Jess, and her husband, Nick, Milo, and Gramps are coming to our place for dinner. Grace thinks we are cooking. I, however, knew it would end up being an engagement party and don't want her working. I have Jess arranging for it be catered, and there will be champagne flowing. Tara and Kyle will be there also. I briefly considered inviting Anthony. I am not that big of a man yet, however, but he's a good guy, and I won't hold the past against him.

My parents will no doubt find it odd that the first time they will be meeting my girlfriend will be when I announce our impending marriage. Our romance has never been ordinary though. We do things a bit ass backward, and that's just fine by me.

"Are you ready for tomorrow night?" I ask Grace.

"As ready as I'll ever be. I can't believe we're engaged though! This makes it all a bit different, doesn't it?"

"Just that much better," I assure her.

"I hope everyone else agrees."

"They will. I told Milo and Jess about this, but no one else knows."

Looking slightly worried, she asks, "Do you think we should take down the pros and cons list? You haven't mentioned it to your parents yet, have you?"

"We leave that up. I want to tell them about that too. I'm serious about it, so they need to know sooner rather than later."

"Everything is changing so fast. It's exhilarating." She beams at me.

***

Grace

When Jess arrives early and gathers me into the tightest hug ever, my nerves settle down a little.

"I'm going to have a sister again," she says with tears in her eyes.

"I have two, but they hate me, so I look forward to one that might actually want me," I laugh a bit nervously.

"Ollie has told us about your family, and listen to me, Grace: they are the ones losing out. We are gaining from their loss. They don't deserve you anyway." She shakes her head vehemently.

I feel familiar, strong arms band around my waist, and I'm surrounded by my favorite scent in the world as Oliver comes up behind me. "Damn right."

"Nick and Milo are picking up the food and should be here soon. What else needs doing?" Jess enters big sister mode after kissing Oliver on the cheek.

"I think everything is ready," I say as we head into the kitchen.

She stops in front of our pros and cons list. "I heard about this from Milo. What are the chances we will lose you to the great unknown?"

"Pretty high, I'd say," Oliver answers for us.

"It's very tempting," I admit sheepishly. I hate the thought of stealing him away from his family and worry they will resent me for it.

"What an adventure that would be!" Her eyes twinkle as she smiles at me.

"You would come and visit, right?" he asks her.

"Try and stop me. I will be on the first flight I can get! Don't get Nick started either; that man is such a *Lord of the Rings* geek. He will try to move to Hobbiton." That makes me laugh. Maybe his family won't take this as badly as I feared.

When the doorbell rings and I open the door to find Tara and Kyle outside, I feel my forehead wrinkling in confusion.

"What are you doing here?"

"Well, I feel so welcome," Kyle huffs.

Tara just chuckles and comes in. "We are here for some special surprise thing that Oliver wouldn't give me answers about." She lifts my left hand and waves it around. "I do believe I understand it now though." I'm quickly squished between the two of them in a huge hug as I get kisses and congratulations.

"Ugh, stop it, you two." I push them playfully.

"Cat's out of the bag?" Oliver asks.

"Yes. The ring gave it away."

"Now we know what the party is for."

I pull Tara away and into the bedroom then, telling everyone I just need a minute with her. "Are you going to be OK hanging out with Milo all night? What happened with you two?" I worry about any hurt feelings that I'm unaware of there.

"It's fine! We talk sometimes and maybe have made out a few times…nothing serious. Look, tonight is about you, Grace. Stop worrying about me. I can handle Milo; I have no doubt." She pushes me back out to the living room firmly, and I am clearly not getting any more information about that situation.

When Milo and Nick arrive, I notice he keeps surreptitiously stealing glances at Tara. I decide he is the weaker link of the two and make a plan to corner him for the answers I seek. I loop my arm through his and steer us toward the balcony. Once out there, I shut the door. "Spill. I want to know exactly where you and Tara stand. No bullshit." I leave no doubt that I'm serious in my tone of voice.

"Should have known you were up to something," he mumbles. I just stare and wait. He puffs out his cheeks with a big breath and blows it out. "Fine! Look, after I met her that night at Glory Days, we sort of spent the night together. It was supposed to just be nothing, a drunken hookup…one-night thing. But we talked and texted a few times, and I keep thinking about her. I just don't know what I can do about it. I don't really do 'serious,' Grace."

I rub my forehead in frustration. "Milo, she isn't a twenty-something-year-old bimbo. She is a great woman who deserves someone nice. I love you, you know that, but if you don't want serious, then maybe leave her alone? I know her well, and she isn't the hooking-up type. Even if she might try to act like she is."

"Yeah, I am aware. That's why I attempted to not see her again. Only I couldn't stop thinking about her and talking to her. She is special; I know that, but I'm not necessarily ready for anything big and serious. I'm trying to do the right thing here."

I hold up my hands. "OK, I'll try and keep out of it then. As long as you're aware."

"I am, believe me. It's part of my dilemma."

"One day you should try a grown-up relationship. You may actually like it." I poke him in the ribs to lighten the mood. He grabs my hand then and checks out my ring.

"Yeah, but they lead to this kind of thing. Then you're tied down to one person forever." He shivers in fear.

"It's better than you think."

"Come on, sister-to-be. Let's get back to your party before my brother thinks I'm trying to steal you away from him."

"Jackass."

"You love me."

Soon enough Benjamin and Molly Bekker arrive with Molly's father, Grant. He isn't in his wheelchair anymore but using a walker instead, I'm glad to note. They immediately hug and kiss me, treating me like a long-lost daughter they already know and love. It warms my heart immensely. The atmosphere is so pleasant and genuine that I understand why Oliver is the man that he is. Coming from a family as real and affectionate as this could only produce good people. There is no fakeness, coldness, or passive aggressiveness, all the hallmarks of my childhood. When Oliver tells them about our engagement and shows them my ring and his tattoo, there is nothing but legitimate joy and celebration. The champagne is popped and poured.

Molly comes to my side and wraps her arm around my waist. "Thank you for bringing him back to us," she whispers to me. "This is the Oliver we all thought we would never see again after Ally died. Just look how happy he is!" She is beaming at her son, and the fact that she is crediting me for his happiness causes a lump to form in my throat.

"I just love him so much." It's all I can think to say.

"I can tell. I see it in the way you look at him." She smiles warmly. "My father has been so excited to meet you. Oliver and he have always been close, but they grew even closer after Ally was gone. Did you know Oliver went and told him he was falling in love with you before you two even got together?"

"No, I had no idea."

"It's Dad's favorite story to tell lately. He feels so privileged." She laughs.

"I will have to get him to tell it to me."

"He'll be thrilled!"

Grant and I find comfy seats in a quiet corner so he can tell me his story and all about Oliver as a little boy. Soon Jess and her husband join us, and our little group is laughing merrily. Tara, Kyle, and Milo have drifted out onto the balcony, and I hope all is well there, but I try to keep my word and mind my own business. I notice that Oliver and his parents are in the kitchen looking at our list. He must be explaining our idea about possibly moving far away. At least they don't look upset as they listen to him intently. My level of contentment is so high I wonder at myself. Grace Murphy the misfit, the black sheep, the crazy girl…how did you get so lucky?

**

Oliver

Watching Grace gradually let her walls down around my family was fascinating. I doubt she was even aware it was happening. My grandfather especially turned on the charm, determined to make her giggle and blush. Mom and Dad adored her, something I never doubted but know she did. When I talked to them about New Zealand, they each added their thoughts and ideas for the pros and cons; overall they are supportive. They always have been. They want her kids to follow their dreams and experience all that life has to offer. Dad said he would be visiting to take advantage of the beautiful golf courses, and Mom wants to go to the beaches. My biggest concern is leaving Gramps. He's the one I worry something will happen to and I'll be on the other side of the world. He would hate the idea that he is holding us back, so I don't tell him this. As much as I enjoyed the evening with everyone, I was most happy when they finally all left, because I need to be alone with my girl. It was only hours ago that we were last in bed making love this afternoon, but I need her again.

Lying here holding Grace against my chest, I feel the urge to start our future together as soon as humanly possible. "When can we get married?" I say as I kiss and nip the back of her neck hungrily. She squirms against me, the feel of her ass causing me to harden even more than I already am.

"Whenever you want. I'm already yours," she says breathily. My hand drifts up to the curve of her breast and I palm one, my other hand going down to where I know she wants it most. I rub her hard, grinding her body back against me.

"I want to make you fully mine, baby. Let's do it soon." I suck on her earlobe. Her moans are growing louder, and I feel her wetness. I adore how her body reacts to my touch every single time.

"Yes, soon," she agrees, panting heavily. I push into her then, needing to be one again. Her leg lifts on top of mine, and we are wedged together so tightly there is no knowing where one ends and the other begins. Reaching her arm up to grip my neck, she turns and kisses me fervently. Our tongues tangle as much as our bodies as I grind and pump into her.

"I can't wait to spend the rest of my life with you, Grace." I can barely grit the words out as I lose control. I circle her clit, making sure she comes with me.

"Yes, baby, yes, I'm coming." Her soft cries are the sweetest music to my ears.

As we lie there still deeply connected, I gently stroke her body, and we come down from the high of our orgasm. "God, Grace, you are the most amazing thing I never knew I needed."

"I always knew I needed you. I just didn't think you could possibly be real."

"You know, I am not the paragon of greatness and virtue you seem to think I am," I tease her.

"I think you want to pretend you have a bad side, but I still haven't seen one."

"I can be a bad boy. In fact, I have another surprise planned for you soon, then you might just have to admit I'm a little badass."

She laughs, "I will believe it when I see it!"

I pull her tighter into me, biting lightly down on her shoulder. "Yes, you will."

Happily Addicted

Grace

Neither of us want to wait long before getting married. I don't want a huge, overblown affair. I want something intimate and special. The first place I visit is the florist shop where I went the day I visited Ally's grave. Luckily the same kind woman is there. I learn her name is Mary, and she is thrilled to hear about my engagement.

"I knew you and your man would last. No one has that kind of love and lets it go." She gives me a knowing smile.

"Will you help me with the flowers for the wedding?"

"It would be my honor!"

I show her my white lotus tattoo and explain how much it meant to me that day when she gave me the single bloom. "I would like to have white lotus flowers at my wedding, but I think I want to carry poppies."

"Have you ever seen a Royal Wedding Oriental poppy?" she asks.

"No, never."

"Come, I'll show you." Pulling her eyeglasses down from the top of her head, she motions for me to join her at the computer, where she pulls up pictures of beautiful, delicate white poppies with deep-violet centers.

"Those are so beautiful," I gasp.

"Is your dress going to be white?"

"No, I don't know what it will look like yet, but I know I don't want white. It just isn't me."

"Then white flowers would be perfect. I would ideally pair these with some cream and blush colored peonies for a bouquet." She shows me an example of what she means, and I love it immediately.

"Yes, that's perfect, as long as it's small. I want it to feel simple. We haven't got anything planned yet. I came here first, but I'm glad I did. Now I feel full of ideas."

"Peonies are always good for a wedding. They mean good fortune." She winks at me. "Also, I do know a few places that do weddings if you need any suggestions. What sort of feel are you looking for?"

"Maybe a loft or warehouse feel. We want it to be soon, and it will be small. Around fifty people. With wanting it soon, we may not have many choices, I know."

She scrunches up her face in thought. A minute later she snaps her fingers. "Oh my goodness, I have an idea. It isn't exactly a wedding venue, more of an empty space. I never thought to use it that way, but it could be perfect."

"What is it?"

"Well my husband was a photographer. I never could get rid of his studio after he died; it's here in Brooklyn. It's small but might be big enough for fifty people, and there is a rooftop area also. I would need to clean up some of his old equipment and things, but that is something I need to do anyway. I just keep procrastinating."

"Are you sure? I wouldn't want to put you out at all."

"I want to at least show it to you. Will you let me?"

"Of course, if you really are sure."

"I am. It would be the most amazing thing if his space could be used to make someone happy." She clasps her hands together in front of her, and her eyes glisten with unshed tears.

"You are very kind." I can't help but say it. I am still unused to the kindness I keep finding in people lately, and it touches me deeply.

"Oh, nonsense. I am a lonely widow who is sticking my nose in your life," she laughs it off.

"How long has he been gone?"

"It's been almost a year, but it feels like forever. Every day is an eternity without him."

I cover her hand with mine. "I'm so sorry."

"Thank you. It's nice seeing other people find love though. That's what makes life worth living, if you ask me."

"I think I have recently come to understand that," I agree.

"Well, give me a couple of days to make it look presentable, and I can show you and your fiancé the studio. Write your number down for me."

We exchange numbers, and once again I can't stop myself from hugging Mary before I leave. When did I become such a hugger? I wonder as I walk away from the shop, smiling to myself.

***

"You do know I'm taking you shopping for a dress?" Jess asks me. We are curled up together on the couch talking about wedding ideas.

Oliver is in the kitchen pouring us wine. As he brings it in, he looks at his sister, one eyebrow raised. "You do know you can't just boss her around?"

"I am the big sister, so yeah, I can," she points out.

"I don't mind. I hate shopping for dresses, honestly, so I need someone to force me."

"You could show up in pajamas, and I would think you're the sexiest bride ever."

"Ugh, puke, Ollie! When did you become so sappy?" She gives him a look of total disgust that I have to laugh at. He throws a cushion at her, and she squeals. "Have you at least picked a wedding song?"

"We haven't talked about it." I admit as we share a guilty look. The truth is we haven't talked about many details. Every time we start talking about wedding things, we get excited, start making out, and one thing leads to another, and…yeah, this is why I need help and a chaperone. We must be staring at each other a bit too long, based on what we hear next.

"You two really are sickening, you know that?" Milo walks in. I had no idea he was coming over, so it's a pleasant surprise.

"How's Tara?" I ask him pointedly. He gestures zipping his lips shut and throwing the key away.

"Oh, you don't have anything to say now, huh?" I tease.

"I have a private, private life, Grace. If I were to tell you all the sordid details, you'd probably just be jealous and realize how boring this guy truly is." He points his thumb at Oliver.

"If you only knew all the filthy things your brother does to me, your tiny little brain would explode, Milo." I tell him.

He chokes on the wine he was sipping as Oliver, Jess, and I all burst out laughing at the shock on his face.

"Changing the subject quickly, let's find you guys a song." Milo says at last when he can breathe again.

"Well Kyle is dating that DJ now and said we get a friends and family discount, so at least we have the music locked in." I point out.

"I do have one song I'd like." Oliver surprises me with that.

"Do tell." Jess looks as taken aback as me.

"'Collide' by Howie Day. It's always made me think of Grace and how I fell in love with her. It wasn't easy at first. I was being stubborn and fighting my feelings because of Ally, but it was inevitable, and it was a collision, really. We were meant to be." He threads our fingers together as he speaks.

Jess puts her hand over her heart and looks like she wants to cry. "That's so sweet."

"I love that song, and we heard it that first night we spent together in the Hamptons. It's perfect," I say and kiss him for good measure.

"Yeah, don't remind me of that singer. He was trying to get you to pay attention to him like I wasn't sitting right next you," he growls.

"OK, I want to hear about this night. How do I not now you guys slept together in the Hamptons?" Milo interjects.

"We didn't," we both say at the same time.

"We just shared a room—well, and a bed, and maybe kissed a little," I add.

"After you tried to feed me to the sharks," Oliver remarks.

"Oh, now I really want to hear about it."

"No, we need to focus on the wedding. Milo, if you aren't going to help, then leave." Jess is back to planning mode.

"I'll just be quiet and drink my wine," he swears, holding his hands up in surrender. Having picked a song, knowing my flowers, and even having a possible venue, things are starting to feel a lot more real. I make a plan to take Friday afternoon off and go dress shopping with Jess. She wants to come with Oliver and me to see the studio in Brooklyn on Saturday, and then of course Milo gets offended that he is being left out. So I guess it will be four of us going. I'm secretly overjoyed at how much I feel a part of Oliver's family.

*** ***

Oliver

I swear my siblings like Grace better than they have ever liked me. Suddenly they are always around, constantly popping in, tagging along, and making plans. I can't help but feel a bit guilty at the thought that we might soon be moving very far away, even if it still isn't one hundred percent set in stone yet. My grandfather is doing OK lately, but I want to make sure his health remains stable for a few more weeks before deciding anything final. Besides, we have the wedding to plan. I try to visit him as often as I can in case we do move away.

This morning we saw the empty photography studio in Brooklyn, and it was perfect. Small but not too small. Exposed brick walls that have been painted with whitewash and gorgeous original hardwood floors. It has a whole wall of large windows and French doors that open to a rooftop area that is mostly empty except for some planted hedges. We just need to bring some rental furniture and outdoor heaters in, and it will be ready. Mary was so thrilled that we liked it that I thought she might cry. She kept trying to say she wouldn't let us pay to use it, but I absolutely insisted. She gave me a ridiculously low price. I will just add in a tip when I pay her for the flowers.

Now it's time to bring Grace for her next surprise that I planned a few days ago. Milo is coming with us since it's his idea of fun too. We say goodbye to Jess and head out of the city.

"Why do you always insist on telling Milo what you plan and not me?" Grace pouts.

"Because then I can torture you with the fact that I'm in the know and you aren't," he pipes up from the backseat.

"That right there, that's the problem." She points at him, giving me a look of consternation.

"Behave, you two. I like surprising you. How would I do that if I told you?"

"I don't mind you not telling me, just don't tell him either," she grumbles.

"Next surprise I won't tell Milo, I promise."

We pull into the speedway, and Grace shrieks in delight. "Racing!"

"Happy? Little speed demon." I grin at her reaction.

"I'll be happy when I beat both your asses!" she challenges.

"Ha!" Milo barks. "Don't count on that. This isn't our first rodeo, little Miss Gracie. Ollie and I have been here before."

"That's true. We may have an advantage." I just have to egg her on, knowing how competitive she is.

"Lead the way," she says full of confidence, jumping out of the car.

When I booked this outing for us, I also arranged for a motorcycle driving lesson for Grace. I have learned to drive one in the past, but it's been too long for me to teach her. I know she will get a thrill from it. That part will come after the fast cars though.

The professional stunt driver that is working with us gives Grace lots of extra-special attention, which my little brother happens to find delightful since he can tell it irritates the hell out of me.

"I have never seen you so jealous. It's great," Milo points out, leaning against the barrier next to me while my eyes are glued on the instructor helping Grace get ready for her first time around the track.

I give him the evil side-eye and just shake my head. "Glad you're entertained."

"Seriously, dude, for some strange reason, that woman is crazy in love with you. You have nothing to worry about."

"I'm not worried. I just don't like creepers near her."

"Should we beat him up in an alley later? I hold him down and you punch?"

I shove my clown of a brother. "I'll let you know."

Grace makes good time but never beats mine or Milo's… to her extreme disappointment. However, the thrill of the speed has her cheeks flushed, and she is clearly loving it.

When the motorcycles come roaring up, her eyes light up, and she walks over to admire them, still not knowing that she's going to learn to drive one.

"You like them?" I ask.

"Oh my god, yes! I always wanted to drive one."

"Which one you want to ride?" I ask her.

"What do you mean?"

"These are part of your surprise. You're going to learn to drive one today if you want to." Before I even know what is happening, she has leaped into my arms, wrapped her legs around me, and is kissing me like there's no tomorrow. When I finally catch my breath, I give a small laugh. "So you want to then?"

"You really get me, babe. No one has ever known how to make me happy the way you do," she tells me seriously with wonder in her voice.

"I will do whatever I can in my power to make you happy for the rest of our lives."

I feel a hand on my shoulder then and turn to see Milo. "Put the girl down, Oliver. We're in public." Grace giggles as she slides down my body. Well shit, now I just want to take her home as soon as possible.

I only release my hold on her because we need our hands free for the motorcycle lessons. For her first ride around the track, I have Grace behind me on one bike. Having her thighs gripping me tightly, feeling her breasts pressed firmly into my back and her arms wrapped around my torso, I decide I really like the idea of having a motorcycle. When she finally does her first solo ride, the excitement is practically rolling off of her.

"Oh my gosh, that's the best thing ever! What an addictive high," she spouts as she removes her helmet.

"You want a bike now?" I grin at her.

"I just might trade in the Mini!"

All this adrenaline flowing through my veins and her tight jeans are really getting my blood racing. I need her as soon as I possibly can get her alone.

Heading back inside, I feel like a horny teenager as I look around for somewhere I can sneak away with her for a quick make-out session. There is a long hallway where the bathrooms are, and while Milo is talking to the drivers, I pull Grace in that direction.

"You are so sexy, Grace. I want you now," I tell her as I try a few doorknobs, looking for a supply closet or something we can use for privacy.

"Yes please, baby," she agrees quickly. The third door we try opens. It's nothing more than a broom closet, but we rush inside, and I'm delighted to find that the doorknob locks. Immediately I have her back against the door as I hoist her up and devour her mouth. She reaches down, tearing into my pants, whimpering with desire.

"What do you want, Grace?" I tease her, nibbling on her lips and dipping my tongue in.

"If you don't fuck me right now, I swear to god I'll scream," she demands, grinding her hips into me. I love when she is in this type of mood: demanding, wanton, and completely mine.

I decide she needs to be bossed around a little. "Open those pants for me, and I want you to stay quiet while I make you come, baby." I use my roughest voice. She quickly opens the skintight jeans she's wearing, sliding them and her panties down out of my way.

"Good girl." I brace myself, caging her body in against the door as I hold her legs around me and slide into her balls deep. A groan escapes her lips, and she looks at me, apologizing for making noise. I place one hand gently over her mouth to stifle the rest of her moans as I begin pumping into her with abandon. Her eyes tell me everything I need to know as they roll back in ecstasy. I may be managing to keep her somewhat quiet, but I can't stop my own grunting as I come fast and hard. We never have boring sex, but even for us that was intense.

"How do you get better every time?" Her breathless question makes me need to kiss her again.

When we emerge from our little escapade in the broom closet, my brother's look tells me we weren't quiet enough. No one else makes any reference to it, though, and we have finished here anyway. Besides, this woman makes me lose all my common sense, and I wouldn't care if I got arrested for public indecency right now. Totally worth it.

On the walk back to the car, Milo finally breaks his silence. "Well I'm officially scarred for life. I guess you aren't as boring as I've always assumed, Oliver. My poor ears." He cringes.

"Oh my god, are you serious?" Grace spins around to him with her hand over her mouth. "You heard us?"

"Grace, New Jersey heard you," he says flatly.

She slaps his arm. "How? We were as quiet as possible!"

"If that's you being quiet, I feel really bad for your neighbors." He raises his eyebrows at her. I can't help but laugh. My poor little brother will never be the same. He has always imagined he's the only wild one in the family. Guess he doesn't know about "The Grace Effect," as I like to call it. It makes me do unimaginably insane things with zero regrets, all for the wild woman I love. She's my drug, and I'm happily addicted for life.

Looking Forward

Grace

"I'm here to see Grant Merchant." I check in with the receptionist at Oliver's grandfather's care home. I haven't told him that I'm coming; in fact, no one knows. It's something I've been planning to do for a while. I have something to discuss with him, and I hope it's an idea he agrees with.

The nurse shows me the way to his room. "Hello?" I knock lightly on the open door.

Grant is sitting in an armchair by the window, reading a small paperback. He turns to me, a smile lighting up his face. "Grace, what a very pleasant surprise! Come sit with me." He motions to a chair next to his.

"Thank you. How are you doing?"

"I'm well. A bit tired from water aerobics in the old folks' pool this morning."

I can't help but smile constantly when I'm around him. He's always cheerful and sweet.

"What are you reading there?" I point to his book.

"Oh, this? It's an old novel. *Lost Horizon* by James Hilton, I've read it many times but always enjoy it."

"I've read that—the original story of Shangri-La. In fact when I was younger, I had a bit of a crush on Hugh Conway. It's a very good book. Have you seen the movie?"

"The one with Ronald Colman?"

"Yes, I had a thing for him too." I have to laugh a little at the look of shock on Grant's face.

"That movie is from 1937. I can't believe a young thing like you knows it!"

"Well, I've always been a bit of an old soul," I admit.

"I can't tell you how grateful I am that my grandson found you, Grace." Grant lovingly takes my hand in his large, soft, age-worn ones.

Tears spring up into my eyes because the way Oliver's family has embraced me and welcomed me never ceases to affect me. "Thank you."

"Are you ready for the wedding?" He beams at me.

"Almost. Actually, that's part of the reason for my visit here today. I have a favor I wanted to ask you."

"Anything."

"Well, as you know, I am estranged from my family. So I haven't got anyone to walk me down the aisle. I was wondering if you would honor me by doing it?" I hold my breath a little, hoping that I haven't presumed too much. He reaches up and wipes the side of his eye, and I notice then there are tears there.

"I can't imagine a greater honor, young lady." His voice is full of emotion. "I'm not always so good at walking these days, but with you on one side and a cane on the other, nothing will stop me."

I just have to throw my arms around him then. The tears come to me when I do, because he hugs me back with genuine love.

"I can't thank you enough Grant. It means the world to me. I used to feel all alone in the world. Now it's like I have a real family at last." He just holds me while I cry. I never expected to feel so affected, but it overwhelms me.

"You are one of us now, Grace. We've got you," he whispers.

I stay there all afternoon. We talk about our favorite old books and movies. We also decide to not tell Oliver about Grant walking me down the aisle; it will be a nice surprise for him. He thinks I plan to walk alone. When they bring Grant his dinner, they ask if I'd like some, too, and I agree and stay and eat with him.

By the time I leave, I think I finally know what it feels like to have a loving grandfather. I never knew my own. I make plans to come back soon and watch *Lost Horizon* with him. It's one of the best days I can remember having in a long time.

Arriving back home, I find Jess is there waiting with my wedding dress that she picked up for me from where it was being altered. We lock ourselves in the bedroom so Oliver can't see it, and I try it on again. When we went shopping, I told her I didn't want white or anything too gaudy. We eventually came across a gown that stole my heart. It's made of pale-pink chiffon and lace, with a Queen Anne neckline and sheer lace sleeves. The flowy chiffon skirt is a modified A-line that makes me feel like I'm floating when I move. The back dips low and is scalloped with more delicate lace. My bouquet of the white poppies with deep purple centers, along with blush and cream peonies, will look lovely against it, I think.

"Oh my, it's so beautiful," Jess gasps when I have it on. "Even better than I remember."

"What do you think I should do with my hair?" I think out loud as I stare in the mirror. Standing behind me, she takes my wavy hair in her hands and makes a large braid on one side, twisting it all together and securing it in the back beautifully, then she pulls pieces out here and there, and suddenly I feel like a real bride.

"Wow, you're good." I admire her handiwork.

"Of course, we can do better on the day, but this style will look perfect. So soft and feminine, just like the dress." She gives me a kiss on the cheek then and squeezes my shoulders. "My brother won't know what to do with himself when he sees you."

***

Oliver

I knock on my own damn bedroom door again. "Jess, go home, I want to be with my fiancé," I yell.

Suddenly it's pulled open, and I swear, if looks could kill, Jess's would turn me to stone. "You are so impatient, Ollie! We are finalizing her bridal look."

I just give her an unimpressed look and cross my arms. "You have been in there for almost an hour. I know you, Miss Bossypants. If I don't rush you, you will monopolize her all night."

She huffs at me. "So possessive. Is this why you're trying to move to New Zealand?"

"Not the main reason, but privacy is definitely a perk." I wink just to irritate her some more. They both have emerged finally, and I take Grace into my arms, murmuring into her ear, "Where were you all afternoon?"

Looking over her shoulder at me, she has an impish grin. "It's a secret. You'll find out on our wedding day." Now I'm extra curious, but if she is trying to surprise me, I won't pry. Our wedding is two weeks away, and though my family doesn't know it yet, we have made the final decision about the move also.

Because we are moving to the other side of the world, we aren't doing a large honeymoon. Instead we have a secret plan to hide out at The Plaza Hotel right here in the city for a few days of completely uninterrupted alone time. I have already completed my final interview for my new job in Queenstown, and we are narrowing down which part of the city we want to live in. I have arranged to purchase a motorcycle for us when we arrive also, but that will be a surprise for Grace. We have worked out a way to tell my family all at once at a dinner soon. I have a feeling they expect it, but the confirmation will still be hard on them. They have grown especially attached to Grace in a very short period of time, but it won't be the end of their relationship with her.

We are both beyond excited about this new adventure that we will be beginning as husband and wife. In all honesty, I cannot wait to be her husband. As close as we are, I want to be closer. I want to have every possible connection we can have.

"I guess I'll get going, since I'm apparently a third wheel." Jess pointedly looks at me.

"You don't have to go. I just don't want to be locked out of my own room and away from Grace," I concede.

"No, it's fine. I need to get home anyway. I'm just teasing." Walking her to the door, I confirm that she remembers the family dinner I have planned at one of our favorite Italian restaurants.

"It's the move, isn't it? That's what the dinner is about."

I'm not in the least surprised that she has figured it out, so I just nod.

"I'm happy for you two. It's so exciting. Even if I hate that you're taking her away just as you gave her to us." She gives me a bittersweet smile.

"Thanks, sis. I wish I could bring you all with us. It's going to be an amazing adventure, though, and she deserves it." Nodding, she just squeezes my hand. I can tell she is fighting back tears, so I hug her tightly. Feeling immensely grateful to have the family that I do, I say good night.

"You told her?" Grace asks as I come back into the living room.

"She guessed it, yeah."

"I will miss her."

"Not changing your mind, are you?"

"Not a chance. I'm on cloud nine with all the things we have to look forward to. Just because some of the things we leave behind will make me sad doesn't mean I don't want to go." Her arms come around my waist, and she lays her head on my chest.

"Good, because I can't wait to marry the shit out of you and start our first big adventure together." I kiss the top of her head.

***

Grace

Gianni's is one of those places where you feel like the Mafia is definitely making deals in a back room. The food is so authentic I swear it could give you an Italian accent. As we all sit together in the dimly lit place and enjoy the jammy wine, amazing cuisine, and romantic music, I lean into Oliver and observe this group of people that have become my family, too, in such a short period of time. His strong arm wrapped around my shoulder is the truest form of home I've ever experienced.

"We wanted to get everyone together tonight to officially announce our decision to move to Queenstown." Ollie squeezes my shoulder comfortingly as he speaks.

"You're moving to Queens? What the hell happened to New Zealand?" Milo looks genuinely confused, and I can't hold back my laughter.

"Queenstown, New Zealand, you clown." Oliver grimaces at him.

"Oh." Milo goes uncharacteristically quiet then, looking sullen.

Oliver continues, ignoring that. "I officially start my new job three weeks after the wedding. We are going to keep the apartment here and lease it out for now until we know for sure how long we will stay. My initial contract is for two years. After that we'll see where we're at."

Everyone starts talking at once, offering congratulations and opinions—well, almost everyone, that is.

Milo is sitting on my other side, and he is completely silent, so I take his hand.

"You going to come visit us?"

Looking at me, he nods. "Yeah, for sure." He clutches my hand even tighter but says nothing more. As much as I will miss my own friends and all of Oliver's family, it's Milo that I will miss more than all the others combined. His humor and easy acceptance of me have meant so much.

"Hey, you OK?" I lean closer to him and lower my voice. Oliver is talking to his parents now, so I can focus fully on Milo.

"For some reason I didn't really think it would happen; silly, I know." He gives a small, humorless laugh.

"I'm going to miss you so much. You better come see us."

"I'll miss you too, Grace. I feel like I have another sister now, and a good friend that I'm losing too soon."

"You aren't losing anything. Don't you remember our song?"

He furrows his brow in confusion. "We have a song?"

"The one we danced to when you kept me out of prison." I nudge him with my shoulder, finally getting a smile out of him.

"Ah, 'I'll Stand by You.' Now I remember."

"Yeah, and I will. You can't lose me. I hate to tell you, but you are stuck with me forever, buddy." I never in a million years would have expected to see tears in Milo's eyes, but that's exactly what I see when he turns to me and envelopes me in a bear hug.

"I cannot wait to find my badassery again in New Zealand. I swear your family has turned me into a sappy chump. I'm always hugging people and crying," I tell Oliver as he drives us home that night. It's possible I'm a bit drunk on all that wine, but the words I speak are still true. My whole life I have prided myself on being completely independent, distant from others and happy that way. Now suddenly I have so many connections and feelings for all these people.

Oliver is laughing at me. "Aw, my poor baby. Have we melted your ice-cold heart?"

"Don't mock! I was perfectly happy alone in my ice palace like Elsa. Then you came along, and suddenly I'm turning into Anna…caring about everyone and their snowman."

"You are drunk if *Frozen* is the best pop culture reference you can come up with, babe."

"I know, it's sad." I close my eyes, falling asleep in the big comfy seat. I hear a very sexy, deep chuckle as I drift off.

***

Oliver

My phone rings with a number I don't recognize. I'm swamped with work, trying to wrap up all my projects in New York before leaving, but I answer it anyway. "Hello."

"Is this Oliver?"

"Yes, who is this?"

"Maureen, Grace's mother." I feel my jaw tense up, and my hand becomes a fist just thinking of Grace's family.

"What do you want?" I grit out.

"Is it true you are getting married?"

"It is." I won't give this woman anything more than facts.

"I heard that through the grapevine, but I couldn't believe Grace would do that without letting her family know." She sounds petulant and whiny.

"Maureen, I was standing there when Grace made it very clear that she was cutting you all out of her life. I know her reasons and support them one hundred percent. It astonishes me that you still aren't getting it."

"Well she acts impetuously; she always has. I would assume given time, her common sense would return. Not that I expect an apology ever. I know that's too much to hope for—"

And there I reach my fucking limit. "I need to cut you off right there. You are obviously delusional to a degree that needs psychiatric help. Stay away from us. I don't know how you got my number, but I will be making sure you are blocked from calling it again, just like I know you are blocked from Grace's. If you or anyone from your family attempts to show up at our wedding, I will call the police and have you carted away in the most embarrassing way I can. Have I made things clear enough for you, Maureen?"

There is silence on the other end of the phone for a long minute, then she says, "You two deserve each other," in a voice I've heard her use before: one full of venom and hatred.

"Yes, we fucking do." I end the call there.

I don't know if I will ever tell Grace about her psychotic mother's phone call, but if I do, it will be after we are on the other side of the world. For now I will simply make sure I prepare some of the male members of the wedding to be on the lookout for any trespassers and to call the police on them. I will allow nothing and no one to ruin that day for her.

I'm meeting Mary, the florist, at the studio after work today to help put together a surprise I ordered Grace for the wedding. We are installing a large fountain in the brick wall on both sides of where we will say our vows. It will have two waterfalls cascading down into twin pools full of floating white lotus flowers, with a stone arch connecting them over-head. The plumbers have already been there, working on the pipe installation all morning. Tonight Mary and I will make sure everything looks perfect. The string cafe lights need hanging over the rooftop area, too, so I am getting Milo, Nick, and Kyle to give me a hand with that tomorrow. Grace deserves the most beautiful wedding I can give her, so that's what she'll have.

Those We
Leave Behind

Grace

Tara and I are having lunch alone as our own special goodbye before things get too busy with the wedding and the move.

"I know you never want to talk about Milo with me, but I just need to know if you two are an item. He is practically my brother, and you are my best friend; it affects me." I really need to insist at this point because I will be gone, and I worry about both of them. If I should be worrying about them as a couple, I need to know that also.

"I like him, like, a lot. But I don't know if he's ever going to want to settle down. I do want to. I want a husband and kids, and I'm too old to pretend I don't. So I try to keep him at arm's length. I just don't always succeed, that's all." She sighs deeply.

"OK, so you've gotten together again?"

"We have. You know, I'm sure I don't have to tell you how charming he can be, not to mention persuasive."

"Yeah, I can imagine. But he knows you want something serious, so what does he say about that?"

"He says maybe he can try. Then I kick his sorry ass out of my bed and tell him I don't need a trier; I need a real man. And a few days later, we repeat the cycle. I swear it's like he's brainwashed me or something. I keep saying this time is the last time. But no, I always end up going back for more."

"Wow, at least you know there's no problems with the chemistry," I chuckle.

"Yeah, we get an A in chemistry for sure, and biology. I just don't want to keep wasting my time. I need to meet the person who can give me all the things I want. Can't really do that with him distracting me all the time, can I?"

"I'm sorry. I wish I could help, but it sounds like a real dilemma. You have a guy in your system; believe me, I know how hard that is to get rid of."

"Yeah, I hate to tell you, Grace, but you didn't get rid of yours. You're tying yourself to him for life." We both laugh at that. She's been pushing the food around her plate the whole time we've been here, and I recognize the signs of complete and utter distraction. Now that I know Milo is the source behind it, I can't help but be a little happy. These two people mean a lot to me, and if they could find a way to make things work, I would be over the moon.

"When are you going to come visit me in New Zealand?" I decide she will probably appreciate a subject change.

"As soon as I can afford a flight. They are no joke."

"We can do all kinds of fun things while Ollie works. I can't legally work there yet, so besides writing, I'll be a lady of leisure."

"Lucky woman. I'd ask if he has a brother, but I already know the answer."

That afternoon I'm back home separating things into piles for selling, storing, and packing. We aren't bringing much with us at all. Just what we can pack in a few large suitcases, really, so there is a lot to be put into storage. We are leasing the apartment to a man that Oliver works with, he also needs the furniture so it is staying put. I sold my car already, and after the wedding Oliver plans to do the same. It still feels surreal to think we are going to start this new adventure so soon. There's a knock on the door, and I go see who it could be.

"Milo, what are you doing here?"

He comes in and flops onto the couch in his usual manner. "I don't even know. I just keep thinking about you guys leaving, and I don't like it."

"I know, we're going to miss you a lot."

He huffs out a breath. "You won't though. You have each other. Who do I have?"

"So you came because you want to talk about Tara, I see." I give him a smug look.

"Grace, you think you're so smart, don't you?"

Getting up, I head back into the bedroom. "Come on, I have to keep working. If you are going to be here listening to my pearls of wisdom, make yourself useful and pack." I hand him a box and tape.

"Fine. But this is just going to depress me more, you know."

"I know, sorry. It has to be done though." I wait for him to start talking after that because I know that he has something specific on his mind, and I want him to spit it out.

Eventually, as we work, he starts. "How did you know Ollie was the one?"

I think on it for a minute before answering him. "I guess I just couldn't imagine wanting anyone else anymore. No one ever understood me or cared for me the way he does. We never had to pretend with each other. From the first time we talked, we were so open with one another. It was like I found a matching puzzle piece, and all the edges I had slid into place next to his. Does that make sense?"

Sitting down against the wall, Milo puts down the box he was assembling and starts playing with the roll of packing tape. "Yeah, actually, it does. But doesn't it ever scare you? How can you commit to someone forever?"

"What exactly do you mean?"

"I mean, you may be crazy about him now, sure, but say you meet some hunky rugby player out in New Zealand that gets your heart racing...what then? I understand that people fall in love, of course. I just don't get how they think that's it for life."

"It isn't about never seeing another attractive person again. I'm not naive. I know that is going to happen, for him too. There is so much more to love than that though. Oliver is irreplaceable for me. There will never be anyone who can come close to him in my heart. I'm not going to let some fleeting attraction mess that up. I have been hurt enough and treated badly enough times to know I have something of extremely high value with your brother. You don't just trade that in for something of no value."

I go and sit down next to Milo, taking his hand in mine. "If you never let yourself really love someone, really be open and fully vulnerable with them, you will be missing out, Milo.

That's what it takes to get to the point where you know they are the one. It is scary, of course, because in doing that, you give them the power to potentially hurt you. Life and love involve risks, but they are worth it."

Taking in a deep breath, he blows it out slowly.

"I'll think about it," he says finally.

"Come on, let's order some dinner before Oliver gets home." I pull him up.

***

Oliver

When my brother tells me he wants to take me out for a bachelor party, I have to give him a look.

"I don't trust you for a second."

I arrived home from work to find him there helping Grace with packing the apartment, and now we are all having dinner together. It's no surprise to find him here these days; he is like a sad puppy who won't leave.

"Why does everyone assume I'm immature and irresponsible?" He puts his fork down, offended.

"Um, because that's all you've ever shown us?" I say.

"Yeah, well, maybe I don't show you anything else because you're all judgmental assholes. Except you, Grace, you're an angel." He gives my fiancé a sweet smile, and I give him the usual smack to the back of his head.

She just laughs and asks, "Then tell me what you plan for his bachelor party?"

"Fine, I will. I simply wanted to rent a private driving range booth and invite a few select guys for a classy, private night of drinks and conversation before my only brother gets married and moves very far away." I feel skeptical, but his hurt tone convinces me he's sincere.

"Seriously, man? Nothing sleazy?"

"Seriously. I wouldn't do that—I'm Grace's number one fan. I'm not that bad." Now it's his turn to look stern.

"Well I apologize, then, because that sounds perfect."

"Hmph, I have to reconsider if you're worth it now. You keep smacking me." He rubs the back of his head.

"You keep flirting with my fiancé," I point out with a laugh. I really will miss this crazy clown.

"If you think that's flirting, I guess you've never actually seen me in action."

"How is Tara doing?" I ask.

"What have you been telling him, Grace?" he demands.

"I haven't said anything!" She gets up with the dishes, laughing.

When she returns, I pull her onto my lap. "I hope no one plans on trying to do anything crazy for your bachelorette party."

"Jess and Tara said they have it in hand." She shrugs.

"Uh-huh. I'm just going to call my sister and lay some ground rules."

"Your mother is invited. I doubt there will be male strippers," she laughs, wrapping her arms around my neck.

"I don't know, Grace. Our mother is pretty crazy when she has champagne. And she has seen *Magic Mike*; that is a conversation I wish I could forget," Milo says, throwing back some beer.

Her eyes go huge at that. "No! Molly has seen Channing Tatum's junk? I never even got around to watching that movie."

"Good! You never need to either," I put in.

"Oh my goodness, you are so adorable when you think you can boss me around, Mr. Bekker." She plants a kiss on my forehead. This gets a guffaw out of my brother.

With that, I decide to show her just how bossy I can be. Standing up, I haul her over one shoulder in a fireman's lift and give her ass a loud smack.

"And you, soon to be Mrs. Bekker, only need to watch one man strip from now on." I throw her down on the couch and hover over her menacingly. The fire burning in her eyes tells me just how much she enjoys the Neanderthal act. My eyes wander down her body as I watch her bite her lip and clench her legs tightly together.

Gagging noises from Milo stop me from taking this any further until we are alone.

"You could just ask me to leave. You don't have to drive me away with all this disgusting PDA, you know."

Grace looks over my shoulder then. "You don't have to leave. He will behave." I grunt at that and sit down.

"You can have one more hour, dude. Then go find Tara and do your own romancing."

"You two are very pushy about my love life, you know that?"

"We want you to be happy, that's all," Grace tells him.

"I'm not convinced that happily ever after is real, at least not for me."

"That's no way to live. What are you going to be, old and still trying to play the field in bars one day?" I turn to confront him.

"I don't know what I'm going to be. Let me figure that out in my own time." He starts for the kitchen then, putting his dish in the sink. "I'm going to get going so Oliver can finish ravishing you or whatever was about to happen. I think I will give Tara a call after all. You guys might be a bad influence."

"Alone at last!" I sigh as I hear the door shut. I lean my head back all the way so I can see, just to be sure he's actually gone. When I do I feel warm, soft lips start working their way up the column of my throat.

"Mmmm." I rumble, closing my eyes. Grace's small hands are moving up my chest under my shirt while she nibbles my neck.

"God, you're so sexy. When you smacked my ass, I almost came. I'm soaking wet for you, baby." She tells me in a seductive voice.

"Someone likes being punished?" I grab her ass, pulling her onto my lap fully.

"By you, yes I do. You know I'm a bad, dirty girl. I probably need some spanking."

"Fuck, Grace! You're trying to kill me, aren't you?" I lift her up roughly and head into the bedroom, kissing and sucking at her neck, ears, and lips the entire time. I reach for the tie I discarded when I got home from work earlier and take her wrists, lifting them over her head and securing them to the headboard with it.

Her smoldering look and heavy breathing tell me how much she is anticipating what I will do to her next. She is wearing a thin old T-shirt. I reach for the neck of it and rip it straight down the middle. Her squirming body is trapped between my legs, and I hold her in place as I slowly open her front-clasp bra; her nipples are always so responsive. Sometimes I can get her off from touching and kissing those alone. I tease them lightly this time, barley touching them as I hold the mounds of her breasts firmly in my palms. Her panting gets heavier and heavier.

"Please, Ollie," she begs.

"Please what, bad girl…tell me what you want."

"Touch them, please!" She is thrusting her chest up into my hands, trying to get the contact she craves. I lean forward slowly and lick one nipple, then the other. Her moan is so loud and guttural I feel it vibrate through her body. I lean back and lock eyes with her as I finally take them in between my fingers, rolling them hard.

"Oh yessssss, fuck that's it!" she screams. Her hips buck up, and I lock my thighs tighter around her. Moving down her body, I peel her shorts and panties off completely now and take her with my mouth, deciding I've teased her enough. I bring her to orgasm soon with my tongue and thrusting fingers. Lapping up all the delicious juices that flood my mouth, I savor every tremor her body makes. I watch her satiated body relax back as I lean forward to untie her hands and cradle her while I kiss her deeply.

"Oh my god, what did you do to me?" Her voice is husky and dazed. "I've never come so hard in my life."

"I lose my mind with you, baby. I just needed to show you how crazy I am about you." I smile over her lips between kisses.

After that we don't leave the bed for the rest of the night. It's like we can never get enough of one another. I sometimes wonder how I got to be the luckiest bastard in the world to have this woman in my bed and heart. The spark of attraction that I felt when I first met Grace is a raging forest fire that only grows bigger daily. Who would have thought that a second chance at love could be so mind blowing? We always think that it's the young people that have the wildest love lives. I'm learning that is the furthest thing from the truth.

***

Grace

Since I already left my job, I have more time to visit with Grant during the day. Today we played backgammon for almost two hours and practiced our walk down the aisle for Saturday. I can tell he's feeling worn out, so I just double-check that his suit is ready for the big day before I get him his book and settle him into his favorite chair for the afternoon.

"I'll be wearing my dancing shoes Saturday, Grace. If you think you can hold me up, I'd love a dance with the bride."

Leaning down, I kiss his cheek. "I will reserve you a prime spot," I promise.

My next stop involves another surprise that I need to have done before the wedding. Elvis greets me at the top of the stairs in Dragonflame Tattoo. "You ready to do this, bride lady?"

"I am. Are you and Monica ready for the wedding?" I give him a hug because I'm a hugger now, apparently.

"She spent a buttload of money on a fancy dress, so I guess we are," he snorts.

"She will look so beautiful you'll realize it was worth every penny."

"Yeah, yeah, that's what she said." I settle in, and he gets his equipment ready. "So a matching tattoo on your ring finger, huh? You two sure are sappy," he teases me as he cleans the skin in preparation.

"We are, aren't we?"

"Seriously though, I'm really happy for you guys. When I inked him after Ally died, I was really worried there for a while. He was lost. Now he's like a whole new man, so fucking happy," he laughs.

"He's not the only one."

"I can tell."

The small tattoo of the name "Oliver" around my ring finger doesn't take long. When I try to pay, Elvis insists that it's part of his wedding gift to me.

"You can't keep giving me free tattoos. I'll get spoiled!"

"Well soon you'll be in freaking New Zealand, and you'll have to pay for them there."

"That's true." I acquiesce.

***

Unlike Oliver, I don't know what to expect for my bachelorette party tonight. He already knows exactly what his party entails. I was simply told to look good and I would be picked up by Jess at six. As I get dressed, he keeps trying to distract me, holding me from behind, nibbling on my neck and shoulder.

"I can't do my hair if you don't let go of me," I point out.

"I don't think you need to look too pretty for a night without me."

"So you're trying to mess up my hair?"

"Maybe." He gives me a sly grin.

"I thought you gave Jess ground rules?"

"I did, but when does she ever listen?"

"It will be fine; stop worrying." I give his chest a reassuring pat and sneak past him to lock myself in the bathroom to finish getting ready.

"Sneaky," I hear him grumble as he heads out of the bedroom.

When Jess arrives, Oliver tries to pump her for information. She simply ignores him and ushers me out the door.

"You handle him well," I point out, laughing.

"He is a bit of a control freak. I mean especially after Ally, I understand that he worries, but for goodness sake, we are all adults and can take care of you for one night," she huffs. When we reach the street, there is a hot-pink stretch limousine SUV with the song "Girls Just Wanna Have Fun" blasting out of it.

Opening the door, Tara pops her head out and smiles broadly. "What do you think?"

"I love it!" I say, getting in. Inside is a group of people that makes my heart happy: Jess; Tara; Ollie's mother, Molly; Elvis's wife, Monica; Mary, my unofficial wedding planner, and…Kyle?

"What are you doing here? You're supposed to be with Oliver's party."

"Hey, I am your friend first and foremost. Plus, they are golfing." He makes a gagging gesture with his finger down his throat. "I begged Jess to let me pick which party to attend, and she gave in." That gives me a case of the giggles, and someone hands me a glass of champagne, so I'm sure that will only get worse soon.

"So who is with Oliver tonight, then?"

Jess ticks off fingers as she names the people. "Dad, Milo, Nick, Gramps…they snuck him out of the care home for the night, and he is thrilled! Two of his coworkers, Elvis, and some guy named Anthony he said he's friends with."

I spit my champagne out at that.

"What! Are you sure he said Anthony?"

"Yesss…he said he's a friend of yours and his, so you must know him."

I feel my cheeks getting hot. "Yeah, I do know him. I just didn't realize they were close. Weird." I turn away so she doesn't inquire more about my reaction.

Of course there on my other side when I turn is Molly, my future mother-in-law. Smiling sweetly, she says, "Is Anthony a close friend?"

"Um, just someone I've known for years, and Oliver met him a little while ago. I guess they've talked more than I thought." We need a change of subject stat, so I ask quickly, "Where are we headed?"

"We are going to a boutique lingerie and adult toy store that I rented for the night. And you have a five-hundred-dollar budget to pick out stuff for the wedding night, Grace. Besides anything you may want to spend yourself, of course; that amount is from all of us." Jess winks at me.

"I'm so excited." Molly claps her hands together. "It's called Madame Aphrodite's, and I've heard amazing things about it."

"Wow, that's….something," I say taking a big gulp of champagne because I'm about to be adult toy shopping with my mother-in-law and Kyle. Oh my god, who in the world thought this was a good idea? Tara and Jess, obviously. I'm going to kill them.

As we drive to my party, the music blares, and everyone is drinking and laughing. I use their distraction to pull my phone out and send Oliver a text.

—I'm going to kill your sister and my best friend. How's your party?

—Mine is pretty nice, actually. Milo did an amazing job for once. What did they do to you, poor baby?

—First, they let Kyle come; don't ask me why. Does no one realize he's a man? Second, my party is at a lingerie and adult toy boutique…so I get to shop for sex toys *with your mother…and Kyle*. Why????

—Babe! I literally just spit out my beer all over Milo (he's not thrilled). That is actually hilarious. I'm sorry, but also I want you to know I fully support this shopping, and I can send you my credit card number.

—Oh, that reminds me: I also spit my champagne out earlier. When Jess told me you invited Anthony tonight…is there something I am missing?

—Oh yeah, well I don't really mind the guy, as long as you are not around, that is. And I did invite him to the wedding. Sorry, I meant to tell you. It's a complicated thing to explain. I haven't told you, but he and I talk sometimes, so we are tentatively friends…weird, I know. Is it OK?

—I'm shocked, but yeah, I guess so. Just no talking about me, right?

—He knows better, believe me.

—OK. I better go. They are yelling at me for being on my phone too much. Love you.

—Love you too. Buy lots of sexy things!

***

Oliver

When I heard where Grace is heading for her party, I had a hard time getting my attention back to my own party. Turning to Milo, I ask, "Did you know about the shopping Jess had planned for tonight?" He's still glaring daggers at me and wiping the beer spit off of his shirt and face.

"You mean Madame Aphrodisiacs, or whatever it's called? Yeah, I knew. I gave Tara three hundred dollars to spend there. I hope she gets something good."

"So you two are dating?" I raise an eyebrow at that.

"'Dating' is a very formal arrangement sort of word. I try to keep her monopolized; let's just say that. If she is always with me, she can't meet anyone else, can she?" He looks triumphant at that, like he's solved the world's greatest mystery.

"You are such an idiot, you know that? So she might spend three hundred dollars of your money on lingerie and toys, but you guys aren't exclusive. Which means some other guy can enjoy the benefits. You do realize that, right?" I watch as his ears turn deep red and pure rage fills his face.

"What the actual fuck, man? Why on earth would you say that to me?" He practically yells.

"Because you need to hear it! I'm giving you a reality check before life does. She is a beautiful, amazing woman. Someone smart enough to value her will come along one day, and if you aren't in a 'formal arrangement,' as you call it, then you can kiss it all goodbye."

I shake my head at him and continue, "You see that guy Anthony." Milo looks at him and back at me, confused. "I met him when he came out of Grace's bedroom with her after he spent the night with her. That was how life gave me my reality check. I almost lost her because I was so stuck in the past and afraid to say what I was actually feeling. Is that what you want to see coming out of Tara's room one morning? Because let me tell you, nothing will ever hurt like that, and she wasn't even mine yet." His look of incredulity almost makes me want to laugh. The memory is still too painful for that though.

Pointing over to Anthony, he simply says, "Why in the hell is that guy here?"

"Because he didn't do anything wrong, in all truth. And he happens to be a decent guy that I can't help but like. I have had a few talks with him, and believe me, we both know very clearly where everything stands. That isn't my point. I care about you, and I'm trying to help you out by explaining that you aren't going to have forever to get your head out of your ass about Tara. I have met some of your competitors, and I have to say, they aren't messing around."

That gets his attention. "Wait, competitors? What the fuck are you talking about now?" His anger is back. Good. I take out my phone, remembering the picture Kyle posted of our little paintball team. When I find it I show Milo. In it Sean is holding Tara up in his arms with a huge smile. "Who is this joker?"

"A friend of Kyle's, but that day he was only interested in your girl. I'm not trying to be a dick, honestly. I love you, and I want you to be happy. I think she makes you happy. I just need you to understand that you have to figure out what you're doing. Are you ever going to grow up and take things seriously?"

"You sound just like Grace." he groans.

"Maybe because we both care about you. I think with our move looming, we worry about everyone we're leaving behind."

After my little reality talk with my brother, he gets rather quiet. We all enjoy another hour of hitting balls, drinking beers, and eating gourmet wings and pizza. Abruptly Milo announces that we are moving to our next stop. Everyone is confused at that because this is the party, but I have a sneaking suspicion I know where we are going. We summon two large Ubers and pile in. Milo won't tell anyone where we're heading, so there is a lot of speculation. When my grandfather, of all people, says he hopes it's a strip club, I burst out laughing. The cars pull up in front of a fancy building with the name "Madame Aphrodite's" in fancy lettering, and I smile to myself, knowing that I really got to him.

***

Grace

The guys showing up to my party is the best part of my evening. Honestly, if I had to explain how one more rabbit vibrator worked *to my future mother-in-law*, I might die of embarrassment. Everyone is apparently having a ball with this situation, Kyle included. He gives us the "man's perspective," as he calls it, and has everyone laughing and fawning over him. Honestly tonight is like a sitcom, I swear. If I wasn't the person it all revolved around, I'd likely find it extremely entertaining. Molly had just finished examining various-sized glass dildos, exclaiming over their beauty and craftsmanship, when the pounding on the door started. Thank god for distractions.

When the owner of the store opened the door and we saw all the men gathered on the sidewalk, I breathed a deep sigh of relief and pushed my way to Oliver.

"Baby, you're here!" I grab him and drag him in. No way am I letting go of him now.

"We couldn't stay away." He kisses me, then starts looking around a bit too happily.

"We are not doing this shopping in front of your entire family," I hiss firmly under my breath.

"They are distracted; we can just be discreet," he says, a little disappointed.

"Why did you guys come here, anyway?"

"I scared Milo straight. I'll explain later." He winks at me.

I lead Oliver to the food spread at the back of the store and pour us each a flute of champagne. "Did you eat? We have tons of food left."

"We had pizza and wings. This stuff looks good though. I can eat again."

I look around at that moment, at this room full of happy people, and realize how lucky I am.

"I'm really going to miss them all," I say. I feel the big, familiar arms I love so much come around me.

"We aren't losing anything, babe. We're just expanding our world."

"That's true. I can't wait to see all the new things we discover together." I lean into his embrace with so much contentment I wonder at myself. Grace Alice Murphy...the damaged, sullied, beaten down, and discarded. Look at what life has given you.

Tara marches up to us, breaking my happy trance. "Oliver, can you explain why your brother is acting so strange, please? He said something about competitors and Anthony coming out of my bedroom. I don't even know Anthony! What the hell?"

Oliver holds his hands up in a gesture of defense. "OK, he might be a little worked up. Plus he's had a few drinks, so maybe he isn't making sense. I just had a talk with him about growing up. I tried to help him see that life isn't going to give him forever to man up."

"What the hell does that have to do with Anthony in my bedroom?" Her brow is still furrowed.

"Ugh...he said that wrong. That was another story he's confusing with yours. Look, just forget that. Will you just give him a chance to stop being such an idiot, please? I think he really cares about you."

Blowing a breath up into her hair, she just stares at us for a minute.

"I care about him too. He better not be messing with me right now."

"I don't think he is. I think it's more like he's scared straight," Oliver assures her.

"OK fine, I'll take your word for it." When she turns on her stilettos and marches away again, we look at each other and just grin.

"They needed a push," I say.

"I gave him one, a big one," he replies.

We rejoin the group just in time to hear Oliver's father, telling his wife, that they need a rabbit. I have no words; I just look at Oliver pointedly. "You see what I've been dealing with?" The look of horror on his face is priceless. I will never forget that as long as I live.

"Oh no, that's so wrong. I can't listen to this." He places his hands on my shoulders and steers us in the opposite direction, whereupon we see Milo and Tara in a rather heated discussion.

"I hope we didn't make things worse for them," I comment nervously.

"Enough worrying about everyone else. I want to see what you have picked out."

Jess comes up to us just then and swats Ollie's arm. "No sir, that is for the wedding night and honeymoon!"

"She's right, it would probably be bad luck or something if I show you," I agree, simply because I know how much it will irritate him for me to agree with his sister.

"Fine, I will just go look around and make some of my own purchases for you." Putting his hands in his pockets, Oliver heads over to fancy display of furry handcuffs and various leather whips while he whistles to himself.

"We should probably wrap this night up soon," I tell Jess. "I can't imagine what your grandfather is going to think of half of the things in this place. Not to mention I really don't want to know all of your parents' kinks."

"You are probably right, although I'm going to kill Nick for letting Milo bring the guys here. He should have stopped him or at least called me so I could make sure the door stayed locked when they arrived."

I can't help but pity Nick a little for the chewing out he might get later, but I also saw the things Jess bought, so I know he will have plenty to be happy about too.

Elvis Has Entered the Building

Oliver

The day of my second wedding feels nothing like my first. I'm not a kid this time around, with no idea what married life is really like. I'm not in a church with hundreds of guests. Instead I'm almost forty. I've lost one wife and soulmate only to find another. I know that marriage can be tough but is ultimately wonderful with the right person, and I love Grace more than I ever imagined possible. This time I'm in a small studio loft space in Brooklyn with about fifty guests; it's more intimate and simple. The tinkling sound of the waterfalls is soothing, and the DJ has some classical cover versions of popular songs playing low in the background while we all wait for the bride. Mary, the florist, is doing one last check on the lotus ponds and all the table arrangements. Outside the lights are sparkling over the many velvet sofas we rented and have scattered over the rooftop in seating areas. The heaters are on full blast, making it feel cozy in the middle of winter.

Milo comes and checks if I need anything. "How about a quick drink at the bar before they get here?"

I give him a smirk. "For me, or for you before you see Tara?"

He adjusts his suit jacket for the hundredth time. "Just so you know, we are exclusive now. I talked to her." It's not much information, but it's a lot from him. He never talks about his private life much.

"Congratulations, little brother." I put an arm around his shoulder and pull him in for a hug.

"It's not that big of a deal; don't be a dick." He shoves me a bit, but he has a broad grin on his face that he can't hold back.

Anthony is in charge of patrol duty, watching for any signs of Grace's family trying to make an appearance, even though I doubt they have the nerve. He comes up to reassure me that everything is kosher so far. Placing one hand on my shoulder, he gives me his genuine wide grin.

"You did it, man. You two lovebirds are going to be sickeningly happy together; I can just tell. I'm happy for you."

"Thank you. You played your part. I wish you hadn't, but in the end it's all worked out how it should. Who knows? Maybe I would have wasted even more time and eventually lost her for real if it weren't for you." I give him a hug. We've come a long way; I don't hold the past against him. Milo still thinks I'm insane for this.

The music stops, and Elvis makes his way to the front. Elvis got ordained so he can marry us. He watched me go through the grief of losing Ally and saw me come back to life because of Grace. He was there when I proposed, and he inked my ring finger. We couldn't think of a better person to marry us. Everyone makes their way to the chairs, and a hush falls over the room. It's time. I look to the back of the room where the gauzy curtains hang, where I know my soon-to-be wife will come through any minute now. I see Jess, Tara, and my mother all coming through them and taking their seats. They were her helping committee today. I breathe in deeply and let it out slowly as I wait, and this moment feels suspended in time.

Kyle and his DJ partner start up the song that Grace chose to walk in to, "Creep" by Duomo. That brings a smile to my face, my crazy girl. What other bride in the world would walk down the aisle to that? The curtains are pulled back, and I see not only my girl but my grandfather. The tears come then. He's got a cane to help him, and he leans on Grace's arm as they begin walking. I can't take it all in fast enough. Her beauty is overwhelming, but seeing the way she helps him walk, the way he's beaming with joy and pride, and the serenity on her face. It's all too much. Her eyes lock with mine, and I'm lost to her. Utterly lost, heart and soul. She reaches me, and we help my grandfather to his seat. He gives Grace one last kiss and whispers something in her ear. We face each other in front of Elvis.

The three of us stand under the stone arch that Mary has white orchids and moss hanging from. On either side of us the waterfalls tinkle and the lotus flowers drift through the water. Tara takes Grace's flowers so I can take both her hands in mine. We each wrote our own vows for each other. Elvis begins, and we prepare to say them.

"Grace, I have never met anyone as authentic and beautiful as you, inside and out. Your patience with me was far more than I deserved. You came into my world and changed it in all the best ways imaginable. Now there's no looking back. I can't wait to start this journey together. You are my heart, my oxygen, my life. My vow to you is this: no one will ever hurt you again. I will be your shelter, your rock, and your defender. I promise my eternal love and faithfulness, come what may."

"Oliver, for the first time in my life, I found out what true love was when I found you. You see me…all the good, the bad, and the ugly, and you never turn away. I never knew safety until I was in your arms. With you I have truly found myself at last, and I have found peace. I know that whatever comes in life, I will be OK because I will have you by my side. I swear that nothing will ever shake the foundation we have. Storms may come, but we will stand strong because we stand together. I give you all that I am from this day on."

Milo and Tara step up to hand us the rings we will exchange. When I take Grace's hand to put hers on, though, I notice she has a new tattoo on her finger. The matching one to mine, my name. I look up, and she is grinning from ear to ear, having surprised me with this. I look to Elvis, who obviously is in on it, and he winks.

"I love it," I whisper. Once the rings have been exchanged and we are officially married, I kiss my *wife*. My wife. I will never be tired of looking at her and saying, "That is my wife." The music starts back up with "Happy" by Duomo coming on loudly, and everyone is clapping.

***

Grace

The night before the wedding I spend at Tara's apartment. I'm not usually a traditional sort of person, but sleeping apart from Oliver feels right for this night. I will need someplace he can't see me to get ready anyway. In the morning Molly and Jess join us also, and I think about how they probably want to get to know Tara more since Milo and she seem to be an item. It's odd how a year ago, Tara and I wouldn't have known Molly or Jess if we passed them on the street. And now the four of us are practically one little family, chatting away while we get ready for my wedding. My wedding...wow, I really love hearing those words.

Today is the first day I'm getting to see the dresses they have all bought to wear, and they look so beautiful. Tara is wearing a mint-green tea-length strapless gown that really shows off her long legs and auburn hair. Jess is in a long pale-blue Grecian-style dress. With a plunging V-neckline and a banded empire waist, the skirt is split and flowy, and she basically looks like a blond goddess. Molly is in a pale, buttery-yellow-colored pencil skirt and matching fancy top, and I realize with my pink dress and all their pretty colors, we make a virtual rainbow. It will be lovely in the pictures. Oliver and the men are in light-gray suits and will be very complimentary to the palate. It may seem odd for my wedding to be full of such bright spring colors, seeing as it's taking place in winter. However, I feel like I'm bursting with sunlight inside, and it seems absolutely perfect that the colors are reflective of that. Jess's husband, Nick, is in charge of getting Grant and making sure he is ready for the important walk he will take me on.

I will forever treasure the look in Oliver's eyes as he watched his grandfather and I walk toward him. The photographer assures me he got plenty of shots of that, and I can't wait to see them. I never thought I would be the type of person who even had a wedding. I pictured myself as more of the spontaneous, Vegas-chapel type. But having people you care about to share this day with makes all the difference, I have found. And this will be one of the last times we are all together before we leave for Queenstown. There is a bittersweet feeling when I think about the move. Today, however, is a day for happiness.

I found a cover version of the song that Oliver picked, "Collide." It is more acoustic and romantic. As we have our dance together, each word is perfect and makes me reminisce about all the things we went through to finally come together.

"What's that look on your face?" Ollie asks, looking down at me.

"I was just thinking that I sometimes thought I'd never get to have this, have you. I still have to pinch myself sometimes to believe it's real."

"Me too. I thought I would be sad and lonely for the rest of my life. Until a little tornado named Grace blew into my life. Now I have more than I ever have before."

"I'm so glad my family isn't here to ruin this day. I just know they would have."

"That reminds me—I have to tell you a story about that." He gives a wry chuckle. "Later, though. Even talking about them is more than they deserve today."

I have to agree with that.

"What did my grandfather say to you earlier?" he asks.

"It's a secret. Maybe if you're a good boy, I'll tell you one day." I smirk at my husband.

I make sure to have my dance with Grant before he gets too tired. We dance to "Dream A Little Dream Of Me" by

Mama Cass. Milo surprises me by having "I'll Stand by You" played for us to dance to, and I have to try really hard not to cry until he starts being his usual ridiculous self, and then I'm just laughing.

"Don't tell Jess, but you're my favorite sister," he tells me.

"That's awful, and I like it." I smile wickedly.

"What am I going to do when you guys leave?" he says more seriously.

"You will call and FaceTime for advice on your love life, for one thing. Then you'll come visit, and I'll take you bungee jumping. But mostly you'll be with Tara, I have a feeling."

"That doesn't sound so bad," he concedes. I hug him tightly as our dance comes to an end. "Love you, little brother."

"Are you ready to head to The Plaza, wife?" Oliver's arms slip around me, and his voice is low in my ear.

"Very, husband," I reply.

Epilogue

Oliver

About six months after our move to New Zealand, Grace started a charitable foundation to help children and adults dealing with the aftermath and long-term effects of abuse. It was something she had been planning and working on for a while. It gave her a sense of peace to use the money from Ronan to help others. When she showed me the paperwork and what she named it, I told her it was perfect: The Phoenix Foundation. She splits her time between working with that, writing, and chasing down her next thrill, of course. We explore our new country together, and the natural beauty and majesty of it all has given us both a sense of renewal. I doubt we can ever go back to living in New York.

One day Grace came home on her motorcycle and told me that we needed to trade it in for a safer vehicle. I looked at her like she had lost her mind. Knowing how much she loves that thing.

"Well apparently, car seats don't fit on them," she simply said.

"What?" I was absolutely dumbfounded. We never planned on having children. Her childhood and family life had made her reluctant to. And as for me, I just thought the time for that had passed me by, and I was perfectly content with my life as it was.

"Please don't be upset, OK? I flaked a little. Remember when I was sick with that sinus infection and on antibiotics? Well I forgot that they nullify my birth control. So yeah, we have a surprise on the way. You are going to be a dad, old man," she told me nervously.

"I have no clue what to say…are you OK with this?" I asked her, still stunned out of my mind.

"I am, actually. I never thought it was something I wanted. Until I found out what a safe, fulfilling, and happy family life actually felt like. Now I am surprisingly excited about this. I think you are going to be the most amazing father ever." Her face was beaming, and suddenly I felt a rush of joy so strong I couldn't contain it. Lifting her into my arms, I spun her and kissed her all at once.

"Baby, we're gonna have a baby."

***

Grace

I lean back in my lawn chair, watching Oliver lying out on the blanket in the evening sun with our twins sleeping on his chest. We often take a walk with them on the beach after dinner. We have moved out of Queenstown and to a smaller coastal town near Dunedin. I will never tire of watching the sun rise over the waves and feeling that breeze come through our windows. When we found out we were having one girl and one boy, I told Ollie I would like to name them Harper and Grant. Harper for Ally, since that was her maiden name, and Grant for his grandfather, who we lost a year after we left New York. They each have a special middle name too: Harper Lotus and Grant Phoenix. One day they will probably be annoyed that they are named after their old mother's tattoos, but they can just deal with it. Since the arrival of the babies, my in-laws visit a lot more often, so it's a good thing we got a larger house now instead of the urban apartment we started off with when we first came out here.

As I close my eyes and drift off slightly, I can't help but think yet again that life can take such unexpected turns. When I walked into that Whole Foods in Brooklyn on a Sunday afternoon, I had no earthly idea I would be running into the man who would change my world forever. The only one I can ever imagine giving my heart and soul to. The one who gave me not only love but a real family.

Just then my phone rings, which is odd since I usually only get texts mostly. Even odder when I see that it's Tara, considering the time difference. It's early for her to be calling me on a Sunday in New York.

"Hello?" I can't hide the trepidation in my voice.

"Grace, I don't know what to do….."

The End

9 781685 153328